I0451779

I DO
TERRIBLE THINGS

BY JOHN GOODRICH

She grabbed his hair with one hand. Before he could turn or fight, she jammed the jagged stem of her decapitated glass into the side of his larynx. She pulled it out, and his breath whistled through the new hole in his neck. He lurched forward, hands on the wound. Donna yanked him backwards, stabbed the sharp pick of her glass stem into the side of his neck. Blood spurted from the ragged hole, smothering the woodlands with the hot, coppery reek of the abattoir. She could just see the dark blood that hosed from his neck, pattering on the undergrowth like rain.

He struggled, but she gripped his hair tight, directing the welter of blood away from her. With one arm trying to cover his spurting neck, he tried to grab at her, but she kept out of his reach. Still he pumped buckets of blood, more and more pouring out of him. The ground to her right was soaked dark in a wide arc nearly two feet broad. There seemed to be no end to the pumping, spurting spray. How much blood was in him?

After what felt like hours, Michael's knees bent, and Donna shoved his body forward so he fell on his face. The blood no longer even burbled from his neck, but leaked in a slow, constant flow.

After a crushing silence, the noises of nature returned. Bugs buzzed and whined, frogs peeped in the background. The smell of blood was overpowering. How would she get it out of her clothes and hair?

Copyright © 2019 by John Goodrich
ISBN 978-1-949914-17-7
All rights reserved. No part of this book may be used or reproduced in any manner
whatsoever without written permission except in the case of brief
quotations embodied in critical articles and reviews
For information address Crossroad Press at 141 Brayden Dr., Hertford, NC 27944
A Macabre Ink Production -Macabre Ink is an imprint of Crossroad Press.
www.crossroadpress.com

First Trade Edition
Previously published in limited edition by Thunderstorm Books

*Dedicated to the late, great Bob Booth,
the wonderful Mary Booth,
and all of my NECON family*

CHAPTER 1

SHOVEL

Donna stood still for a moment, contemplating the sad-looking old man before her. Then brought the shovel down on his face.

The impact was loud enough that she almost didn't hear the snap of bone, and the old guy collapsed into the manicured grass. Donna assumed that this was his yard. She wasn't sure how she had gotten here. Or why she was winding up to bash him again.

She slammed the flat of the shovel down in an overhead arc that smashed his nose. Blood spurted out of the sides of the spade.

The old man was weeping, but his voice only came out in odd grunts. He brought gnarled hands up to his ruined, bloody head. She'd flattened the left side of his face, tearing the skin. Blood welled out of rents in his cheek, like lava from a craggy fissure. One of his eyes was a ruined hollow, a gout of clear liquid from the empty socket had washed down his face.

Donna shifted her grip and slammed down on his forearms. Bone crunched and he folded over, curled around his crippled hands, face a mask of agony.

Why was she doing this? If she'd wanted to murder someone, there had to be more efficient ways to go about it. It seemed cruel. A gun or a knife would have been faster, and what was the damn point of murdering this guy? He was going to be dead of old age in a couple of years anyway.

As she was thinking, he rolled over on his front, crawling

on his elbows, grunting and whimpering in pain. She couldn't imagine how painful it had to be to crawl with broken arms. And yet, he was trying. She could see the dark stain spreading in his pants where he'd shit himself. How terrified he must be.

She didn't recognize him, did she? Before she could come up with an answer, she had placed the shovel on the back of his neck, the point digging into his skin. She held it a moment, letting the man know he was about to die.

She leaned on the shovel. It dug into the skin, but didn't cut through the way she thought it would. She brought her boot down on the shovel head, and was rewarded with the pop of ligaments, but the bone stopped it short. She shoved a couple more times, each time eliciting a moan of agony from the man she was killing too slowly. She brought the shovel up, and with all her strength, brought it down. Bone crunched, and he stopped moving. He didn't even spasm, and lay still on the short-cropped grass. Dark blood oozed out of the wound, turning the grass black. With a wrench she pulled the blade out and dropped it to one side. She'd had the foresight to wear gloves. Leaving her fingerprints on the handle would have been awkward.

Donna looked at the immaculately maintained lawn, now ruined by the body lying on it. The street lights cut through some of the night gloom, lending a surreal atmosphere to the whole thing.

Donna woke up, in her familiar bed, Jim sleeping next to her. He turned over. She must have woken him up, too.

"Fuck." Her shoulders ached. It had been a dream. Had to be. The old man covered in blood, the reek of shit and piss, all of it. Sleep-murdering wasn't a thing. Was it?

"What's up, sweets?" Jim's calm voice grounded her. She was here. In her bed with Jim Corey. Even just waking up, he was good-looking. Well-muscled, tousled brown hair, kind brown eyes set in a handsome face. She hadn't killed anyone.

"Bad dream," she said.

"Tell me about it."

"I don't want to talk about it," she said. That got her The

Look. The one he gave her when he thought she was being irrational. The condescending one.

"Come on, a little something. Tell me about it."

"No." She waited for a moment. "What do you want for breakfast?"

"Donna, seriously. Tell me about your dream. Talking about it will help get it out of your head. Tell me."

When she needed to talk, Jim was there. Still, she hesitated.

"I don't know. It was a dream, and that's just random shit my brain is throwing at me." But her arms ached, as if she'd gripped something too tightly. Today was going to be tough. She had three massages on her calendar, and a cardio class to teach first thing. "Talking about it will just make it easier to remember. Let it fade."

He shrugged. "If that's what you want."

"It is." She kissed him. "I'd rather think about something else. You got anything that needs doing this morning?"

"Nothing I couldn't postpone." He wrapped her in his arms and kissed her again.

"Weird shitty dream last night," Donna confided to her best friend over the best caramel coffee in Oakham. "My shoulders are tense all the way down my back."

"Honey, you're twenty-four. You'll bounce back in the time it takes me to drink my coffee. You're a massage therapist, isn't there someone who helps you when you're tense?" Mildred Davies refused to be the victim of her unfortunate name. In her fifties, she was frumpy, but her vitality made her easy to get along with. She and Donna shared a schedule, so they met for coffee most mornings at Café Gitan.

"I've got a tool for that," Donna said.

"I thought you had Jim for that," Fierce said. Donna's convoluted play on Mildred's name came from a Carol Burnett sketch, 'Mildred Fierce' which mocked the classic Joan Crawford film *Mildred Pierce*. Fierce loved her nickname.

"I never dream about that kind of thing," Donna said. "The only dreams I ever remember are where I'm teaching a class I'm not prepared for and then look down and realize I'm in my underwear. Stupid stuff like that."

"I once dreamed that Carl had left me in the mud at the side of a dirt road. I hated him all morning, and let him know it."

"This wasn't about Jim, though. This was about killing some old guy. Usually I know the people in my dreams. This was weird, I didn't know the guy at all. I hit him with a shovel, just over and over." Donna's mouth twisted in distaste. She flexed her hands, feeling the tension in her forearms. "I don't like horror. Why would my brain do that to me?"

"Honey, have you had any bad clients recently? Someone try to pull something on you?"

"No, Fierce, nothing like that. Life's been pretty quiet, if anything."

"Too quiet? Maybe you need a little spicing up?"

"I really don't. I'm liking the quiet. I'm financially solvent, business has been good. Jim doesn't steal my money. Everything's better than it was two years ago.."

"Sometimes your brain does brain stuff because it's got brain things to work out." Mildred paused to let that sink in. "Sometimes it's weird, but really, unless you start getting these every night, I wouldn't worry about it. It sucks, but you're just going to lose a night's sleep. Have a second coffee, and thank Jesus you're young and don't need two huge ones every morning. Get good sleep tonight, and you'll be over it."

Donna took a swallow, savoring the contrast of sweet caramel and bitter coffee.

"Could it be your agoraphobia?" Mildred asked.

"I'm not agoraphobic," Donna said, nettled. "I've just, you know, never been out of Oakham."

"Honey, that's not normal. Most people travel."

"Mom used to try to take me places, but she tells me I would cry, just screaming like I was being tortured. When she turned around, I would calm down. So I don't even try any more. I can't leave Oakham."

Fierce shook her head in amazement. "It's just so weird that you've never been anywhere else."

"I dunno, why would I want to? UMass Oakham is pretty good, we've got Chinese and Thai, a couple of good gyms, damn close to perfect coffee, and the Internet for everything else. What more could I want?"

"You're kidding, right? Donna, there's a whole state, a whole country out there. Lots of things to see, lots of different people to meet. Oakham's a pretty good town, but to have lived here your whole life? Crazy."

Donna shifted in her chair and said nothing.

"Have you tried to leave town?" Sometimes, Fierce wouldn't let something go. Her tenacity was a good thing, most of the time. "Surely it's time to figure out what all that screaming was about?"

"No, and can we drop it?"

"Yes, sorry." And she meant it. "I think we've got a raccoon in the attic. And my big client's being a dick again. If he wasn't such a big deal, I'd tell him to stick it. He cracked a dumbass joke about lazy Mexicans, and I just wanted to knock him down. He inherited his money, so while you go out build your own business, the old hypocrite's criticizing you for slacking. He thinks I can't see him staring at my ass like he's a fourteen-year-old." She shrugged. "Dick."

"He wasn't talking about me, Fierce. He doesn't even know me."

Fierce's smile was thin. "Oakham isn't all that big, but I doubt you'll ever cross paths. I can't see him coming to a cardio-boxing class."

"I hope not, it's hard enough to get people to come to something that challenging, without dealing with some creepy old guy."

"We should go out for drinks Friday. We haven't had a girls' night out for a while."

"A week."

Fierce smiled. "Yeah, but I like to look at Rich. And Peter. Either one, really. The whole tattoo thing. And they're muscular without being bulky. I figure either one would be fun in the sack. And Peter brings some color in this town, which desperately needs it."

"You do remember they're married to each other, right?" But Fierce wasn't listening.

"So drinks, Friday night?" Fierce asked.

"You're on."

Donna mangled her cardio-boxing class. Still distracted by the memory of the old man's agonized face, she rushed her warm-up, and cramped up thirty minutes in. She pushed through, but the class could tell she was covering something.

"You should relax a bit, Donna." Brittney was seventeen, outgoing, and loved to chat after class. "I thought you were going to pop a forehead vein."

"Had to work through it," Donna said, taking a moment away from her breakfast smoothie. "Can't expect the class to fight through the hard bits if I don't."

"You're such an inspiration," Brittney simpered. "Hard work makes a hot bod."

Donna was used to Brittney's compliments, even if she wasn't sure how to take them. Brittney herself was lean and sculpted, the result of long hours of work at the gym. Her outfit was, in Donna's opinion, too tight. But she came to class regularly, and Donna would be foolish to alienate her.

"I look at it as a better life: more energy, more strength, and I'll admit, keeps me trim. We gotta do what we gotta do, Brittney. Hard is always good for you."

Brittney giggled, and put a warm hand on Donna's shoulder.

"You're such a great teacher."

"It helps that I've got dedicated students." She gave her most winning smile. "But I need to run. Lots to do, not enough time."

Brittney nodded, smiled, and turned her pert self away. Donna had a half-hour massage in an hour. She had to get prepared.

Between the cardio class, two single-hour massages and three half-hour massages, Donna was dragging by the time she opened the apartment door at 7:30. But the smell of cooking pork and onions tickled her nose. Jim stood in front of the stove, shirtless, wearing an apron. Small medallions of pork sizzled in the frying pan.

"Salad is in the fridge," he said with a pleasant smile.

She hauled her bag of crap past him, into the dining room. The table was set, the black dishes on crimson placemats. A couple of candles stood, unlit, in the center of the immaculate table.

"This morning was fun," Jim was behind her, his fingers tracing lines down her back. He smelled very pleasant, his light musk combining with the smell of the pork and onions. Food and manliness, the two scents twined into her, irresistible. She turned.

Jim's smile was warm. She was an awkward, sweaty mess and needed a shower. He leaned down and kissed her. She melted against his hard body, his heat leaving her breathless when they separated.

"Ready for a rematch?" she said.

Donna didn't dream that night. She woke, feeling rested. Distance made the frightening dream less immediate. Still, she got online and looked at the obituaries for Oakham and the surrounding towns. Nobody looked like the man whose face she'd smashed in her dream.

Not that she had expected to find him. It had been a dream. Nothing more. But just to be on the safe side she did a broader web search for any murders that might have happened in the county in the last two days. Nothing came up, certainly no old men who had been bludgeoned and decapitated, with or without a shovel. She shuddered, the man's pain-wracked face swimming up in her memory.

It had been a dream, she reminded herself. *Just a dream.*

CHAPTER 2

TEETH AND CLAWS

Donna dreamed she'd been sitting for a long time. Darkness clustered around her, with it the scent of pine trees, and the sound of men talking, punctuated by the occasional crash of a bottle being broken. Earlier, she'd heard dogs snarling, barking, and tearing at each other, followed by whimpers of pain, quickly cut off. She should have been sick to her stomach, but the disconnect from her body was a yawning chasm.

Cars were being started, and she roused herself. She must have been sitting for hours, and she wondered what she'd been waiting for. She walked on the blanket of pine needles until she came to the edge of the trees.

A line of red taillights receded into the night, and a grizzled man in a baseball cap, filthy jeans, and a red plaid shirt closed the gate behind them. His silhouette was rail-thin, the shirt loose. Before her was a flat expanse of dirt, like an unpaved parking lot. The sides were hemmed in by stands of trees, like the one Donna was hiding in. In the center of it all slumped a dilapidated barn, once painted red but now silver with age. Now that the cars were gone, the only light came from a ring of naked bulbs that hung on the exterior of the barn.

She hugged the trees in the dark, moving slowly. A man stood in front of the closed gate. She could see the cherry-red glow of his cigarette and after a few moments, smelled the reek of burning tobacco. Away in the dimness, she heard the husky breath of the dogs in their pens. Now she could smell blood and urine.

Donna didn't like dogs. When she was a child, an over-friendly lab had knocked her over in the middle of a street. She felt that panicky nausea in the pit of her stomach, remembering the hot, strong dog above her, hyperactively sniffing at her as she tried to scrabble away, terrified a car would kill them both. She didn't trust dogs. But no dog deserved this.

She edged toward the barn. The figure with the cigarette stayed close to the gate. She wondered what the sick motherfucker was thinking. Probably about his winnings. Shitbag. She put her back against the wall of the barn, glanced up, and positioned herself just below a bare bulb.

Way to sneak, she thought to her dreaming self. *Right under a light source.*

Not that it mattered to the figure. He turned away from the gate and headed toward her, head down, hands in his pockets. She watched, incredulous, as he approached. Her hand touched something heavy but supple hanging at the back of her belt.

"Woah there, missy. I didn't see you there." He was a small man, probably six inches shorter than her. His fifty years had been hard, his dark beard gray in patches, his face sunken and lined. Hair sprouted from his ears, peeked out from under his shirt sleeves. Quite the miniature Sasquatch.

"You looking for some after-party action, that it? The dog-fightin' get you all wet?"

She sidled away, not speaking, keeping her back to the barn.

"If you run, I'm only going to follow." He snickered.

She retreated, which he interpreted as a coy come-on. He followed, licking his lips. She'd seen this scene on TV. All she had to do to make it complete was run, stumble, and fall into his strong arms. Donna wanted to throw up inside her own brain. She wanted to wake up. She remembered the shovel and the old man. What was wrong with her head these days? As she was thinking, she reached the barn doors. A tug, and one opened just enough for her to squeeze through.

Inside, the barn reeked of blood and fear. Bulbs had been strung across the bare rafters, casting a pitiless light on everything. Dogs lunged against chain-link gates, their scarred muzzles pressing against their prisons. Donna's hands fumbled at her waistband, found a pair of heavy leather gloves. She pulled them on by feel, keeping her hands behind her back. Sap gloves. People used them for exercise; the backs of the hands and fingers were covered with steel plates, pouches on top were filled with lead shot. Realization ran through her like an electric shock.

Dog Killer muscled the door open in what he probably thought was a manly way.

"Where are you, girly?"

She stood, hands behind her back, a pose that emphasized her tits.

No. What the hell was wrong with her? She wanted to wake up. She didn't want to even dream about fucking this animal-abusing shit bag. Why would she dream this stuff?

"Dunno if you're the real deal, but I don't fucking care."

The hands reached for her, and she danced out of their grasp, retreating past the kennels. The dogs snarled and barked.

"Fuckin' tease." His flannel shirt made a pile on the floor, revealing a wife-beater covered in crusty black and yellow stains.

He grabbed at her, but she connected with a heavy-gloved wallop that rocked him.

They glared at each other. He was reassessing the situation. Donna let out an internal sigh of relief. She'd rather murder this bastard than let him touch her.

She squared off in a weird boxing stance, like she was Muhammad Ali. It was all wrong; too much weight on her front leg, her arms held away from her body. She was going to get tired fast, especially with the extra weight of her gloves. Why would she stand this way?

He spun away, ran to a corner, where he picked up an aluminum bat. He hefted it, and she could see the dark stains, the rough patches from hard use.

"Don't know who you are, bitch, but you are fucking with the wrong guy."

Blood thundered in her ears, louder than the mad barking of the dogs. He could kill her. If this wasn't a dream.

He feinted once and she didn't react. He tried again, but

she could read him well enough to know he wasn't serious. He didn't commit his shoulders or his feet.

He stepped in for the real thing, a side-swing like a lumberjack going for a tree. She punched at it, and the bat spanged off her glove like she was made of stone. Her wrist sang. She backhanded him, the heavy glove lending her some punishing power. He went down, the bat ringing on the concrete.

She was on him, heavy fists hammering into his unprotected ribs. The dogs went insane, as if the violence was catching, scrabbling madly at their prisons. She knelt astride him and slammed furious fists into his face. His lip split, his nose gushed blood, and still she carried on, one strike followed by another. Her shoulders and back ached, but still she worked his face. It was now a river of blood from cuts to his scalp and under his eyes. Red clotted his beard, flowed off his face, soaked into his filthy undershirt. Red spattered the concrete as if she'd dropped a melon. The reek of blood was overpowering. He stopped trying to raise his head, and still she pounded his face, pushing her exhausted shoulders. Then, apparently satisfied, she stood, her breathing heavy.

His unresisting body was difficult to move, awkward and boneless. She dragged him across the floor to chain-link cage of a starved-looking mutt. The other dogs were still barking like mad, but this one squatted and snarled at her, then launched itself against the side of its cage, barking like mad. She could see every rib on its wasted flank, the chewed-off ear, the mass of scars down the top of its muzzle, the heavy chain collar. Letting the dog out of its cage would be suicide.

She grabbed Baseball Cap by the waistband of his dirty jeans and pulled his unresisting form onto her shoulder. She heaved him up, pressing him against the chain fence that kept the dog imprisoned. The caged dog wasn't barking, just letting out a low growl, showing teeth. She kept levering his unresisting form up. He must have become conscious enough to realize what was going on. But his struggles were too weak, and she had his torso over the bar. With a shove he went in, and Donna turned away, to find herself facing the pit where the dogs fought. She walked to it, leaving the sloppy sounds of the dog at its meal behind her.

The ring was a concrete depression, four feet below the rest of the floor, surrounded by yet more fencing. Spattered blood, dried and fresh, made a Jackson Pollock painting of the walls. The floor was caked with it, with lumps of shit scattered here and there.

She crouched. Beneath the layers of dried fluids, the drainage channels looked wrong. Not all of them led to the drain. Without touching the filth on the fighting pit, she followed the grooves with her finger. Several of the lines didn't lead to the drain, even indirectly. Weird. She walked over to one of the strangely curving channels. Then she stood, went back to the chain-link fence, and climbed it. From her high perspective, the channels made a strange, swirling pattern that made her head spin.

She walked back to the cage where she had dumped Baseball Cap. The dog had torn his throat right down to the vertebrae, chewing a bloody gobbet. *Bastard. Fucking asshole dog-abusing bastard.*

Donna jerked awake, breathing hard. Her clock face glowed 4:37. She ached. Her shoulders were so tense she thought her neck was going to snap off.

"What is it?" Jim asked. She must have woke him when she jerked awake. "Another bad dream?"

"Yeah." It was out of her mouth before she could stop it.

"Were you killing someone again?"

How had he known? She couldn't say anything, just stared at him. How had he known?

"Come on, tell me. I need to know."

She found her voice. "Need?"

"OK, I *want* to know. If it's bothering you, it bothers me."

"Back off a second." Donna was still trying to get the images, the dogs, the crunch of bones being crushed by strong jaws, out of her head. She couldn't do that and talk to Jim at the same time.

He stroked her shoulder. "Baby, I just want to know what's upsetting you."

"Can I have a little space? Having you get on me about these frikkin' horrible dreams the minute I wake up messes with my head."

"Tell me." He was gripping her arm hard enough to hurt.

"Back off." She didn't mean to snap. She brought up her hand and pulled his hand off her arm.

The back of her hand was developing a rectangular bruise. Where the hell had that come from? In an instant, she knew. The steel plate that had been in her SAP glove. In her dream. Her guts turned to liquid, and the room spun around her. It was real. She had done it. *Shit oh fuck oh hell*, she'd murdered two people in her sleep in the last week.

Why? She hadn't recognized them. Were their places within walking distance? Why hadn't there been any announcements of murders?

It all ran mad circles around her head. Could she possibly be committing these murders? How could she? Why would she? It made no sense, and yet, the bruise throbbed, accusing her.

Jim all but forgotten, she threw off the covers and charged out of the bedroom.

Was she going insane? Donna walked through the quiet house, frightened and confused. What was happening to her? She tried to figure out the possibilities. One, she could have gone out and murdered this guy. Two, she could have hit her hand in her sleep, and dreamed about hurting it. *Oh shit*, was that all she had? She shook her head. She wanted to believe the second, but she had to be totally certain the first wasn't true. She wasn't a murderer. She couldn't be a murderer.

The madness of it scrabbled inside her head like a squirrel in a washing machine. This sort of thing didn't happen here. Oakham was a nice little town. The people were friendly, the streets were clean. Serial killers didn't come from small, nice towns; they came from big, impersonal cities. She wasn't a serial killer. She just wasn't. She would know if she was that crazy. She didn't have any reason to kill people. She couldn't think of anyone she wanted to murder. And definitely not in a drawn-out messy way.

She shuddered, remembering the dog tearing chunks out of its former master. As if beating his face into hamburger hadn't been bad enough. She felt so alone.

Passing by the dining room table, she saw her phone. She picked it up and made a call.

"Mom?"

"What's wrong, Donna? You sound worried, honey." Donna wanted to hug the phone. Her mom always paid attention, knew what she was thinking.

"I've…" Was honesty the way to break this, telling her Mom everything? If she was a murderer, telling her would make her an accessory. Ah shit, what should she do? "I've got a problem."

"You're calling me at quarter to six. I know it's a problem. Is it Jim?"

"No Mom. I've just been having some really bad dreams—"

"Bad dreams? Having a hard time with the business? Someone get creepy again?" The line was dead for a couple of breaths.

"Are they about your father?" Donna's mother's voice trembled.

"No. At least, I don't think so." Donna didn't know a damn thing about her father. Her mother never brought him up. She had never seen a picture of him. Why would she be having dreams about him?

"What's this about my father? Why would I be having dreams about him?"

"Nothing, dear, nothing." Donna knew when her mother was bullshitting her, but that would have to come later. "Tell me about your dreams, then."

Donna hesitated. She could tell her mom anything, but right now, she was keeping something back. What was this sudden wall of secrets?

"I'm doing… stuff I don't want to be. Bad things, terrible things. I feel like I don't have any control over my body. And the dreams are just gruesome. I have no idea what's going through my head. I've never had dreams like this before. They've been weird, and sometimes I wake up shaking my head, but not like this. Never like this."

Her mother was silent for a moment, and Donna was afraid she'd scared her off, told her too much. She should have been more tactful, broke this to her more gradually.

"Donna, honey, are you doing anything you shouldn't?"

"What? No. I'm taking care of myself. Jim's been a pillar of support." A small lie. Mom had warned her against Danny, but she hadn't listened. "But have you ever had really weird dreams? Anything at all?"

Again the silence, which was not like her at all.

"When I was in college, I had some very vivid dreams after finals," Her mother sounded distant. "Are you having some sort of stress? Coming off it maybe?"

"No. I mean not anything strange." Donna thought for a moment. "I'm a little low on cash right now, with the student loans and all, but I'm not missing any payments or anything like that. Just… having ugly dreams." The dreams were causing her stress, which was causing her to have bad dreams? That made no sense.

The line was quiet again.

"I wish I could help you." Her mother said it slowly, as if she had to pick just the right words. "You'll want to keep an eye on any new men who have come into your life recently. Someone might have some malign influence over you without you knowing it."

Malign influence? Donna almost shouted the words back into the phone. What was this shit? What was this shit from her Mom?

"Sometimes we meet someone who seems like a good person," her mother went on. "And it turns out they're not what they seem."

"You mean like Danny?" Donna was weirded out at the conversational turn. Her mom never talked around stuff like this. "Mom, this is really strange. You're being distant, and I could really use a shoulder right now. And why bring up my father?"

"Dear, I have to go. You… you take care of yourself, OK?"

"Sure." Donna was numb, her voice expressionless as the line went dead. Her own mother had just blown her off. Her *mother*. She cradled the phone to her, wishing for some comfort. Mom was acting weird. Was it her? Was she going nuts and alienating everyone around her? She hated thinking Jim was right and her Mom was trying to undermine her.

She held her head in her hands. What next? Who was there to talk to? Fierce?

Tia Ana. She could call Mom's sister.

Her hands were shaking as the punched the numbers. After three rings, someone picked up.

"Tia Ana?" She tried not to sound desperate.

"Donna? Donna it's really early."

"What do you know about my father?"

Silence on the other side of the line, then: "You called me at six thirty for that?"

"Some frightening things have happened to me," Donna said. "Really bad dreams, don't ask about them because talking doesn't help. So I called Mom and, she brought up my father. And that was just completely out of the blue. She's always shut me down when I've asked about him before."

Ana was silent for a moment, and Donna imagined she was going to say any one of a dozen horrible, cutting things. Or worse, say something weird and shut her out the way Mom had.

"I never met him. I don't think anybody did."

"So he was a one-night stand?" Donna had never gotten the idea that her Mom was angry about her. Or her father. Just that she didn't want to talk about him, that she'd put that chapter of her life behind her. She didn't seem to resent Donna. Far from it, Mom made it clear that she loved Donna. They could talk about a lot of things. Or used to. She thought of the comments Jim sometimes made, that her mother didn't support her, and that Donna didn't see it because she was too emotionally close.

Ana sighed into the phone. "Not exactly. Your mom was in college, and she said she met this guy, and said he was neat, and that he was going to take care of her. But she never brought him home. I know I never got to meet him, and I don't think your grandparents got to, either. Never even saw a picture of him. He must have been loaded, though."

"What? Why?"

"Sylvia dropped out of school to have you. And once you were born, she went straight back to college, and wasn't borrowing money to do it anymore. I assumed her awesome guy dumped her as soon as he found out, because the day we found out was the last day she ever talked about him. Which makes him irresponsible trash, but he must have found a conscience somewhere, since he paid for the rest of her degree."

Ana's voice was soothing, but Donna's mind was going faster than ever before. What the hell did this have to do with her blood-soaked dreams? Why would her mother associate the two?

Could he have been a rapist? Forced her mother into something, got drunk and regretted it later? It would explain why her mom associated her terrible dreams, if they were dreams, with her father. But that didn't explain why she was having the dreams.

Maybe it was nothing.

"Donna, what are you thinking?"

"I don't know. I don't think this is helping." Donna wanted the blood to be gone, for the dreams to stop, for people around her to stop being strange.

She looked at the clock. Six forty-five. She had to get her shit together. She was teaching kickboxing at seven thirty, and she hadn't eaten, stretched, or managed to get any peace of mind. She stared down at the square bruise. What to do?

"Are you still there?" Tia Ana asked from the phone.

"I have to go in a couple of minutes." She winced, realizing this was almost the same phrase her mother had used to brush her off.

"If you've got some trouble, let me know. Boston's not that far away."

Donna let out a breath. Her world wasn't completely off.

"Thank you. I can't tell you how much it means to hear you say that."

"You've always been a smart, determined girl," Ana said. "You might need a little help, but you can handle whatever gets thrown at you."

"Thank you. That means a lot. And thanks for listening. Like I said, Mom's been strange."

"Give her a little space. She's always been touchy about your father."

But she brought him up, Donna thought.

"I need to get my head clear before I go to class," Donna said. "Thank you again. I'll call you in a couple of days."

"Take care of yourself until then."

"You too." She hung up.

She was still sitting on the floor of her dining room, in her underwear. Time to put the night behind her and face the day.

"Ha!" Donna hammered her knee into the air in front of her, followed up with a kick from the same leg, planted her foot, and drove her fist into the imaginary opponent. Kickboxing class wasn't as cool as it had once been, but she had an enthusiastic core that let her keep teaching it.

"Ha!" She slammed her knee into the imaginary target, kicked again, punched. Six women and a man mirrored her combination. The dreams still bothered her. The bruise, the damned bruise ate at her. What if she was committing these murders?

"Ha!" She kneed, kicked, and drove the punch from her shoulder into the problem that refused to resolve itself. She hadn't committed murder in her sleep. Someone would have noticed. The police hadn't knocked at her door.

"Ha!" Knee. Heel strike. Fist. Nobody just casually murdered people and got away with it. Although Donna had to admit that she hadn't had any brushes with the law—outside of a traffic ticket a year and a half ago.

"Ha!" She drove her knee into the lack of answers before her. Kick, strike. What else could she do? She didn't know what was going on, and that scared her.

"Ha!" Knee, kick, strike. What if she was killing people? Why would she do that? She'd always felt normal, like a regular person. She didn't want to kill anyone.

"Ha!" Knee strike, heel strike, fist. Even if they were dreams, they were strange like nothing she'd ever had before. Vivid. She remembered the smell of fear and filth in the dog's cages.

"Ha!" Knee. Foot. Strike. She came around to the bruise again. She hadn't dreamed that. It throbbed now that her heart was really going. It was real.

"Ha!" Knee. Kick. Strike. She couldn't figure out what she might have hit, either the day before, or in the night, that would give her a square bruise on the back of her hand.

"Ha!" Knee, kick, then fist. She couldn't have murdered those people. She didn't know them. How had she even gotten to wherever they were?

"Ha!" Knee strike, foot strike, punch. What was going on in her head? She didn't know these people, she didn't recognize where they lived.

"Ha!" Knee. Kick. Strike. It had to be a dream. How could she possibly go out and kill, especially with the amount of premeditation she had shown with the asshole with the dogs, in her sleep?

"Ha!" Knee strike, knee strike, punch. Where did she get all the details, then? Her dreams were usually surreal, vaporous, set in shifting locations that changed as things progressed.

"Ha!" Knee. Kick. Strike. She could remember details of the people, the unfamiliar surroundings. But how could she be killing people? She had no evidence, other than a bruise she couldn't explain.

"Ha!" Knee. Kick. Strike.

"Donna, stop!" Donna was suddenly aware of the class. Most of them were standing, or bent over, catching their breath. All of them were staring at her.

"Ah shit." She could feel the leg she'd over-kicked with beginning to tighten up.

"Sorry, forgot where I was. Let's do some stretching and cool down."

She'd never gone so far into herself, certainly not in the middle of a class. How many reps had they done? She eased the class into stretching, concentrating on the right side, where she'd performed all the kicks. She let out a large breath. She really needed that drink with Fierce tonight.

The Horn was Oakham's Viking themed bar. A few steel shields hung on the walls, but no axes, for which Donna was grateful. The real selling points were music that wasn't deafening, and Fierce liked to look at the bartenders.

Peter and Rich owned and worked The Horn. They looked like they came from a set, both with shaved heads, both clearly on the same exercise routine. They were handsome, in their thirties, and solidly muscular. The Horn was as creeper-free as they could make it, which was a lot better than the other bars in town.

"You're not wearing kilts today," Fierce complained as Rich shook her a Dry Manhattan.

"If we did it every day, it wouldn't be special." Rich said with a warm smile as he poured the concoction into her ice-filled lowball. "If it's any comfort, we do get a big tip boost the nights we wear them. But we don't want that well to run dry."

"I'll bet you do," Fierce cooed. Donna resisted the urge to kick her barstool.

"Anything for you, Donna?" Rich asked.

"Harvey Wallbanger."

Rich left to get the orange juice, and Fierce put her hand on Donna's.

"That's a little out of character for you, dear."

Donna sighed and looked away.

"It's been a bit of a week, Fierce."

"You want to talk about it now?"

"Let me get a drink in me first."

Bless her heart, Fierce shut up about it. They nattered away about nothings, and Donna felt the knot between her shoulder blades start to ease.

Donna left the Wallbangers behind and moved on to a whiskey sour. Fierce was nursing a snifter of absinthe before Donna felt like she could talk.

"I'm having weird dreams. Like I'm getting up and doing stuff. But I'm not sure it's not actually happening."

"Are you sleep-humping Jim? I think Carl had some trouble with that when we were first married. He'd get on top of me and grind away, never remembered it in the morning." She cocked her head. "I kind of miss those."

"Yeah, I kind of wish." She was going to add something more, but it died on her lips.

"Come on, Donna. If you're coy, I'll just have to drag it out of you."

Donna sighed. No one was sitting on her other side. Peter walked by, nodded, and continued on his way. The Horn was humming with chatter. Friday night in Oakham. She lowered her voice.

"I think I'm hurting people. Like going to their houses and… and beating them up."

Fierce's mouth set itself in an odd quirk.

"How much have you had to drink?" she asked.

"Not enough to make that shit up."

Fierce looked at her glass.

"How many of these have I had?"

"Just the one absinthe. There were a couple other things before it, though."

"Well, shit." Fierce put her hand on Donna's. "Do you think you're really doing this stuff?"

Donna moved Fierce's hand, showing the square bruise.

"I dreamed I got this."

Fierce took her hand, got it right up close to her face as she examined it. She took a moment to prod the bruise.

"Hey, quit that. What?"

Fierce had an odd expression, as if she was weighing something. Then she reached into her purse, and pulled out a pair of lined handcuffs.

"Hon, if you think you're sleepwalking, maybe you need these."

Donna shoved the handcuffs, along with Fierce's hand, back into the purse.

"OK, I can't believe you were carrying those. That's really creepy. And I can't believe you think that I need a pair of *handcuffs*!" Her last word was a hiss.

"You need to relax, Donna. These aren't your style, I get that. But here's the thing; you won't be able to get out of them in your sleep. If you've got a bedpost, or even if you just do your hands together, you'll know that you won't be able to get out of them. Just leave the key on your bedside table. As a bonus, they're lined, so they aren't going to dig into your hands the way regular metal cuffs will."

Donna didn't like the thought. Danny had tried some

bondage with her, and she'd hated the feeling of being a side-character in his power trip. A little while later, she'd realized the entire relationship was a power trip for him, and threw him out of the apartment she paid for. Donna hammered the rest of her drink and raised a finger for a refill. Rich was there in a moment, and poured her another whiskey sour.

"You OK, Donna?" His concern was touching.

"Thanks, Rich. I got booze and I'm good for the night."

Someone wanted his attention, and Rich hurried off to fill another glass. Donna watched him go, wishing she didn't have to return to her conversation with Fierce.

"If you're worried, take them," Fierce said, as Donna turned her attention back. "You don't have to use them, but I want you to have the option."

"I don't want them," Donna said. At least Fierce hadn't taken the cuffs out of her purse again. "I'm not going to use them, so you go ahead and take them home and do whatever you were going to. I'm not interested."

Fierce's face softened.

"Donna, honey, I'm sorry. You just seemed really frightened, and I thought I had a solution."

"Danny handcuffed me a couple of times." Donna felt the words spilling out of her. She wouldn't even be talking about him if she hadn't drunk so much. "Just another way to show me that the relationship was all about him. He pretended to be interested in me, and then did whatever the hell he wanted." The memory of helplessness lanced through her. "Fucking prick."

"And that's what I want to hear," Fierce said with a drunk but triumphant grin. "You can be so uptight, I think it's good that you can get it out."

"I am not uptight," Donna muttered. But she couldn't stay mad at Fierce. She'd been nothing but a good friend. They went places together. They talked about stuff, even if Fierce talked a lot about kinky sex.

Two faces floated into Donna's memory. The terrified old man, his face smashed in, blood pouring from his nose and ruined face. And the skinny, skeezy guy, leering at her like she was a piece of meat. Her hands balled into fists. She'd hated that dirty bastard, but not enough to feed him to his dogs. Not really.

Donna held out her hand to Fierce. "Give me the damn cuffs."

"Kinky," was Jim's reaction. Donna had made sure he saw the cuffs before she put them on. She wanted to have this discussion when she wasn't manacled.

"I don't think so." She forced a smile. "I'm just worried about the dreams, you know?"

Jim nodded, then sat on the bed next to her.

"I know they've been disturbing you, but they're just dreams." His voice was soothing, understanding.

"I know. But what if I'm wrong? Someone dies, and they die badly."

"I think you're overreacting. You're having some bad dreams, and this one was like that other one. So that sort of says it was a dream. I mean, how likely is it that you dream-killed someone, didn't get caught, and then just a few weeks later, did the same thing? Oakham PD is pretty good with their investigation. I'm sure they would have caught you if you were murdering people."

His kiss on her forehead was chaste, undemanding. Donna could feel herself unclenching.

"The worst part is that it's winding you up. You're worried enough that you think the handcuffs are necessary. Dreams are dreams, and they aren't the real world."

She went to hug him, but she was shackled by her cuffs. She considered taking them off, but decided not to. The memory of the redneck and his dogs was just too horrible.

After the first sleepless night, Donna decided to cuff her hands in front of her, rather than latching herself to the bedpost. She bolstered her pillows into a mostly-upright sleeping position, and went to sleep with her cuffed hands in her lap. In the morning, she would get the key off her nightstand, and unlock herself. In two days, she was completely used to it, and slept well. The process seemed to work. For a time.

CHAPTER 3

STEMWARE

Donna was at a party. She could tell by the wash of conversation over the European techno music. She was wearing her slinkiest outfit, a red, one-shoulder dress that hugged her form. Jim's favorite, he always asked her to wear it when he wanted to show her off. She didn't know where she was. She looked at the drink in her hand, a martini glass full of something red. A cosmopolitan? She tried to take a drink, but her hand didn't move.

Shit. She was dreaming again. Her body didn't respond. Was she going to kill someone? Maybe this was just a pleasant dream about being at a party. Conversation hummed around her, guys in business casual, women in expensive dresses. Gold hung off women's wrists, diamonds and pearls on their ears. She wasn't used to mingling with this set, except once when she'd tagged along with Jim.

She was leaning on something, a table perhaps, her drink in her hand. She watched the little knots of conversation break up, then re-coalesce over some fifteen minutes. A few people tried to talk with her, but she managed to brush them off. This was boring for a dream. Usually something happened. Here, she was just lingering in the backwater of someone's house party. Donna started to relax. She didn't seem intent on murdering anyone.

Still, she couldn't control her actions. That drink that hung in her hand might as well have been a thousand miles away. Was she here to steal something? She clung to the hope.

She was watching people. No one specific, but when

someone would walk by, her head would turn.

She didn't see any wedding rings, but she caught intimate touches happening between couples. She'd never been to a mixer like this, but she knew men and women on the prowl when she saw them. At least she wasn't dealing with any wolves hitting on her. Why was she being left alone, then? She would be insecure later. Right now, she needed to figure out what was going on. Why was she here?

She tried again to bring the drink to her mouth. Nothing. Dammit. Alcohol could only help.

Her head snapped around, and seemed to focus on a man. He was handsome, slender, short brown hair with a slight curl to it. Nice brown eyes, expensive jacket, and he looked her in the eyes.

"Hey," she heard herself say. Was she drunk? She sounded drunk. How long had she been at this party? "Been waiting for someone with a little spice to show up." She took a slug of the Cosmopolitan like it was a shot of gin. And Donna could taste it. It was good.

Donna remembered the guy at the barn, how she'd led him on. This seemed more intimate, more likely to become mutually sexual. She exploded with rage, shouting in the echoing confines of her own skull.

Her hand flicked nonexistent lint off his lapel, then gave him a proprietary pat. He worked out. His shirt was silk.

"I don't think we've met," he said.

"I'm Yolanda," she heard her mouth say. At least she hadn't called herself Juanita.

"Michael," he said. She pushed her face close to his and snapped her teeth, as if catching his breath.

"This party was boring until you got here," her voice was breathy. "Now all I want to do is leave."

Michael's laugh was uncomfortable. "I just got here. I haven't even had a drink."

"But you've found what you are looking for." She said the words slowly, licking her lips like she was getting ready to suck his cock. Donna screamed silently. Was she going to kill this guy? Fuck him?

She knocked the rest of her Cosmopolitan back. "We should go somewhere more private."

"You're very... sure of yourself," he said. She wanted to scream into his stupid face that he was going to end up dead if he followed his dick. Her body shrugged, then looked him up and down.

"I know what I like," she said, laying a finger on his lips.

He blushed, which she found oddly endearing. He placed a hand on her bare shoulder, took a moment to study her.

"I just want to make sure you haven't been roofied or anything like that. You sound like you've had a few."

"I'd think a handsome man like yourself would be more used to women who know what they want. I mean, if you prefer women who come on to you and then run away and leave you hanging for half an hour and change their minds..."

"No no," he said with a throaty chuckle. "I just want to make sure our signals are straight, is all."

"Let's go somewhere private and have some fun, how's that for clear?"

Michael glanced at the party swirling around them.

"All right."

His arm settled on her hip, but she shifted it off. Holding his hand, she led the way to the front door, past the other party people. Again, Donna didn't recognize the neighborhood. The house was a bright spot in the middle of a dark copse. Knots of people stood and conversed in pools of light that huddled near the house. She wondered how many others had already slipped away into the darkness. What was she doing? Michael seemed like a nice guy, but she was with Jim.

They walked, hand in hand, into the darkness. Somewhere ahead of them, frogs peeped, trying to get laid. Similar to the conversations she'd heard in the house, really.

"So what..." Michael started, but Donna shushed him. She gave his hand a squeeze. With the other, she snapped the top off the Cosmo glass with a *crink*.

"What was that?" he asked. "Did you just step on something?" She could barely see his face. The night was moonless, the stars bright but remote.

"I might have kicked something," she said. "It's kind of hard to see..."

He pulled her close to him. "We should be careful." He moved in to kiss her, but she dodged him.

"Not yet," she said. "Save that for later."

He pursed his lips.

"Further away. I'd prefer not to be seen, or heard," she said.

His hands found her shoulders, came down and fondled her breasts through the thin fabric of her dress. Her nipples stiffened.

"A little off the road," she whispered. Michael moved in to kiss her again, and again she dodged him. She let go of his hand, gave him a gentle shove into the bracken.

Her other hand held the stem of her glass.

The carpet of sticks and underbrush wasn't quiet. Michael crashed ahead, sounding like an elephant on the rampage. Donna thanked whatever dream she was having that her body had decided to go to the party in flats, rather than heels.

Michael seemed to think he'd found the place. He stopped, and Donna walked up behind him.

She grabbed his hair with one hand. Before he could turn or fight, she jammed the jagged stem of her decapitated glass into the side of his larynx. She pulled it out, and his breath whistled through the new hole in his neck. He lurched forward, hands on the wound. Donna yanked him backwards, stabbed the sharp pick of her glass stem into the side of his neck. Blood spurted from the ragged hole, smothering the woodlands with the hot, coppery reek of the abattoir. She could just see the dark blood that hosed from his neck, pattering on the undergrowth like rain.

He struggled, but she gripped his hair tight, directing the welter of blood away from her. With one arm trying to cover his spurting neck, he tried to grab at her, but she kept out of his reach. Still he pumped buckets of blood, more and more pouring out of him. The ground to her right was soaked dark in a wide arc nearly two feet broad. There seemed to be no end to the pumping, spurting spray. How much blood was in him?

After what felt like hours, Michael's knees bent, and Donna

shoved his body forward so he fell on his face. The blood no longer even burbled from his neck, but leaked in a slow, constant flow.

After a crushing silence, the noises of nature returned. Bugs buzzed and whined, frogs peeped in the background. The smell of blood was overpowering. How would she get it out of her clothes and hair?

What was she going to do now? Her body's need to murder assuaged, she just stood in the clearing, away from everything but Michael's corpse. A strange calm pervaded the clearing, but Donna could feel her heart hammering in her chest.

Donna started awake. She was in her bedroom, her hands cuffed in front of her. Did she smell blood, or was it just a memory?

"Go back to sleep," Jim mumbled next to her. She looked at the clock. Five twenty-eight. Early. Another dream. She wasn't getting back to sleep.

The cuffs were a failure. If these were more than dreams. What else could she do?

Jim was asleep again. Donna uncuffed herself, walked into the living room and turned on the computer. Oakham hadn't had a newspaper for three years, but the *Oakham Advertiser* lived on as an ad-heavy web page. Donna went straight to the obituaries.

Oakham's population was large enough that they listed at least one death a day. Donna went through the previous three weeks, hoping, and dreading that she would see someone she recognized. She almost hoped she'd find the shitbag dogfighter, but none of the pictures matched her fuzzy memories. Were they dreams? They were so specific. She was always a passenger in her body, always murdering some guy. Young guys, old guys, it creeped her out. They were so specific, always bloody and horrible. She'd never dreamed anything so disturbing before.

She'd been at it for fifteen or so minutes when Jim walked into the room.

"Obituaries," he said. "Did you have another one of those dreams?"

"Killed some guy in the woods." She shuddered. "Cut his throat and he took forever to bleed out. Funny thing is I talked to this guy, his name was Michael. Seemed like a nice guy."

"Well, he couldn't have been all that nice if you felt the need to kill him." Jim put his hand on Donna's back. He was warm and real. Her dreams seemed distant and foggy.

"I'm having some kind of breakdown here. Could you not make fun of me?"

"Hey," Jim crouched next to her. "I'm not making fun of you. You're having dreams, and I think you're giving them too much credence. They're dreams, Donna. Just dreams."

"They don't feel like dreams," Donna said.

"Found anything in the obituaries yet?"

"Nobody familiar," Donna conceded.

"Look for as long as you need to."

For the first time, Donna really looked at him. His certainty was so tempting, she wanted to cling to it, let the worries go away. But he didn't know what the hell he was talking about, and she knew it. *He* wasn't dreaming about stabbing people in the forest or feeding scumbags to ravenous dogs.

Jim stood, and kissed her on the forehead before he left. Donna watched him go, her emotions in even more of a mess than they had been. She couldn't resist Jim when he was charming, and she so wanted to just fall into that absolutist mindset of his, knowing that these were just dreams.

But that wasn't her. Struck with a thought, she got up and ran to her closet. Was it as she had left it? She shuffled through the hangers until she found her slinky red dress. Was it hanging oddly? Had she put it back like that?

She buried her face in it, inhaling deeply. The scent of the spray-cleaner overwhelmed her senses. But there was another smell in there, something rank. Sweat? Blood? She pounded a fist into the back of the closet. She couldn't identify it. She didn't know.

No evidence.

"So how are those cuffs working for you?" Fierce smiled over her coffee. Donna had come in late, dragging this morning.

"Not so good," Donna said. "I had another murder dream last night."

"Well that sort of proves it's a dream, doesn't it? You couldn't have sleep-escaped from those handcuffs. And if you had, I think we could totally get you your own TV show."

Donna knocked back a slug of Café Gitan's Big Bruiser, an overlarge tub of coffee that she seldom felt she needed.

"They still feel real, Fierce. I wake up and I can smell the blood. There's got to be something I can do. I hate waking up like that." She took a long, angry gulp of coffee.

Fierce was quiet for a moment, then swallowed some of her own coffee.

"Have you considered sleeping with Prince Valium?"

"I don't know. I try to stay away from medication."

"Sister, you stay away from it until you have a problem. You have a problem."

Fierce had a point. Did the dreams frighten her enough that she wanted to drug herself? She wanted the dreams to stop. What if they did? Would they reappear when she stopped taking the meds? Would she have to take them for the rest of her life? She'd heard about the people who sleepwalked, even drove, when they were taking some sleep medication.

What if she was already being drugged? Who could be drugging her?

"I don't think it's that big a problem," Donna mumbled, looking into her half-full Big Bruiser. "Besides, where am I going to sample something?"

Fierce was uncharacteristically coy, examining her napkin for wrinkles or imperfections. Donna stared at her.

"Tell me you don't just happen to have some in your bag."

Fierce laughed. "I don't carry my meds with me. The stronger ones need a prescription. I could probably get you a sampler, if you thought that was what you needed." She saw Donna's face. "I'm not talking about anything hard, just sleep aids. They really do work."

Donna pinched the bridge of her nose.

"Not right now. I want to see if I can find another solution before I start messing with my head."

"You don't get any prizes for being strong and not getting help," Fierce said. "You get crazy and breakdowns for that.

Believe me when I say I know."

Donna nodded, accepting her friend's wisdom. She should talk to her mother again. Maybe her auntie, as well.

Fierce looked at her watch. "Shit, I gotta hustle to get to BedMart. Alan worries if I'm only five minutes early. Won't pay me for extra minutes, mind, but he's such a basket case that it's worth getting there early so he isn't pacing and sweating."

"I always thought accountants didn't have to hustle." Donna wanted to give Fierce something cheery as a farewell.

"That's what I thought when I started," Fierce said with a sigh. "People just got so impatient in the last decade."

"I'll see you later, Fierce."

The kickboxing class went well. Donna didn't space out, and the exercise lifted her mood. She was feeling the warm glow of a good morning. She had lunch early, and went to her office. Her office at the gym was medium-sized, which let her have her own massage table, and small desk. She also had her own bathroom, which was a fantastic perk.

Danny had helped her set the place up, lay the carpet, hang the sliding door, and she always felt just a twinge of guilt about using the location. Danny had his moments. He'd been useful and handy, and he'd also stolen from her. No man was perfect, but she'd deserved better than him.

Donna draped clean sheets on the massage table. Her phone sang a little ditty, letting her know it was five minutes before her appointment. This was a new client, Nick something or other. She smoothed down her shirt, wondered if she looked professional enough.

She heard a knock at the door.

"Come in."

He was short, maybe a little on the heavy side, Italian or some other Mediterranean background. Greek, maybe? Short black hair with a bit of wave, a pinched mouth covered by a mustache and poorly-kept beard. She extended her hand.

"Hi, I'm Donna."

"Nick." They shook. His hands were cool, his grip limp.

"Have you ever had a massage before?"

He looked her up and down, with special attention to her hips and chest.

"I've had a couple." Which meant that she probably would only have to explain how it worked once.

"So, has anyone ever chased you around your massage table?" He asked.

Donna could feel her jaws clenching with the effort not to tell this asshole to fuck himself.

"I keep a hammer in my bag, just in case something like that comes up." Well, she'd managed to keep her voice level. She wanted to scream at him that she wasn't a sex worker, that what she did wasn't about sex, and that he was soft and she really would go after him with the hammer if he even looked at her funny.

"I was just kidding, heh." His eyes darted to her bag, and then back to her.

"I'm glad that we both understand what massage is and what it isn't," Donna said.

He didn't give her any more trouble. But she took a long, hot shower afterward.

Fierce was off at something, Jim was at White Guys' Club. Every now and then his job required him to spend an evening with his co-workers and talk business, just not on the clock. The skeeviness of Nick hadn't washed off by evening. So Donna was at The Horn by herself. Thus far, no one had hit on her. For that, she was grateful.

Anticipating a long evening alone, she skipped the hard drinks, and stuck to Modelo Especial with lime.

"Drinking alone tonight?" Rich asked. "Where's Mildred?"

"I dunno, maybe writing a letter to one of her kids or something," Donna said. Fierce was right. Rich's well-muscled body was quite lovely. She could imagine the power of his arms, the security of being held by him. She didn't even mind the shaved head, it made him more manly. She also liked the fact that he was brown, too. Oakham was very New England.

"You look tired." He said it with sympathy, or maybe it was just the beer talking. She looked into his eyes, and saw concern.

She was going to say something, but Barry, one of The Horn's regulars, took the moment to signal for a refill.

"Be right back," he said. Donna sighed. The Horn wasn't busy, could she bend Rich's ear? What would she tell him? She took a swig of her beer.

When had she become the sort of barfly that needed to talk to the bartender? Where had all her friends gone? She'd had a lot of them, Eva, Tammy, Lavender, and Angela. Where had they all gone? And when?

"Sorry about that." Rich was back. She'd never noticed how quietly he could move when he tried. "You looked like you were going to say something when I was called away."

"I don't know."

"I wouldn't be a good bartender if I didn't know when someone was having trouble. You're a good customer, and you look like you need someone to talk to."

"Does it show that much?"

"I'm a professional, I watch a lot of people who a little dunk and have their guards down."

"How did you know?" Did that make her sound paranoid? Was she paranoid? Could he tell that she was feeling paranoid?

"It's a trade secret," he said. "They tell you this sort of thing in Bartender school. It's a whole ceremony and a process, and if I tell anyone, the Brotherhood has promised to hang my intestines around my shoulders and bury me a cable's length from shore." Macabre as that was, it broke Donna out of her cycle of worry. She laughed.

"That's weirdly specific. What do they do if there's a Brotherhood violation in Kansas?"

"I suspect we'd fly him, at Brotherhood expense, to the nearest shore with a tide. Colorado's not nearly as problematic as some of the more remote parts of Alberta. There's a movement afoot to dump people at the nearest lake or river, but that seems lazy to me."

"Well, I dunno about that. Breaking with tradition just because it's expensive? There's no worse reason."

"I agree," Rich said. "Sacred trust and all that. It's a small price to pay for the privilege of pouring drinks for drunks, antisocial types, and pick-up artists."

"Can I get a refill here?" The demand came from Ross, three stools down. His tone made it clear that this was not a request.

"See what I mean?" Rich winked at Donna before going over to serve Ross.

He was back after a minute, replacing Donna's dead soldier with a fresh bottle.

"Are we going to flirt all night, or are you going to tell me how you know so much about my day?" Donna asked.

Rich's smile was warm, comforting.

"Usually, you're wearing a top that's a jewel tone; green, blue, or that red that looks so good on you. Right now, you're wearing khaki. You're trying not to be noticed. And that's not like you. You're outgoing, pleasant, with a very generous nature. If you're hiding that under a bushel, then something is wrong."

So simple. Donna shook her head.

"So, are you going to tell me about it?"

Donna covered her hesitation with a swig of beer. Did she want to open up to Rich? She took another swallow of beer, knowing it would help the inevitable.

"First of all, total asshole today. Thought I was a hooker." She was trying to keep her voice down, but the anger made it a fight. "As if I was some sort of compliant piece of meat he was renting."

"Sounds like a real dick. Sorry that happened to you."

"Ruined my day."

Rich was quiet for a moment. "What else?"

"What do you mean?" Donna asked, startled.

"You said 'First of all.' You're strong enough that one jerk didn't ruin your day. What else is going on?"

Donna pursed her lips, letting him know she wasn't pleased.

"I'm having weird dreams. Disturbing dreams." Why did she say that?

"I have one where I'm climbing up a pyramid when a gigantic bloodshot eye appears over it and then tentacles grab me."

Donna's laugh was more an involuntary bark.

"I fucking wish they were like that. No, I've had three

dreams where I murder people. And they're horrible. I can smell the blood, I can see them suffering, hear them screaming."

"Are they people you know?" His question was mild.

"No. I mean, they're all guys. But they've been young and old. One guy was real pond scum, another seemed like he was classy. I mean, why am I dreaming about killing guys?"

"How's the relationship with Jim? You could be displacing, killing guys in your dreams that represent him, but aren't him so you hide your resentment from yourself."

"I didn't realize you went to college," she said.

"Because I work in a bar?"

"I guess I never thought of you studying. You seem more like a go outside and do things sort of guy."

Rich's grin was wide and bright. "I bet I've got a couple of secrets that would surprise you."

"Probably do." Donna could feel herself blushing. She really didn't want to be thinking about the size of his dick.

"Hey Rich?"

"Be with you in a sec, Laura." And he turned back to Donna. "I've got business, and this isn't a good place to talk about secrets. But what do you know about how Oakham was settled?"

"Random much? I dunno, I sort of assume pilgrims settled here because they didn't have the stick jammed up their asses as firmly as everyone else in Boston."

"Well, sort of. The Devil, as they say, is always in the details. You're not entirely wrong. Makepeace Humberton was the leader of a group of well-to-do second and third sons of wealthy Puritans in England, weird as that sounds. He established Oakham to be a haven for alchemists."

"Alchemists." Donna was lost. Where was this going?

"They're a little like occult bartenders. A little of this, a little of that, and soon you've got a magic drink."

"Rich?"

"Yes."

"Is today the day that all men agreed to go totally pants-on-their-head crazy? Was there a meeting where you all got together and said it's time to fuck with Donna?"

Rich nodded, his smile kindly without being condescending.

"There are more things in heaven and earth, if I may quote."

Donna stood, pulled out her purse and slapped money on the bar. "This hasn't been the right day for cryptic bullshit. Sorry, Rich."

She wanted to scream as soon as she was clear of The Horn. Why did people want to fuck with her today? And how had Rich known about Jim?

Somehow, Donna managed to have a normal week. Her classes went fine, her massages went without a hitch. Jim was sweet and thoughtful. Rich at The Horn stopped talking in riddles, and she enjoyed her drinks in peace. Fierce and Café Gitan remained staunchly drama-free.

She realized that she was counting the days since her last dream. She was waiting for the other shoe to drop, for her life to fall apart again. The realization depressed her. She was hiding from… from what? From gore-filled nightmares that came from… where? From herself, that could be the only explanation. No one else could influence her mind in her sleep.

Still, the anxiety built. After a week, she still couldn't relax.

Why did she dream of murder? Was there some sort of lack in her life? A week after the dream of the party, Donna started watching *Friday the 13th* films, to Jim's delight. They seemed most likely to resemble her experiences, a series of murders that had little or no motivation behind them.

She and Jim watched them, one a night. He liked slasher films. She didn't. She hated the victims' roles, the casual interest the camera showed in them until they were murdered. And then it was loving close-ups of their spattery deaths. The gore was tame compared to her dreams. Sometimes, though, the setup, the music, the sudden bloody murder, somehow all resonated, and she felt sick to her stomach. Usually just once in a movie.

Still, she dreaded the next nightmare. And kept wearing the handcuffs at night.

CHAPTER 4

GAS GRILL

Donna knew immediately she was in one of her dreams. She was skulking around a house she didn't recognize, darkness pressing in on her. She went to pull her phone out and see what time it was, but her hand didn't respond. Again, she was a prisoner in her own body.

She knew what was coming. Death. She was going to murder someone in some horrible fashion. Was she possessed by the spirit of Jason Voorhees, randomly killing until someone stopped her? What had she done? Had she read a forbidden book or touched a cursed item? She had to sin before she was punished, wasn't that how these things worked?

Despite her inner turmoil, she was moving. With slow deliberation, she stalked across the yard. She saw a lot of room between this house and the next, a well-to-do house, if this was even in Oakham. Where else could they be? She'd never been anywhere else.

She crept her way into the golf-course perfect backyard. Bark mulch surrounded each tree trunk in a precise wheel. She could see no garden, but the house had a deck. And she seemed to be headed in that direction. Four flagstones led to the stairs, and then she was standing on the deck.

Before her stood the most impressive gas grill she had ever seen. Immaculate burnished steel gleamed, even in the cloudy night. It had more knobs than the stove in her apartment. A broad hood, four feet wide, covered the burners. Her hand flicked a switch, and the temperature gauge lit up, as did the back-lighting on all the knobs. Donna would have gasped, if she could control her breathing. This thing must have cost a fortune.

She knelt, and opened the valve for the gas. With a twist and a click, the burners lit. She set the hood back down, turned, and banged on the glass door that led into the house. The interior looked pleasantly appointed, with a leather love seat set in front of a monstrous flat screen. She pounded on the glass door again.

The man who appeared was probably forty, with a mustache that didn't distract from the bald spot in the middle of his brown hair. He wore a monogrammed blue bathrobe that looked very comfortable, but did little to conceal the paunch beneath.

He put on his glasses and peered at her through the glass door. But his eye caught on something behind her, the illuminated grill. His cheeks flushed with rage, he slid the door open and stepped out of the house.

Her fist hammered into the side of his face, slamming him into the doorframe. He screamed as he went down, his glasses clattering to the deck. He scrabbled around for his glasses, but her fist smashed into his face, sending him sprawling. She brought her booted heel down on his hand as he tried to get away from her. She ground her weight into the hand, and heard the crunch of bones.

He screamed and curled into a ball, cradling his broken hand. Donna brought her heel down on his face once, twice, three times. He shrieked his pain out of bloody, broken lips. He spat out a tooth. As the breath burbled from his swollen mouth, she crouched, whipped the belt off his robe, gagged him, tying it tight around his head.

He tried to bring his hands up to untie the knot, but the fingers on his right hand wouldn't work. Grabbing him by the back of the collar, she hauled him to his feet. In the dim light, the unrestrained robe fell open, his flaccid penis flapping, a comic counterpoint to his struggles.

One hand on his collar, the other forcing the broken hand behind his back, Donna frog-marched him across the deck. He started to resist when he realized he was headed for his gleaming silver grill. Donna just tightened her grip, grinding the bones in his hand together. The pain dropped him to his knees, sobbing. She hauled him back to his feet. With a grunt, she shoved him hard enough that he fell to his knees in front of his monstrous grill.

He looked up at her, the gag still in place, eyes imploring.

She grabbed the collar of his bathrobe, and pulled him up. With her other hand, she opened the hood, freeing a burst of burning hot air. They looked at each other, just for a moment. She saw nothing but fear. She slammed his head down on the grill. The black smoke of his burned hair wafted, acrid, into her nostrils. His screams were no less piteous, muffled by the gag.

He flailed a hand onto the grill, trying to lever himself off the burning metal bars, but his hand sizzled and his muffled screaming got worse. He didn't have the strength, or the resolve, to press himself up.

She lifted him up, as if checking to see if a steak was done, and Donna screamed inside her own head in horror. The right side of his face was a horror show, blackened like an overdone porterhouse. His right eye had shrunk in on itself, recessed into its socket, the eyelid charred closed. Even if she stopped now, he would never look normal again. The reek of burned hair and seared flesh was nauseating.

He groaned, his breathing coming in wheezing gasps. His knees almost buckling, some horrible survival instinct keeping him upright.

She shoved him down on the hot grill. His arms tried to find purchase, to push away from the heat, but Donna used both hands to keep him down, one on top of his head, the other on his shoulder.

The end was quick. His tortured breathing got shallower, and he stopped twitching and moaning. When she finally let the body slump off the hot grill, the right half of his face was a charred ruin. The skin had burned away, roasting the muscles into a horrific mummy's mask of cooked meat.

Donna tried to close her eyes and wish it all away. Nothing worked.

She woke in bed, in her familiar bedroom, the stench of charred meat filling the apartment. She ran to the bathroom, almost missing the toilet as she heaved up what little was left of last night's dinner. The scent clung to her, filled her nostrils. When she closed her eyes, she could only see the charred face, the dried-out eye socket. And the reek of burned flesh wouldn't go away. She washed her mouth out with water from the sink, but the smell of burned meat still clung to her.

"Hey, you OK?" Jim was at the door. One hand held a spatula covered in grease. "I thought I'd…"

She barreled past him, away from the horrifying stink of seared flesh. She ran out of the apartment, into the hallway. It wasn't far enough. Outside, she leaned on the side of the building. The summer sun dappled the ground through the open leaves overhead. It was quiet out here. The scent of pine washed over her, purging the smoke, and Donna could think again.

This was getting worse. The intensity of the dreams, the brutality of the violence. She couldn't take it. What could she do? She looked at the grass, the blue sky, felt the brush of wind on her face. This was real. The ground under her feet, the sky above her. They helped chase the fear and the pain away.

"Hey." Donna jumped. Jim had managed to sneak up on her. "You alright?" He tilted his head. "Another one of those dreams?"

Donna nodded.

"I cooked us some eggs and bacon for breakfast."

He stopped when Donna held up her hand.

"Not the right morning," she gasped out.

He tilted his head again.

"What's up?"

"Some really horrific shit, OK? Bad dreams, really violent dreams." Unbidden, the image of the man's face surfaced in her mind, the charred skin, the burned hair. She shuddered.

Jim moved in to hug her, but the stink of charred meat clung to his clothes. She tried to move away, but he grabbed at her. She struggled out of his smothering grasp.

"Fuck off," she said. She felt bad immediately. It wasn't his fault. He didn't understand.

"What did I do?" He stood back, arms at his side.

"Not you, it's me," she said. "Still too involved with the dream."

"Do we need to do something about them? How can I help?" And her heart melted right there. He cared. He cared so much. He wanted to help, he was there for her. She turned around and hugged him, fighting down her nausea.

"Hey, what's that all about?"

She stepped back, allowed herself to breathe again. The stink of bacon faded.

"I know I've been difficult for the past couple of…" months? How long had this been going on? She was losing her sense of time. She'd drifted off mid-sentence. Jim was staring at her. "Weeks. Sorry. I've been difficult, and you've been nothing but supportive." A little lie, and she knew it. "I just wanted to say thanks. Because you've been here for me. I'm trying to figure some stuff out, and it's making me prickly, and all too often, I snap at you because you're right there."

Did she really need to apologize? Yes. When you loved someone, you mended bridges.

"Let's go get some breakfast," he said.

Donna let him lead her into the apartment. She nibbled at the generous portion of eggs he slathered into her plate, but let him have all the bacon. She couldn't watch him as he ate, the sound of his teeth gnashing together on the fried fatty bacon unsettled her stomach. It wasn't long before she had to concentrate on her breathing to fight off her rising nausea. Her eggs were not going to stay down if she kept smelling the cooked meat.

She pulled out her cell phone.

"I have to go. Gotta have coffee with Fierce," she lied.

She stood, and he leaned his face up for a kiss. She hesitated. That grotesque mouth, glistening with the fat he had just consumed. She kissed him, quick as she could. And was out of the apartment before she wiped her face with a napkin.

It was going to be a tough day.

At ten minutes past eleven, Donna was sitting in Tim's office, nursing memories of being in trouble in middle school.

"Are you doing OK, Donna?" Tim sat behind his well-ordered desk, armored by space and neatness.

"How do you mean, exactly?"

"Has there been stress in your life, recently? Have you lost a relative, moved, or anything like that?"

Donna hesitated.

"I'm only asking because I care," Tim said.

"Jim and I have been going through a bit of a bad patch," Donna said. It wasn't entirely a lie. But she didn't like confiding in Tim. Work was work, and home life should be home life. Tim taking an interest felt intrusive.

"Trish Camroux said you freaked out this morning," Tim said.

"I think she overreacted."

"She said you screamed 'fuck my life' in the middle of class." He waited for Donna to respond. She couldn't remember doing it, but had little doubt she had. When she didn't say anything, Tim continued. "You are, and continue to be, a tremendous asset to the gym. If there's any way I can help, let me know. You know I value you as a teacher…"

Donna could smell the 'but' coming on.

"… but we can't have you shouting at the clients."

Tim had started using corporate nonspeak about two years ago. The empty words and recycled phrases tumbled out of his mouth. Donna missed the days when she could have a sensible conversation with him.

"I understand, and I'll make sure it doesn't happen again," she said.

"I just want you to understand what's at stake, here. The concepts of individual loyalty, reopportunizing and brand fidelity are essential to our operation. We must maintain best comfort practices in order to incentivize customer return, and our customer resources are increased only by spontaneous report which can only happen if the word proactively increases our brand value."

Donna nodded, trying not to look like a deer caught in the headlights, however much she felt like one. Tim had been good to her, taken a chance in hiring her. Her classes did well, she made the majority of her income from them. Plus, it would be a major pain in the ass to pull up stakes and haul her ass to another gym. But not impossible.

"I get that word-of-mouth is a big part of expanding the business, Tim. And I also know that what I did might hurt business. But I really think they're going to talk a lot more about me than they are about the gym. I... had my little moment, and people are going to associate it with me, rather than the gym." Renee had already texted to ask her about it.

"I don't want you to feel unwelcome. You are essential to this business's operation. You've got the second-largest following of all our personal trainers, and the best attendance rate. I value you, in a business and a personal sense."

Tim thought a lot more of their friendship than Donna did. But she'd had worse bosses.

"Thank you," she said. "I know it's difficult for you to call anyone on the carpet. I really hope that nothing ill comes of it, and that I haven't damaged your good name with my outburst."

Tim liked his apologies grovelly. She pictured his face, broken and beaten with a shovel, the scent of blood filling her nostrils. She snapped herself out of the vision.

Tim smiled, the benevolent boss who could overlook the lapses of his fallible employees.

"I'm sure no harm was done. We can leave this in the past and move on."

"We certainly can, Tim. I'll make sure I don't do that again. I'm taking better care of myself, and I promise I won't drag my private issues into the gym again."

Tim beamed, his stupid fucking smile so broad you'd think he'd actually done something.

"I'm so glad we could come to this agreement."

Donna saw herself out.

Donna's nausea had eased by evening. She'd eaten a few energy bars throughout the day. It was impossible to see the square protein bars as having belonged to an animal. Or a face. Not wanting to go home, she went to The Horn when her day was over. Not to drink, she reminded herself, but to cool off. To be away from Jim. To not be by herself.

She was drinking water. Given her limited food intake, that seemed safest.

"Where's Rich?" She asked.

"Tenth circle of Hell." Peter was a little shorter than Rich, and paler. His lashes weren't as come-hither, either. But Peter shaved his head, like Rich, and they dressed in similar fashion. Some people said they were hard to tell apart, but you could hide a family of rabbits in Peter's bushy beard. Rich kept his neatly trimmed.

"Is that another bar?"

"He wishes. He's in line at the DMV, and his tablet is out of power."

"Harsh."

"How did we all get along before we took our electronics everywhere?"

Donna shrugged. "I sort of assumed people sat like docile sheep while in line, or brought actual books with them everywhere."

"But if you bring the book, people know what you're reading." Peter said it with a smile and a shrug. "Sometimes I don't want people to know I'm reading *Tight Ends in Chains*."

"Is that reading, or more flicking through the pictures?" Donna said.

"Maybe a bit of both. Why, did you want to borrow it?"

Donna laughed. The first genuine one she'd had all day. She could feel the tension in her back start to ease.

"Peter, can I ask you a question?"

"Is this one of those conspiracy questions? No, I'm not a Mason."

"Serious for a moment."

Peter looked the bar up and down. Nobody seemed to need his services right then.

"Ask away."

"Are you and Rich into…" The question ground itself to a halt. What was she going to ask about? *Are you an alchemist* seemed forward.

"Are you into weird stuff?" She knew it was the wrong

question as soon as it was out of her mouth.

"You mean like other than tattoos, bondage porn, and each other?"

Donna knew her smile was weak. Why was she pussyfooting around? Well, she liked them. They were cute together. They had a good bar. Did she think Peter was going to ban her for asking an odd question?

She sighed. "I mean magic."

"Magic." His response was flat. Donna could read nothing in that one word.

"Rich talked about alchemy last week. It was weird."

Peter nodded, frowning into his beard.

"Are you in some sort of trouble?"

"What?" She sounded frightened, even in her own ears.

"Nothing specific. Just if your life isn't going the way you think it should, Rich might bring up magic. Or alchemy."

"What does that mean?"

"He's just talking about being a bartender. You mix the drinks, and a little magic happens.

"Don't bullshit me." Donna's hands gripped the edge of the bar. "He compared it to bar tending specifically. He was not talking metaphorically."

He eyed her from under his brows. He opened his mouth, but Donna held up a finger.

"If you're going to start on another layer of bullshit, think again. There's bad shit happening in my life, and I don't have the time or the patience to fuck up everyone who needs it, but I'm willing to put your name on the list."

Peter raised an eyebrow, and Donna almost apologized. That had come out a bit stronger than intended. But she would stick to it. She was sick of lies and uncertainty.

"I see." Peter was serious, not defensive. "What kind of bad shit?"

"I asked first." He wasn't getting off the hook that way.

Again, the silence, broken by the sounds of the bar, someone coughing from one of the tables, the sound of ice being swirled in an empty glass, the clunk of a bottle being placed on the wooden bar, the murmur of hushed conversation. Donna twirled her half-empty glass of water.

"We are practicing chaos magicians," he said.

"I thought you guys weren't supposed to wear short sleeves."

Peter almost cracked a smile. "It means that we believe that we can influence the world in ways that most people don't think are possible."

Donna took a slug of her water.

"Could you turn my water into a Manhattan?"

"It doesn't work that way."

"So you can only do things that can't be immediately seen or measured."

"Not exactly. It's not something I can do parlor tricks with."

Donna sighed.

"So what kind of bad shit are you experiencing?" Peter's request was as gentle as could be imagined.

Donna considered telling him to fuck himself. He'd beaten completely around the bush when she'd asked him about his so-called magic. But she felt defeated, by the dreams, by Peter, by everything.

"Can you make people dream things?"

Peter leaned over the bar, genuine concern in his eyes.

"Seriously, what are you dreaming?"

She considered him, the desire to talk almost gone. The shift in his attitude frightened her.

"I'm dreaming that I'm killing people."

"People you know? People who have been mean to you?"

"No. They're random; old, young, whatever. It's always at night."

"So it's like a TV killing? Just bang, and they're dead?"

"Jesus, I wish. No, they're always horrible and messy and there's blood and there's always these smells that I hate." She shuddered. "They're never clean, they're always horrible."

"You ever see someone die? Not dreaming it, I mean actually see anyone die?"

Donna shook her head and took a drink.

"What the fuck?" She almost spat it out. She'd been expecting water, not the bitterness she was tasting. What the hell?

It took her half a minute to recognize the vermouth, whiskey, and bitters of a Manhattan.

"You switched my drink."

"If you think that's what it was, then yes, I switched your drink."

She glared at him. Peter crossed his arms.

"I don't know exactly what's going on with your dreams," he said. "But you are mixed up in something strange. There's a couple of people I could talk to. If you want me to."

Donna sighed and rubbed her temples. Why was everyone so determined to make today as surreal as possible? Still, she considered Peter's offer. She'd been unable to do anything to stop her dreams herself. What could she do? Who could it harm? But she didn't know who he was going to talk to. Would they know Jim? Tim, her boss? But the dreams were killing her. She dreaded sleep, she worried all day. This wasn't her life anymore. This was prison.

"Go ahead." She felt a little better just talking about it. Peter was a good guy, but they didn't hang out together or anything. Maybe it was that whole 'telling a stranger' thing.

"What do I owe you?" she asked, pulling up her purse.

Peter's smile was self-satisfied. "On the house." Which wasn't like him at all.

Three days after the horrific dream, Donna was spending the evening watching a film with Jim. Some sort of war picture, Donna wasn't even sure what war it was, but she was willing to bet that the black guy would get it first. Other than that, she was bored. When the phone rang, all she felt was relief.

"I'll be back in just a minute. Go ahead and watch without me," she told Jim.

"Donna, it's your aunt Ana."

"So good to hear from you." Donna's heart leaped at hearing her aunt's voice. Tia Ana almost never called.

"Donna, how have you been?"

"All right. Classes are full. I'm a bit stressed, but it's going pretty well."

"Boston's quite nice. We're only a couple of hours away. You should come see us, if you can get away."

"You know I can't."

Silence from the other end of the phone.

"You know I can't." Donna repeated.

"I wish you would give your phobia up."

"It's not a phobia, Tia Ana. I really can't leave Oakham."

"Donna, you're being ridiculous. It's one thing not to come see us, but to insist that somehow you can't leave that one-Starbucks town is ridiculous. More than ridiculous, it's insulting to the people you never manage to visit."

Donna was quiet, listened to her own breathing, and the silence coming from her phone. What could she say?

"Is that all you wanted to call about, Auntie?"

"I'm sorry, Donna. I haven't been having a good day either."

"What's wrong?" Donna asked.

"Call it guy trouble."

"Carlos? He's usually so good to you. What's wrong with him?"

Ana's laugh was bitter.

"It's your job to be on my side," she said. "You're family."

"That changes nothing. You're my aunt and by definition, a living saint."

Ana's laugh changed. Donna knew how to charm her, turn her mood.

"You are a bundle of trouble, Donna. But it's always good to talk to you."

"I should call more. I love you Auntie."

"Right back at you," Ana said.

Which was just about par for a family discussion, Donna thought. A quick fight and then a makeup almost as rapid.

"Your mother sent me a picture of your father, a long time ago."

Donna's heart somersaulted. *What*? She had never known her father. Why would he be of any use or connection to her? Like so much in her life, when she was growing up, a father was something other people had. But he'd come up recently, and Donna wanted to know more.

Which reminded her. She needed to call her mother.

"Donna?" Tia Ana's voice pulled Donna out of her thoughts. "Could you send me that picture?"

"Sure. I've got your address. I don't think I'm going to need a photo of him."

"I love you and will name my first born child after you."

"What if it's a boy?"

"Especially if it's a boy," Donna shot back. "I would totally ruin my offspring's life because I made an offhand promise. Because I love you so damn much." She drew out the last three words as if she were in the throes of orgasm.

"How did a nut like you ever come out of your mother?" Ana was laughing, and it was infectious.

"Probably because I spent too much time around you," Donna accused.

They laughed until tears leaked out of the corners of Donna's eyes. Ana was truly a lifeline, someone she'd always been able to get silly with. Talking to her made the problems smaller, let her know she wasn't all alone.

Jim came into the kitchen, a frown on his face.

"What's so funny?" Jim asked. "You're making a lot of racket."

The laughter died, and so did Donna's smile.

"I gotta go, Auntie. It was great to talk to you."

"I'll remember to send you that picture," Ana said.

"Thanks. Bye."

And then there was silence.

"I didn't mean to interrupt," Jim started.

"Don't worry about it," Donna said.

"You look a little down in the mouth."

"It was a moment, Jim." One he couldn't share, no matter how much he tried.

"Let's go finish our movie."

CHAPTER 5

NECKLACE

Donna was walking toward a garage. She tried to turn her head and see where she was, but her head refused to move. The darkness was cloying. Was she even in Oakham? She couldn't see any streetlights.

How had she gotten here?

Hunching her shoulders, she walked up to the baby blue garage. She reached down and slowly pulled the garage door open.

The interior was a horror show of potential murder weapons. She couldn't look at the tire irons without thinking about caving someone's head in. The cordless drill was a torture implement in the Middle East, wasn't it? The rows of gleaming screwdrivers were just daggers waiting to be used. Wrenches could be used to bludgeon or crush. Oh God.

She wondered what this gearhead had done to deserve a visit from her. What had any of them done? She looked at the shiny, perfectly-buffed car that took up the other bay of the garage. Some sort of sixties muscle car. The owner probably spent a lot of time talking about his big engine.

Donna was rummaging through one of the toolboxes. What was she looking for? She cringed internally as her hands came up with a roll of duct tape.

She slung it up her wrist like a bulky bracelet, and approached the car. She took a moment to look at it, traced a finger down the meticulous detailing. Someone probably spent more time with this car than they did with their family. She put her palms under the lip where the window fit into the top of the door. She stepped back, squatted, and shoved.

The car alarm screamed like a castrated elephant. Donna stumbled away, shocked by the amount of noise pouring out of the car. She managed to get behind the door before it opened. A white-haired man entered, pushed a button on his keychain, and the silence beat on her eardrums. Her hand was a fist, and she caught him at the base of the skull. He stumbled forward, crashed into his immaculate car. The alarm started screaming again.

With speed and force, she had him face-down on the concrete, wrapping his wrists with the duct tape, then his ankles. When he was helpless, she rolled him over, went through his pockets until she found his keys. When the alarm stopped, all she could hear was the blood pounding in her ears. No traffic, nobody walking by.

She looked down at her victim.

"Who are you?" Those were his last words before she taped his mouth. His eyes continued to implore. She wondered what else he loved, who he had been. He was going to die, and she couldn't do anything about it.

Her movements were more casual, now. She had time. She rolled a spare tire toward him, then lifted it and put it over his head. It dropped heavily on his shoulders, but he remained kneeling.

When she picked up the gasoline, he started screaming through the tape. She could see his eyes, wide and terrified, begging. He could do nothing. She could do nothing.

The gasoline filled the tire, but some of it got on him. He clamped his eyes shut, but it had to sting. Any tears he shed were lost in the dribbles of gas running down his face.

Donna pulled a box of matches out of her shirt pocket. He stopped trying to protest, and just wept. This was going to be it, then.

With slow cruelty, whatever made her body do this horrible shit lit the match, then brought it to her lips, blowing it out. She struck another, and flicked it at the captive man. He flinched, falling over and spilling the gasoline from the tire. Donna watched the liquid flow under the car. At least the two would be united. She wondered if the fire would burn hot enough to fuse him to the machine he had loved so much.

Her fingers flicked a third match, and with a *whuff*, he ignited.

His screams were muffled by the tape, but no less horrible for that. He rolled and tried to scream, unable to escape either the tire or the hungry flames. Greasy black smoke roiled to the ceiling, and the air started to get thick. She watched, covering her mouth, as his skin turned black and cracked. He thrashed as best he could, rolling on the concrete floor in agony. Donna walked out of the garage.

The sound of a car ignition caught her attention, and she woke up.

She rolled out of bed, the cutting stink of burned tire and gasoline filling her nose. She grabbed the key to her handcuffs. Jim was just waking up next to her, but she left the room so fast he didn't have time to say anything.

Donna was in her jeans and a T-shirt, had the keys to the car, and was out the door in less than four minutes.

The rush of the open road was intoxicating. An uncertain future looked better and more inviting than the horrors she was leaving behind. She could still smell the reek of burned flesh and gasoline, and she had to choke back the urge to pull over and be sick until there was nothing left in her stomach.

Acceleration pressed her into her seat and the forested outskirts of Oakham flashed past. The green treetops were rich against the cloudless blue of the unlimited sky. Once she was away from Oakham, she would be free. She could go anywhere.

Something punched her in the back of the head. Her eyes blurred, and she had to fight to keep her gorge down. She took her foot off the accelerator, but she could no longer focus on the road. Her head felt like it had been split open with a hatchet. Screaming the foulest phrases she knew didn't help. Nothing did. Her foot came off the accelerator, unable to deal with the pain and driving at the same time.

She wrenched the car to the shoulder of the road, and barely got out before she heaved the remnants of last night's dinner. The nausea didn't stop. She knelt in the hard gravel by the side of the road, trying to bring up everything she had ever eaten. The tiny part of her that wasn't terrified she was going to start vomiting blood tried to figure out how she was going to get back to Oakham.

Clenching her jaw, controlling the spasms in her gut, she crawled back into her car. Turning the ignition was a chore. She was in such pain that she could only hope that she didn't hit anyone as she pulled a U-turn across two lanes, and pointed her car back towards Oakham. She lost concentration for a moment, gagged hard enough that bile trickled down her chin. She wiped it on her sleeve, trying to keep an eye on her speed and the road, while making sure she didn't chuck over the dashboard. Her ragged breathing frightened her.

"Welcome to Oakham" said the sign ahead of her. The moment she passed it, the headache went away, her eyes focused again. The urge to vomit eased.

Donna pulled over, this time because tears were blurring her vision. The highway was quiet, only the occasional car passing as she wept into her hands. She was trapped. Whatever was happening to her, she couldn't escape.

"Fuck!" She pounded the steering wheel with her palm. "Rat-shit-fucking-assholes and their fucking shit!" What was she going to do now? She couldn't run. She was murdering people. Why her? What had she ever done?

She slumped forward on the wheel, resting her head on her forearms. Enough of the self-pity. She sat back up, wiped her face with the back of her wrist. She didn't know why she was doing this stuff. She had only the smallest shred of doubt, or was it hope, that she was not committing these murders. What was she going to do? What could she do?

Go big or go home, the T-shirt said. Personal restraint hadn't worked. Her life was going to pieces. She couldn't even sleep without fear. What was going on? And why?

She wasn't going to get any answers by the side of the road. With a resigned sigh, she started the car up.

The entrance to the police station was institutional and cold. A few displays in glass cases showed off the gear, but no weapons, of officers past. And Oakham's obsession with its own history was on full display, including pre-World War One constables' uniforms. She looked at the mannequins for advice. They offered none. Which was good. She might be cracking up, but at least inanimate objects weren't talking to her.

The face behind the bullet-proof glass looked bored. He looked up, smiled as he took a moment to look her up and down. Only when he had taken the time to stare at every inch of her did he start to do his job.

"How can I help you?"

"I need to talk to an officer, if I could."

"Can I ask what this is about?"

Fucking small-town Oakham cops. Donna tried not to grind her teeth. What if she was reporting a rape or domestic abuse? Having to admit anything to this stranger with no authority who had just checked her out? Fucking asshole.

"I need to talk to someone *knowledgeable* about the legalities of protective custody." Her voice was more brittle than she'd intended. It didn't help that her guts still hurt from puking.

"Where are you from?"

"Oakham born and raised," she said. He wouldn't have asked a white girl that. Fucking racist prick.

The guy behind the glass nodded, then pushed the buzzer. Donna shouldered the door open. Her cop was older, but fit, bald as a stone, with bad teeth to boot.

He offered his hand. "I'm Officer Kutsenko."

What was she going to say now?

He led her to a claustrophobically brown room with a table and a pair of chairs.

"What can we do for you?" After the experience with the desk guy, Donna found Officer Kutsenko's attempt at friendliness creepy.

"I want to be taken into protective custody." There. She'd said it.

"Who do you need protection from? You'll need to be very specific."

"I don't need protection." Was she really going to confess? She thought of the man burning in his garage, his stifled screams of agony as his skin blackened, and the fat bubbled out of the cracks. "I'm killing people."

Kutsenko blinked and, to his credit, absorbed the information.

"All right. Where have you been committing these murders?"

"I'm not sure, but here in Oakham. I've killed five men." The urge to just blurt it all out was almost overwhelming. Just being able to talk about this with someone, even if this was her last free moment.

Kutsenko's compressed his lips. "How recently?"

"Within the last four weeks. I beat one to death with a shovel, fed another to his caged fighting dogs. I killed a guy by melting his face on a barbecue grill, and last night, I burned a man to death in his garage."

He digested this slowly.

"Five murders, all here in Oakham."

"Yes."

"Why don't you start at the beginning, and tell me who you murdered first, how and why you did it." Officer Kutsenko's attention was a palpable thing. He was listening intently, and she wasn't used to that.

"It was night, and I crept up on this guy I didn't know. He was working in his garage. And I picked up a long-handled shovel and I smashed him in the face with it. He seemed, I dunno, maybe like a nice guy? It was hard to tell."

"What did he look like?"

"He was an older guy, maybe in his late sixties. Had a beard."

"Where did you find him?"

"I don't know. I was just sort of there."

"You didn't know him, you don't know where he lived. Do you know why—"

He stopped when they both heard a knock at the door. They looked at each other. Apparently, he hadn't been expecting this either.

He stood and went to the door. He opened it a crack.

"Yeah?"

"I understand there's a woman in here who's confessing to some murders." Who was Kutsenko talking to? She didn't recognize the voice, and she couldn't see from where she sat. She should do something. She should feel something. She just felt exhausted and unsatisfied, like she hadn't been able to finish what she'd started.

"Yeah." She didn't know Kutsenko that well, but she could hear the annoyance in his voice.

"You better leave her to me."

"Pardon me, sir?"

"I'm pulling you out, and taking this over myself."

"This is a breach of protocol and good sense."

"It is neither, and I'll explain why later."

"Can I at least stay here and observe?"

"You're a good cop, Jerry, and I don't want to see you get all tangled up in this. Step out, and we'll talk later."

The door opened wide. And with a last look at her, Kutsenko left.

The new cop had a bigger belly, a bigger star, neatly-combed salt and pepper hair, and glasses. Meaty hands moved the chair, which creaked in protest when he sat opposite her.

"Why couldn't Kutsenko stay?" She asked.

The new guy extended a hand across the table.

"I'm Peter Schenck, the Chief of Police for Oakham." A frozen chill ran down Donna's back.

"OK." Donna was going to take this slowly. When she did not reciprocate the extended hand, he withdrew his.

"Now, I understand that you're confessing to a series of murders." She didn't like Schenck's condescending tone.

"Yes."

"Right here in Oakham."

"Yeah." Donna already regretted coming here. Kutsenko had listened. Schenck already had a point he was getting to.

"That puts me in a difficult situation, *chica*. You see, there haven't been any murders in Oakham for close to eight months. And we're pretty sure we got the guy who did it. So what I want to know is what a pretty young woman like you is doing confessing to nonexistent crimes."

Donna sat back in her chair, her teeth clenched.

"Could you send the nice officer back so I can speak with him?"

"I've got more authority than he does. You definitely want to talk to me."

"He wasn't a condescending prick."

Schenck's eyes narrowed.

"You're obviously distraught, and I understand that. But there are limits to what I have to take. I want you to consider your next words very carefully."

Donna could feel her stubbornness wanting to tell this asshole to get fucked. But the words died in the back of her throat. This wouldn't get her anywhere. And she didn't want to stay in this guy's local cell. She shouldn't have come here at all.

"I'm sorry, you're entirely correct." Her tone was sweetness and light. She had to get out of here. And the fastest way to do that was to swallow her rage. "It's my time of the month, and I was having a lot of bad dreams, and I think this was a cry for attention."

Schenck wasn't sure what to make of this. But he'd told her that she couldn't have murdered anyone. How could he hold her?

"We aren't here for your amusement, or as a substitute for your therapy, girl. I've got a lot on my plate without you wasting my time on imaginary crimes."

"I see. I'm sorry to take up your time, Mr. Schenck."

He leaned over the desk, pressing his point.

"I'm glad to see that we've sorted this out. If you ever need to talk to the police again, you are certainly invited to call me directly." He held out his card.

Donna clenched her hand into a fist to keep it from shaking. She took the card, waited for him to add something else. When he didn't, she stood, turned, and walked out of the room. Schenck didn't try to stop her.

The hum of the busy police station was like an alien planet after the silence of the interrogation room. Donna could feel everyone staring at her back as she walked away. But she didn't look around. She put one foot in front of the other, fighting the urge to run the whole way back to her car. Even in the car she didn't feel safe.

She pulled into her apartment complex's parking lot, turned off the engine. Only then did she vent her boiling fury, screaming with the windows rolled up. What the hell had just happened? More bullshit piled on top of all the other strange shit that had happened in the last month. When would it end?

She was still swearing at the top of her lungs when a knock at the window made her jump. She turned, ready to tell whoever it was to fuck themselves, and saw Jim.

She opened the door, and was in his arms. She could rely on Jim. Or at least, she could ignore enough of his behavior to cling to him.

"You didn't answer your cell phone, I didn't know where you were." He whispered into her hair as they just stood, holding each other in the parking lot. "I was so afraid." She clung to him tighter.

When she could, she let go of him.

"You left without saying anything," he said. "I took the day off. I don't know if you can, but why don't we spend today together? You've been having a rough time, and I thought we could just bum around the house and chill."

Donna grabbed onto the proffered line like she was drowning.

"I think I need that."

They ordered Chinese for lunch and watched a couple of Donna's comfort movies. The lack of stress started to make her feel normal, safe. Once she was back on stable footing, Donna spent her couch time thinking. What could she do next?

The handcuffs hadn't worked. Maybe if she could put the key somewhere she couldn't reach them in her sleep. Lock them somewhere she couldn't reach? Building herself an actual cage seemed elaborate. She sure as shit wasn't going to sleep in a kennel. But how about a locked room? How much did her sleeping self want to get out and kill people? Maybe a sleep aid, much as she hated resorting to drugs. But every time she tried to keep herself in bed, she failed. And someone ended up dead.

Assuming they were dead. The cop's assertion that there

hadn't been any murders in Oakham had rattled her. She'd searched the papers, on the assumption that any murders in a town like Oakham would be headline news. Nothing.

She poked at the back of her hand. The bruise had faded. Maybe she really was getting worked up over nothing. The faded bruise had been the only evidence she had ever had of the reality of her dreams. Still, she shuddered at her memories.

Two days later, Jim treated them both to a spa. Hot tub soaks, and a couples' massage went a long way to easing her body, and Donna forgot about her troubles for a few hours.

In the morning, after some of the best sleep she'd had in weeks, Donna resolved that she wasn't going to let this, whatever it was, take over. She could control her life.

CHAPTER 6

LOUISVILLE SLUGGER

Wet grass whispered against Donna's boots. She was in her short black dress, creeping at the edge of a well-manicured lawn. Why? Why did she end up this way? What drove her to do this sort of awful thing? She knew these weren't dreams any more. Even if she didn't know who they were, they were still people. They didn't deserve this.

The yard was empty, the sound of cars distant. No headlights swept the yard. The insects were shrieking loudly. She strode across the yard, toward the house. She couldn't tell the color of the house in the night, merely that it was a dark color with no deck or back porch. Two stories, with a small back house. She was making a beeline for the door.

As she wondered about the identities of the people inside, she found herself reaching out and trying the back door. It was unlocked. Goddamn safe, trusting, out-of-the-way Oakham folks. What the hell was wrong with them?

The interior was gloomy, only dim light falling through the door she'd just entered. A baseball bat lay against the door frame. Some sort of home defense system? She picked it up, felt the heft.

Shit.

She crept through the short back house, found the door to the house proper. Another home invasion.

The lower floor of the house was neat and silent, in an abandoned suburban sort of way. This was a kitchen, linoleum on the floor, no dishes in the sink. They took good care of their home, cleaned up after themselves. To the left was a door, and she opened it.

She was in a sort of crafts room. Hanks of yarn spilled out of wide shelves, scissors, a hot glue gun, a sewing machine on a custom table. A wooden chair sat in front of the table. If she did crafty stuff, this was the setup she would have wanted. Of course, she would probably leave the stuff all over the place.

She paused, as if considering. She didn't like the pointy options this place represented. The scissors, sharp needles, seam rippers, not to mention the horrible shit that could be done with a hot glue gun. She still had a decade-old scar on her forearm from the last time she'd tried to glue some rhinestones onto her jeans.

Donna went back to the kitchen, carefully grasped the door, then firmly closed it.

Shit! She struggled to push her feet out the door into the back house, but instead, she sneaked back into the craft room. There, she found a length of clothesline. She dropped it on the floor, then went back to the closed door between the kitchen and the craft room. She stood behind the door's arc, and waited.

After a few long minutes, she heard the quiet tread of someone coming down the stairs. The baseball bat was still in her hand. Why was she doing this? The questions kept on coming, and nothing, not even Rich and Peter, made sense.

The footsteps, trying to be stealthy, came closer. They crossed the kitchen, the slippers making a soft *clack clack* on the linoleum. Then they came back towards the door, and Donna felt herself holding her breath. The door creaked slowly open, and a hand with a pug-nosed revolver came into view. He was leading with the weapon, a flashlight gripped in his other hand. He didn't push the door open enough to press on her.

His mistake.

He moved into the room at a cautious, slow pace. Donna never took her eyes off the gun. He was halfway into the room now, enough that she could see his naked arm all the way up to the elbow.

The bat whipped up, catching him on the wrist. He shouted in pain and surprise and the gun fell to the floor. Donna swung the bat around the door at abdomen height, and was rewarded with a grunt and the sound of a heavy body falling to the ground. Donna stepped out from behind the door.

He was on the floor in his black boxers, short brown hair, wiry arms. He held his wrist, not knowing what was coming next, staring up at her with big, frightened eyes.

In a flash, he was scrabbling away from her, lunging for his gun. She brought the bat down on the back of his calf. Bone snapped. He screamed.

She was on him in a second, gripping the bat in both hands and shoving it against the back of his head. He got his hands under him and tried to twist, but she gave him a vicious kick where she'd broken his leg, and he gasped, unable to fight her for a moment.

She hauled him on his back. He grabbed the bat as she came down with it. He straight-armed the bat and she pressed down. As hard as she tried, she couldn't bend his arms. But she apparently had another plan.

She drew up her right knee and muscled the bat toward it. He put up a fight, but he couldn't shift his torso without using his leg. The bat, and his arm, moved inexorably toward her knee. And then she was pressing his arm, just below the elbow, against her knee. She pushed harder, shifting her weight into it. Poor bastard, Donna thought.

He bent his left arm, and Donna suddenly pushed against that. The arm collapsed, and so did the other. Now she had him, bat across his neck. She pressed down on his neck, cutting off his air.

"Shhhh," she whispered in his ear. "You don't want to wake up your wife."

He stopped struggling. She could see the fear rise in his eyes, the pain, and the regret. He knew what was coming.

She looked down at his leg. It was swelling, turning a nasty shade of purple. She looked around for the pistol, kicked it across the room. He was trying to sit up, turn himself over. Every time he moved his leg, he winced.

She found an extension cord, tied his hands with it. A hunk of fabric went into his mouth. What the hell was she going to do now?

"I need the key of Aros the Philosopher." Her voice sounded odd, strained.

His eyes got wide. She held up a warning finger. The man nodded, acquiescing. Donna pulled the soggy mass of cloth out of his mouth.

"That's it?" He hissed. "You've killed five people looking for the key to Aros?"

The revelation nearly knocked Donna over. They were all linked. They had all happened. Where the hell was she that this sort of thing happened? Had she gone completely insane? She hoped, maybe, she was lying in her bed having a psychotic breakdown. Because that would be better than what she was doing.

Donna's view of his face tilted. "It's important that people know I'm serious."

The man pursed his lips, squinted his eyes.

"I know what's going to happen next, then. You won't get anything from me."

"Stupid," Donna said.

"I've seen your face," he whispered. "You won't let me go."

"How long this process takes is going to depend on how forthcoming you are."

He set his teeth, looked away from her. She lifted her foot and put her great toe on his swelling shin. Without a word, eyes locked on his, she started to push. He ground his teeth, stared at her with defiance burning in his eyes. She didn't press harder, just wait, letting the pain take its toll. The muscles of his jaws stood out, and a cold sweat sheened his face. His lips curled, and still he did not look away.

His leg must have been on fire. His head began to shake, the muscles in his neck standing out. Donna had time. She kept the pressure on.

"Lawrence?" Donna spun. In the doorway was a slender woman, in blue pajama bottoms and a sports bra.

"Get away!" he hissed. Donna took a moment to shove the gag back into his mouth, then turned back to the woman a moment before she crashed into Donna. They went down in a tangled heap of limbs. Donna smashed her elbow into the woman's face, hard enough to bloody her nose. She grunted and clawed at Donna, but Donna caught her hand, and drove her knee into the woman's gut. The air whooshed out of her, and she struggled to take another breath.

Donna took the moment to push away, get to her feet. The man, Lawrence, was struggling, trying to yell something to his wife. A hand gripped Donna's hair and jerked her backwards. Donna pushed herself back, impacting the body behind her, and they were on the floor again. But Donna was on top this time. She elbowed the woman in the ribs, slammed her head back, and heard a crunch.

Donna rolled off the woman, searched. What was she looking for? She saw, lunged for the baseball bat. She came up, bat at the ready.

Her opponent was breathing heavily, holding her elbow. Blood made a mask below her nose, and one of her eyes was beginning to bruise up. The look in her eyes was nothing but fierce anger. She was fighting for her life, and she wouldn't be stopped.

She shot a glance at her bound husband, and in that moment, Donna rushed forward, bringing the bat down. She blocked with her forearm. Bone gave under the bat's force, and she screamed. She held the useless hand to her. Her lips were drawn back in a rictus, her teeth clenched to keep in the pain.

With her good arm, she grabbed a pair of scissors, but Donna swung again. The woman's shoulder crunched under the force, and the scissors hit the floor. Donna followed up with a home-run-strength lick with the bat, slamming into the woman's ribs. She fell with a grunt.

Donna put her foot on the back of the woman's head, pressing her face into the floor. She shot a look at the straining, furious-faced husband. Then brought the bat down, with all her strength, on the back of his wife's neck.

The stillness was instant. She issued a long, final sigh into the floor, with no inhalation. The reek of urine touched Donna's nostrils. She turned, and Lawrence was screaming into his gag, tears coursing down his cheeks, furious.

She waited. His muffled curses and rage continued for

long minutes. When he had mostly blown himself out, she approached, and pulled the gag out of his mouth. He tried to bite her, but she was too quick. The swelling in his leg was now larger than a softball.

"We were discussing the Key of Aros," she said.

"Fuck yourself. Fuck everyone you ever knew," he grated, tears running down his cheeks.

"Mommy?" Donna turned to see a three-year-old framed in the door, a stuffed rabbit was clutched under one arm. "Mommy what's happening?"

Donna froze. Then, slowly, so as not to startle the child, the bat came up.

"What are you playing? Mommy, get up. Get up, Mommy." She toddled over to the slumped corpse of her mother.

She bent down, touched the sticky pool of blood that was oozing from her mother's body. She looked up, wide-eyed, at Donna. She knew. Her mouth was a perfect O of discovery. She might not know the word for murder, but she knew something was wrong.

Donna rested the bat on her shoulder.

"What did you do to Mommy? Daddy, what's wrong?"

Donna felt her grip tightening on the bat.

"No."

She said it. Her word. It echoed in her ears, not just in her own mind. Looking down at the child, she fought whatever was controlling her, pushed with everything she had to not bring the bat crashing down on the child's head.

"No." She grated the word out, pushed her muscles to stay still. She felt the quivering tension of her shoulders and arms.

She spun, and let the man have it to the side of the head. With a sound like a sledgehammer splintering a fencepost, his head caved in. Blood spattered across the room, hitting her across the chest.

His legs spasmed, uncontrolled. She could smell urine and shit. She hit him twice more, until the only motion now was a little quiver in his thighs and biceps.

She turned and the child stood, wide-eyed, staring at her. Donna strode past the accusing eyes, out of the room that stank of death, out into the cool night beyond.

Donna woke, the haunting images of the night refusing to fade away. The woman lying in a spreading pool of her own blood, the man with the side of his head smashed in like a deflated basketball. And the haunting look of the child as she looked at Donna. She put her head in her hands.

The touch of her wet hair made her snap back, to stare at her hands. Why was her hair wet? It had been dry when she'd gone to bed. She grabbed a handful and smelled it. Shampoo and conditioner. She thought about hitting the guy with her bat, the blood spatter that must have gotten into her hair. These weren't dreams. She knew it, knew it all the way down to her bones. She'd been hiding from the reality of it, not allowing herself to look at what she was doing. She was killing people. Murdering them. She shuddered.

"What's wrong, babe?" Jim put a comforting hand on her. She turned to him.

"I've got to do something. This is bad. I don't remember taking a shower last night, and now my hair is wet."

"So you got up in the middle of the night to take a shower," Jim was reasonable, calm. "You've just had another dream."

"Then why is my hair wet? I took a shower and washed the blood off me." She shuddered again.

"Or maybe you don't remember taking a shower because you took it in the middle of the night. You've done stuff in the night you don't remember."

"Or maybe it's because I just tried to murder a child," Donna shot back at him. No, she tried to calm herself down. Her knuckles were white, twisting the sheets into knots. "I almost killed a kid. Beat her parents to death in front of her."

"Donna, you can't have. You don't have it in you. You're no killer. You'll pull off the road before you hit a squirrel. You're dreaming this stuff, and you're freaking yourself out. You aren't killing people. You aren't leaving the bed. I'm here all night, and you don't leave the bed."

"You can't know that," Donna said. "I could be slipping out, and you'd never know. You sleep pretty heavily."

"Every time you get out of bed I wake up. I would know if you were getting out of bed at night, all right? I mean, do you want me to install…" he broke off.

"A Nanny Cam. Yes. On a teddy-bear, or something like that." She laid back, her hands unclasping. Evidence. Why hadn't she thought of a Nanny Cam before? Maybe because it was a little too much like homemade porn, and that reminded her of Danny.

"Well I'm not sure I want to go that far," Jim said.

"You suggested it not two seconds ago."

"And I shouldn't have, OK? It was a bad idea and they make me feel weird. I don't like to be on camera. Especially not in bed. You'll find out I snore or something."

"I already know that you snore, and it's both cute and endearing." Donna didn't like to handle Jim, but he would get distracted if she didn't soothe his ego.

"I don't want a Nanny Cam," Jim was firm. "It says you don't trust me."

"This isn't about you. This is about me."

"And your dreams. Which are just that. Dreams."

Donna took in a breath, held it, then let it out.

"I don't think…"

"I don't want to hear it any more." He threw the blankets off his side of the bed.

"Jim," Donna's stomach turned to lead.

"I said I don't want to hear it." Without looking at her, he stalked out of the bedroom.

She stared after him, the bedspread clenched in her fists. She needed Jim, needed his stability when it seemed like her mind was going to shit. He was a good guy. And if she wasn't good enough, she'd lose him.

Donna didn't have a morning class, didn't have any morning work at all. She sat in bed, head spinning, until she heard Jim slam the door on his way to work. Then she was out of bed, and on the computer in a flash. Alchemy. The Key, the Key of Eros? She typed that into her web search and got way too much porn. Once she added alchemy into the mix, then the hits started getting weird. She discovered half a dozen thriving communities of alchemists.

And there it was. Alchemy, if she could trust the Internet, was a thriving underground she had never heard of before. She thought of what she knew, or thought she knew about alchemists. Weird wizards living in towers with their bubbling concoctions in what looked suspiciously like chemistry glassware. Weren't they all looking to turn lead into gold? What could that have to do with her?

The works of medieval and Renaissance alchemists were available online, but she went cross-eyed after five minutes on their enormous walls of text. Even the modern alchemists loved to write. Just looking at the tiny slider next to the words depressed her. She went on, looking for less popular sites, and found schools of alchemy that would teach their secrets for a substantial fee.

She closed the browser and sat, wondering about what she had just seen. She didn't believe. She only sort of believed in reiki, wasn't too hot on homeopathy or crystals. But she knew people who sincerely believed in them, and she would never make fun of them. People believed, what was the problem with that? As long as they didn't hurt anyone.

Then again, there was belief and there was hucksterism. People were looking for something, and a lot of people were making money off them.

She should talk to Rich and Peter again. They brought up alchemy, and now she was dreaming about it. No, she wasn't dreaming about it. The dreams were real. She was convinced of that now.

Donna looked at her hand. She fanned her fingers in front of the wall. Those rebellious hands had killed, murdered, tortured. What was wrong with them? What was happening to her? She thought of the men whose faces she had ruined, burned, and beaten. They were dead. She'd killed them. Why? She didn't know them. But she'd asked about the Key of Eros. She didn't know what that was. So it wasn't her.

Who, or what, was it then?

In light of weighty questions like these, it was time for coffee.

Donna sipped at her Big Bruiser at the café. The smell connected her to saner days, calmed her.

"You were late this morning," Fierce said. "You're never late."

Donna's smile was weak. Fierce paid attention.

"This has to be the bad morning to end all bad mornings. Honey, what's wrong?"

"They aren't dreams, Fierce. I'm killing people."

"Don't talk like that in public." Fierce covered Donna's hand with her own. "Seriously."

All Donna could do was look at her. She could feel the rush of emotion threatening to burst out of her. She grit her teeth. And nodded.

"Fierce, I can't even get arrested in this town."

"Still, you don't want people thinking you're some sort of homicidal maniac."

Donna subsided.

"What can I do? I've got to talk to Peter and Rich."

"What's that all about?"

"Rich brought up alchemy, then Peter danced around it when I confronted him. And now, I'm dreaming about it. Jesus this is just a huge fucking mess."

"Alchemy. As in bearded old men in robes and pointy hats failing to turn lead into gold."

"I don't know. For all I know he's looking to get laid. I remember something about a Key of Eros, and that sounds odd."

"Sounds like what an alchemist would call his jimmie."

What had been tears erupted from Donna as laughter. Of course, why hadn't she thought about that? Maybe because she was too busy murdering people.

"You know, you're probably right," she said when she'd finished. She wiped away the tears that had run down her face. How long had it been since she'd laughed? Days, at least.

"That's so obvious, I can't believe I missed it," Donna said.

"Well, you've got a good mind, but an insufficiently dirty one," Fierce sipped her latte. "Are you sure that Rich saying something didn't trigger off alchemy in your dream?"

"They aren't dreams, Fierce."

"It's nicer to say over coffee than 'your horrible murder spree.'"

Donna nodded, acquiescing.

"On the other hand, if you really can't get arrested, have you considered a minor crime wave?"

"I really don't want to test the boundaries of what I can get away with. Something like that, once you cross the line, you don't know how far you can go before you run into a wall and get tossed into jail. It seems like the Police Chief isn't in my corner, and this won't work out in my favor."

Fierce's smile was broad. "Oh thank God you did learn something from that catastrophe of a relationship with Danny."

Donna could feel the hot prickle of embarrassment creep up her face.

"Funny you should say that," Donna said. "Jim mentioned getting a Nanny Cam, just so I could sleep easier. You know, make sure I wasn't getting up at night or anything. And all I could think of was Danny. And all that…"

"Hey, it's done." Fierce's voice was sympathetic. "You moved on. Don't beat yourself up about the bad stuff. Leave it on the same trash heap where you left Danny."

"I'm trying. Some days it's not as easy as all that."

"That's why you have friends." Donna's smile was a bit sad.

"Is it bad that I feel like Jim isn't my friend? I feel like I'm fighting with myself so I don't get him mad."

Fierce shifted her coffee to her left hand, took a drink, and shifted it back to her right.

"Is it that bad?" Donna asked again.

"I don't want to tell you how to run your relationship." Fierce was picking her words carefully. "Actually, that's not true, I love giving you advice. But if you don't feel like you can be yourself with Jim, then the relationship isn't working for you."

"But I don't… I don't want to bring a load of crap down on him right now. I mean, he's not being Mr. Supportive, but he hasn't freaked out, either." Not much. "I'm putting a lot of pressure on him with this… dream stuff. Jim's a good guy. I like him. I usually like who I am with him. My life is just going down the shitter and he's not reacting well, and I don't know if I want to be on my own again." She looked at Fierce, fighting back the tears in her eyes. "Not now. Not right now." Donna tried to shrink into herself.

"Donna, you are one of the toughest women, no, one of the toughest *people* I have ever met. A lot of people would have come out of a shitty relationship with Danny, given up on men altogether, and gone straight into the arms of a woman."

"Lesbians don't work that way, Fierce."

"Oh, I know. I'm being funny. And motherly. So back off." Fierce scowled. "Now where was I?"

"Danny."

"Right. Danny was enough to put anyone off relationships for life and make them go live life as a nun. But not you. You got back out there, and managed to find Jim. If it hasn't been your forever relationship, you were on an even enough keel that it wasn't a rebound. You've treated each other decently, from everything I've seen. And if you're having some trouble, maybe it's because *you're having some trouble.*"

Fierce paused for a moment.

"If he's crowding you, not being supportive, or any other kind of shit, you haul off and punch that bastard in his godamn nose. You're a catch, Donna. You're strong, you're smart, you've started a successful business while my kids are still paying off their student loans and moaning about the lack of job opportunities. Take no shit, Donna Otálora. You don't deserve it."

Fierce cocked her head to the side. "Good pep talk?"

"Doesn't actually help me figure out what to do, though."

"I'm good for advice, but bad for direction. I can barely figure out my own life."

"But you listen," Donna said with a sigh. "That seems to be a bit of a problem with Jim recently."

"I know you're feeling like you're off balance, but you deserve someone who respects you."

"Got it. Loud and clear."

"Good." Fierce checked her watch. "And off I go to dig through some books. Wish me luck, 'cause I'm already bored."

"Good luck, Fierce."

And then Donna was alone with her cooling coffee and her thoughts.

At The Horn, Donna didn't remember getting through her day. She knew she'd had afternoon appointments, knew who she'd worked with, but didn't remember the specifics. Maybe it was the three Wallbangers she had in her, but it felt like she'd passed through the day like a ghost.

That wasn't good. She had to keep her life going. She had to be present in the moment. She was out at night, killing people. She had to concentrate on her normal life.

Peter was tending bar tonight. She watched him as he served people, his pale head smooth as a shark's skin, his corded, muscular arms laying down drinks and whisking them away. She liked his broad chest and manly, jutting beard. Why couldn't she find a guy like him, who wasn't involved with another guy, who she sort of liked, too? She sighed.

The bar had been humming with activity, and now it was late, and the night was down to four people. She hadn't confronted him about the alchemy. Yet. She had to. If he had the only key to stopping the madness in her life, they needed to talk.

"Another Wallbanger, Donna?"

She put a hand over her glass. "No more tonight. I already need a cab."

"If you're not drinking any more, you must be here to talk."

Donna looked around. The last hangers-on were familiar faces, people as ingrained into The Horn as the dark wooden bar. They talked amongst themselves, politics, business, and gossip. But how well did she really know them? Who were they really? Did she see one of them give her a sidelong glance? What did they know?

"Are you sure it's safe to talk here?" She kept her voice low.

"We're safe here." Peter said with flat certainty.

"I don't understand any of this," Donna said. "Alchemy? Magic? Murder? I'm lost, like I'm driving down a dark road without the lights, and I get the feeling that something ahead is coming up fast."

Peter's mouth pinched. He picked up a bottle from behind the bar, looked around, then set it back where it had been.

"I know it's scary. You're in deep, and nobody's even taught you how to tread water." He paused. "I wish I could do something for you, but I really can't. This is the sort of thing that takes a lot of time and study to understand. And I don't have that kind of time."

"What?" His refusal made her blood run cold. Why had he even started this with her? Was he playing some sort of manipulative game? Donna ground her teeth, not daring to curse him out for being feckless. "I thought we were friends."

"Donna." Peter moved in close. She looked at his blue eyes, with the small flecks of green and brown in them. "Rich and I have done a bit of snooping. What's happening is serious. Deadly serious. I think you know they aren't dreams."

What could she do? She balled her fists.

"You two were my only hope. The only people who had any idea what the fuck was going on with my life. I'm drowning, Peter. I'm so out of my depth I wouldn't know a lifesaver if someone smacked me in the face with it.

"Hey," Peter's hand patted her shoulder. "I know it looks bad…"

"Bad? I'm killing people. Horribly." Donna fought the tears of helpless frustration. "I wake up smelling the reek of burned people. I beat some woman to death for the horrible crime of not wanting to see her husband tortured. If I had any sense I'd kill myself, but I… I hadn't even thought about it until now." She locked her eyes on his, unwilling to let him get away. "Help me. I don't know anywhere else to turn."

Peter couldn't bear to look at her for long. He dropped his eyes, then looked off toward the other customers.

"I said I can't help. And I mean that. There's nothing that I can do."

Something between a shout and a wail burst out of Donna.

"I know someone who might be able…" Peter started.

"Might? I'm committing atrocities and you *might* know someone?"

"Donna." Peter's voice crackled, bringing her up short.

"Listen to me. Helping you is a lot more dangerous than you think."

"People are dying, Peter. And I'm the reason."

"And this is what I can offer you. There's a guy, and I'm going to ask him if he can give you some time."

"You know it's a damn good thing the fire department isn't as cowardly as you. Can you imagine people dying in a fire and them saying 'I'll ask a guy if he can do anything about it'? I'm not playing around with this."

Peter's eyes were sad, the last thing Donna had expected. She'd always liked him, and despite her frustration and her anger, she felt bad for whatever position he was in.

"I'm doing what I can," his voice was just a whisper.

Donna paid her tab, then left.

Donna had just finished screwing the new, heavy-duty bolt on the bathroom door when Jim came home.

"What'cha doing?" He asked in a playful voice when he saw her putting the tools back in the tool chest.

"I put a lock on the bathroom door," she said.

"I know you like your privacy, but that much?"

"I'm going to sleep in the tub for a couple of nights."

Jim thought about that for a moment. "Is this some sort of health thing? Have you been listening to Dahlia again?"

Dahlia had been a good friend before Jim had crowded her out of Donna's life. Donna should cut him. She stared at the screwdriver, imagined it smashing through the fragile bone at his temple. The gush of warm blood, his stunned look, him folding at the knees and flopping over. He would never look at her that way again, never be mealy-mouthed, never undercut her.

"I still can't believe you listened to her when she said you should abstain from alcohol and keep away from men," Jim was still saying.

How would he look then, the blood pouring from his head, his face slack, never able to give her That fucking Look again? His hair would probably get mussed, and he hated that. But he wouldn't care because those parts of his brain would already be destroyed. And she could get away with it, she reflected. She'd gotten away with a lot of murders.

"Donna?" Jim was waving a hand in front of her eyes. Wasn't he dead? "Earth to Donna," his condescending, sing-song voice brought his inevitable demise that much closer.

She shook her head, snapped herself out of it. What was wrong with her?

"Sorry, just thinking about other projects to do around the house," she lied. Why had she been thinking about killing Jim? Was that coming? Was he next?

"I'm going to lock myself in the bathroom, sleep in the tub," she said.

"Quit talking nonsense. We have a perfectly good bed."

"I'm scared, Jim. I'm scared that I'm killing people and this is the only way I can think of to stop myself."

"The handcuffs didn't make you feel any better, and this isn't going to make you feel any better," Jim said. "And you're going to wake up all cramped. Plus, I won't be there to keep you warm at night."

"Look, it's only for a little while, OK?" Another lie. These episodes showed no signs of quitting. The thought of having to lock herself up for the rest of her life was wearying. So much effort for something she had taken for granted. All she wanted was sleep. Sleep in which she didn't kill people. Had she ever truly dreamed? Or had it always been blood and mayhem? She couldn't remember.

"Did you get the Nanny Cam?" she asked.

"Forgot again," he said, turning away. Ninth time he'd forgotten, or had worked late, or hadn't been able to find them at the store. Jim at his most passive-aggressive.

Donna considered getting one that sat in the belly of a stuffed bear. She hadn't had a stuffed animal in years. She imagined herself, for some reason in one of those lacy teddies Jim liked so much, curled up in the bathtub cuddling a teddy bear. It sounded like the way the victim got found on one of those murder investigation shows.

"Don't worry yourself," she said.

"No, I'll get it. It's just been a couple of busy weeks at work."

"And you think it's silly."

"I think you're worked up about something that's no big deal. And maybe I'm not altogether thrilled to spend money on something that expensive for no reason."

Donna had watched him drop six hundred dollars on a tailored Italian suit because a co-worker had gotten a promotion. Now he was balking at something as minor as a Nanny Cam? They were both telling lies.

"There's a gap under the door, so I can lock myself in, put the key on a piece of paper, and slide it under. And in the morning, you can slide it back to me."

"You really don't need to do that. You're fine. There's nothing to worry about."

"I thought about putting the lock on the outside, but that would look strange for the guests. We can keep the key in the lock except at night." She was talking past him now, plowing ahead and hoping he would agree in her wake, stepping on her anger. She needed Jim. Needed something stable as her life went haywire. And if it wasn't everything she really wanted, she could take some comfort in the illusion of a good relationship.

CHAPTER 7

TWO POUNDS OF FEATHERS

Donna came to herself at night. Not a dream, she knew. This was real. She would not treat these murders like dreams anymore.

She was outside. The air was wet and heavy. She smelled damp grass, wet trees, water soaking into loam. So much of Oakham was still wooded, as the ever-widening suburban sprawl of Boston hadn't yet reached the isolated community.

Donna was walking down a rain-slicked road she didn't recognize. She would have looked around for any sort of street sign, but her head and eyes wouldn't respond. Another night of being front row at someone's murder. By feel, she wasn't wearing anything special; pants rather than a dress, the serious hiking boots. Her arms swung freely, she wasn't carrying any murderous implements. Yet.

Despite the dark, and the lack of streetlights, Donna could still make out the ramshackle house she was approaching. An old saltbox in desperate need of scraping and repainting. Several of the shingles had sprung, which would allow water to seep behind them in the rain. Weeds grew as tall as the sagging porch's support posts. Donna almost expected a madman with a chainsaw to be lurking somewhere in the overgrown yard.

For once, the door was locked, and she exulted in the privacy of her own prison. Couldn't get in. She'd have to go home, lay back down in the tub, and wake up tomorrow morning. Fuck you, whoever was running this horror show. Stopped by a door.

After a minute of stillness, her body began walking around

the perimeter of the house. The pace was deliberate, looking at the peeling window frames. She couldn't tell what she was looking for. The house was dark, and she could see nothing inside.

She found a window that was to her satisfaction. Turning her head away, she elbowed it, breaking the pane. With infinite care that was at odds with the way the intruder generally treated her body, she reached into the broken window and flipped open the lock.

The moment was gone, but as her body climbed through the window, Donna thought about that. Whatever was making her do things cared about whether she got cut. Why? Maybe she had become like a comfortable chair, expensive to replace.

Fuck you, whatever's making me do this! She screamed in the silence in her own head. *I'm not your damned free ride!* But she couldn't do anything about it. She had once, when that kid had been in trouble. She'd stopped her maniac body from beating a kid to death with a baseball bat. So she had some power. Somehow, she'd affected her body. Then again, it had been right after she'd fatally clubbed the same kid's mother to death. What was the difference?

As these thoughts squirreled around her head, Donna's body raised the window sash, and quietly let herself into the rickety house. What was she looking for? Probably someone to kill with their own tools.

I'm bored with killing! She yelled into the unresponsive confines of her own skull. "Can't we ever do something nice like go out for ice cream? What's with the relentless need to kill?"

She waited, hoping, but no response came.

In the dim light from the moon and stars, she could barely see. She felt her way across the wall from the window. Immediately, her hands brushed across the spines of books. She was in a library. Stepping carefully so as not to trip on any unseen obstacles, she felt her way across the bookshelf, encountered another, turned a corner, felt her way past more books, and eventually found a doorknob.

Hand on the knob, she paused for a moment. She could hear something, just faintly. She opened her mouth, put her ear to the door. Everything was so quiet she could hear the rush of blood in her own ears. Beyond that, labored, wheezing breath. She wished she'd heard snoring. Maybe she could make a sleeping man's death quick and quiet. What else could she be here for?

She turned the knob, pushed the door open, and stepped through. The sour smell of someone who spent too much time in one room assailed her. The floorboard squealed as she put her booted foot on it. In the silence, it sounded louder than the scream of an angry cat.

The breathing didn't change. Asleep? A trap? She felt her hand reaching behind her, and then flicked on the light.

The room was a mess. A single bed shoved against the wall, piled high with a heap of quilts and ancient-looking crocheted blankets. Beneath this was a lump of a human, half-sitting on a pile of pillows. His face was creased and lined, hard used for long years. His full beard was white, stained yellow near the mouth, indicating decades of nicotine. One sausage-fingered hand lay on top of a coverlet so faded and stained she couldn't tell the original color in the light of the single bulb.

He didn't rise, didn't bring out a gun to defend himself. Instead, he winced.

"You, huh?"

"Me." Donna's voice still sounded forced.

"I expected you, however you're dressed. You've made a big stir, murdering us."

"They wouldn't play ball. You look like the sort of man who might be persuaded."

The old man coughed, which turned into a wracking hack that left him speechless for a long minute.

"What are you looking for, murderer?"

"We'll start with the Key of Aros the Philosopher."

The old man's laugh was indistinguishable from his cough.

"Ambitious of you, but I suppose anyone who has managed to trans-possess an individual isn't going to bother shooting for squirrels."

"I know your college has it."

"You won't be able to use it. No one can just hand you any of the keys, the process of learning them brings understanding, not only of the key, but also of its proper use."

"Feel better after your sanctimonious little tirade? It's all tradition, control of the students by the masters for no other reason than to keep them hidebound and subservient."

"Is that all the respect you can summon for eight hundred and fifty years of accumulated wisdom? A way to get around it so you may get what you want without having to earn it?"

"Who are you to judge what I have and have not earned?"

"What have you ever earned? As far as I understand, everything has been handed to you." The laugh became a cough again. "If ever I was going to betray my brothers, it would not be to you."

"Am I so hated?"

"If you weren't years ago, you certainly are now. There isn't much decency in you, beating Olivia's parents to death in front of her. But that doesn't make you anything but a monster for what you did to Lawrence and Carol. And no monster deserves the Key of Aros. You're a cesspit someone should have filled in a long time ago."

"Brave words from a man who can't even get out of his own bed."

"I do have to thank you for one thing. The hot brown body you're wearing is just the thing an old man wants to see before he dies."

"See, I'm not so terrible after all."

"You should ask the girl who spends too much time keeping herself fit whether you're a bastard or not." He looked at Donna, truly looked into the *her* trapped inside the rebellious body.

"Tell me of the Key of Aros the Philosopher. I can have you taken to any hospital, given the best care."

"Negotiation, now? Well, I figured it would come around to that sooner or later with you." He speared Donna with his gaze. "There ain't nothing you can offer me. Nothing, you understand? I'm standing at death's door, and there ain't a damn thing you can tempt me with."

In a fury, Donna stalked over to the foul bed. She pulled the pillow out from under his head, and pressed it down on his face.

The gnarled old hands came up, and at first Donna thought he was going to flail at her arms. Instead, each twisted hand curled into a fist, then extended a middle finger. If he said anything, the pillow muffled·it.

It wasn't like the movies. Those defiant fingers remained up for a very long time. Only after three interminable minutes did the hands waver, begin seeking her arms. His gnarled hands fumbled for her wrists, and finding them, grabbed. He was much too weak, from the ravages of his disease and the lack of oxygen, to do any more than hold her forearms with an uncomfortable but less than painful grip. After more long minutes, the grip weakened, and his hands fell lifeless to the bed. But even that wasn't enough. Donna waited until the slight rise and fall of his chest was stilled, and the now-familiar stink of urine filled the air.

She looked down at him, feeling the condescending sneer on her face. She turned on her heel and walked back to the library. With the light spilling from the dead man's bedroom, she found the light switch.

The library was floor to ceiling books. Donna marveled at the riot of old books with cloth bindings, their names picked out in gilt interspersed with a flood of spine cracked paperbacks stuffed between them. If there was an organizational system to the flood of books, Donna couldn't tell what it was. The full shelves stretched higher than she could reach. Like books were not together. Shirley Jackson's *Haunting of Hill House* sat next to a slim pamphlet called *The Long Lost Friend*. The complete works of Charles Dickens, in four green-spined volumes, were scattered among similar-sized volumes with authors Donna didn't recognize like Paracelsus, Galen, and Heraclitus.

Presented with this chaos, Donna's body pulling books down at random, flipping through them, throwing them on the floor. It became clear to Donna that she was looking for something old, because she selected the largest books, choosing the thick ones that smelled of dust. Each one was rejected, and added to a growing pile in the middle of the room.

The pile was close to three feet tall and more than five feet wide before she apparently found what she was looking for.

Donna glimpsed a sepia page with a fascinatingly complex illustration of a labyrinth. She wished she could read some of the Latin, and wondered what the cherubs were doing holding up the title text. Apparently satisfied, she tucked the weighty book under her arm and headed back out the open window.

Donna woke in the bathtub, aching from the cramped position she'd been in all night. Or, at least, as long as she'd been here. Dammit, it hadn't worked.

She checked the knob on the bathroom door. Still locked. She punched the solid wood of the door, and winced. That was going to leave a bruise.

A second later, the key appeared under the door. With a sigh of defeat, Donna unlocked the door.

"How did you sleep?" Jim asked.

"Like shit," she replied.

"Have a dream about killing people?" This was their new morning routine. She pushed out of the bathroom and into the bedroom. She sat on the bed with a sigh.

"Yeah. And it was a weird one."

"Do you want to talk about it?"

She thought about the man who had known what was possessing her. He had recognized it, or known it was coming.

"Why do you want to know about my... my dreams?"

"Because I love you, remember? You are important to me. I want to help. I want you to be happy." His eyes were wide, imploring. And he was right. He only wanted to help, although sometimes he showed it in a funny way.

"This one was about some old man. I smothered him with his pillow, then I ransacked his library. It wasn't as ghastly as a lot of them have been, but it wasn't sweetness and light either."

"Do you know why you killed him?"

Donna shrugged, weary already. "I never do. I just come into these houses, find these people, and do something horrible to them."

"Did you talk to him?"

The fear washed through Donna, her heart suddenly racing. How had he known?

"No." She couldn't look at him as she lied. "It was one of those walk up and kill him things. The only weird part was ransacking his library."

"What book were you looking for?"

She closed her eyes, hoping he would assume she was concentrating. What to tell him? If he knew something about the murders... that was impossible. Jim was a puppy dog. Harmless. Self-centered, but his heart was in the right place. He was kind to animals, bought her unexpected and thoughtful presents.

"Donna?"

"I'm trying to remember, shush a sec." At the same time, his attitude towards her dream murders had been strange from the beginning. And now she was lying to him. After Danny, she never wanted to lie to Jim. He was a good guy. But asking the title of the book seemed too on point, as if he knew something. Especially after he'd asked if she talked to the murdered man. Had she ever told him about talking in her dreams? She couldn't recall.

"I didn't see the title," she said slowly. "I think it was gray, or brown. Big book, old."

"Did you open the book?"

"Yeah. All I saw were words, I flipped through it real fast. Couldn't even tell you what language it was. Might have been Shakespeare."

Jim laughed. "You and your dreams. Killing a guy and then stealing his book."

Donna knuckled under to his conversational shift and managed a tremulous smile. "Yeah." She barked out an unconvincing laugh.

"I was thinking about going out tonight. We haven't been to the Silver Bistro for a while."

He was definitely smoothing something over. She loved Silver Bistro.

"That would be nice," she said, promising herself she wouldn't let it change her attitude. "A little change in the routine, some time out. Probably change my attitude a great deal."

"Good." He bent down and kissed her forehead.

Donna's hands shook as they held her Big Bruiser at Café Gitan. Even a quart of coffee wouldn't put her life back together, but maybe if she could hold on to this coffee, her day might somehow turn normal.

"I don't know if I can do this anymore, Fierce. I really felt like I could drink everything in The Horn, just to get away from the… the reality of my dream last night."

"Aw, honey." Fierce's heavily made-up eyes were all sympathy. "After your, I know they're not dreams, but, uh, experience with the couple, I knew they were just going to get worse."

"It's not that this one was worse. I mean, I just… you know, did for this guy." Donna looked around to make sure no one was listening. "But now, I'm starting to talk with them beforehand. This guy seemed like he knew me. Not me, but was expecting someone to come through the door and knew what it was that was moving me. It was creepy. But for the first time, I felt like someone really saw me through whatever else is happening. It's hard to explain."

"Well, shit. He knew what was going on."

"How come I've never heard of these people?" Donna realized she'd said it too loud, looked around the coffeehouse again.

"Donna, I've only been here like a decade, and Oakham is a weird little town. In Georgia, people are pretty open about what all's wrong with them. But this town has a lot of secrets, a lot of places that nobody talks about."

"Come on. Everywhere's like that."

"Other towns aren't. There's more whispered about stuff going on in Oakham than any city I've ever lived. There's people you never see, in a town of less than fifteen thousand. A lot of strangers live here. It's hard to explain, and a little creepy."

"You aren't making sense." But Donna was fascinated.

Fierce took a big slug of her coffee.

"There's a lot of people in this town that don't know each other. Like in high school. Some people just didn't hang out with other people. But once you get out and into the real world, that goes away. Only it hasn't here. We had a couple of parties at our place, brought in friends and people I knew. Which included two people in the same business, advertising. Two small companies, both in Oakham, and they didn't know each other. Said they'd never heard of each other. And that's nuts. In any sane business, you know who the local competition is. I know who all the other accountants in this town are, as well as the ones in Aylesbury and Bolton. But that's a foreign concept here."

Donna considered. She knew, or knew about, all the local trainers, knew something about the masseuses that worked in Oakham. And there was the professional grapevine. People talked.

"The other thing is that Oakham is so spread out. There's the center, and then there's all these crazy roads that sort of go nowhere until they come out on these hundred and fifty-year-old neighborhoods. I got a job to look through the books of an estate a few years back. I drove around for so long I couldn't believe I was still in Massachusetts, let alone Oakham."

Donna's phone chirped from her bag. She had a message. That was odd. Still a bit early in the morning for anything. Maybe it was Jim.

"Lemme look at this," Donna said. Fierce waved for her to go ahead, then took the opportunity for a long drink of her Middleweight coffee. When had her coffee gotten so much smaller than Donna's?

Donna hauled out her phone, looked at the black screen.

"All magic is governed by the laws of sympathy and contagion," the text read.

She blinked at it. What the hell was this? She glanced over to Fierce, who was dabbing coffee off her blouse. She couldn't have sent it, and she wasn't the sort to mess with Donna. Not this way.

She tried to reply to the text, figure out who had sent it. The reply number came up as invalid.

"Safer for everyone if you don't know who I am." The subsequent text came up with a metallic pling.

Should she show Fierce? Would that put her in danger?

Donna ground her teeth. She hated secrecy, not knowing what she could tell to whom.

"Who the fuck are you?" she tapped in rapidly, but her phone told her again that there was no recipient.

The tabletop was thick, translucent glass, but she was sure she could fuck up her phone by smashing it right on through. But no. It wasn't the phone's fault. Maybe… ah. Maybe it was the guy Peter knew, who was going to help her out. Magical advice through texts? That was weird.

"Someone change their plans?" Fierce asked.

Donna wanted to tell her. But she didn't want Fierce to be in danger. The text, assuming it wasn't someone just messing with her, implied that the situation was dangerous, and Donna had to agree. She'd been murdering people. She had to assume whatever was involved, it was perfectly happy to continue forcing her to kill.

"Massage moved up half an hour." Donna hated not telling the truth. First Jim, and now Fierce. But the anonymous texter was right. This was dangerous.

"Really?" Fierce knew her better than Jim. "That wouldn't be a little tiny lie you just told me, would it?"

What to say to that?

"Yeah. Look, some things I want to keep to myself. I think it's part of the weird stuff."

Fierce tried not to look hurt. They usually shared so much.

"I think this whole thing is dangerous," Donna said. "People are dying. I'm trying to make sure nothing comes down on you or Carl, OK?"

Fierce set her mouth. "You're the best friend I've got that isn't Carl. You're clearly in trouble, and I want to help. So if, when, you need something, you tell me and I'll be over faster than a cat to his dinner."

"You're the best, Fierce."

"I am, aren't I?"

Donna laughed. She'd needed that. Like she needed Fierce.

Two days later, Donna was sitting in front of her computer. Jim was still at work. She'd gone cross-eyed from looking at the online alchemy texts. The roundabout language made her want to scream. Why couldn't they get to their damn point without meandering around a story about two fishermen, and a discourse on the planets? The vocabulary was complex and the spelling wonky. Why hadn't anyone come up with an easy primer on this stuff?

Rather than continue to bash her head against the dense prose, Donna decided to switch to something else. Who had that couple been? The kid had been named Olivia, right? What did the old guy say their names were? Lawrence. She remembered that. She'd called him that the night... the night she'd killed them both. What was her name? Lawrence and Hardy. That wasn't right. Lawrence and Carol. That felt better.

Lawrence and Carol were common enough names. She got more than thirty-seven million hits, including actress Carol Lawrence, who she was pretty sure wasn't involved. She searched the two names again, this time with "+Oakham", and came up with an article immediately. Lawrence and Carol FitzPatrick welcoming a baby girl at the Oakham hospital. And there they were, smiling proudly, holding a tiny bundle in their arms. Donna could do nothing but stare. Lawrence and Carol, alive in the picture, now dead. Residents of Oakham. Carol had been a surgeon. And Olivia, now an orphan. Who was taking care of her now? Donna's face was suddenly wet, and she brushed away tears. Not just dead. Murdered. Protecting something, Donna didn't know what. What was worth so much that someone had beaten them to death with a baseball bat, using her body to do it?

It was all a tangle in her head. All she understood were the stakes, the killing. And that useless cryptic message from the person that was supposed to help her. She pulled out her phone, looked at the message. "Laws of sympathy and contagion."

Sympathy. Understanding someone, right? Being sympathetic, listening to someone, understanding what they're going through. Fierce was sympathetic. So was Fierce magic?

She was on more solid ground with contagion. That meant it spread. When diseases were contagious, you could get them. So contagious magic was something you got from someone who was already infected? She wondered who she'd caught it from.

And how. Airborne? Touch? Body fluid? But no, that was the usual kind of contagion, diseases and viruses and stuff like that. Yawns were supposed to be contagious. You watched someone yawn and then you wanted to do it. It even worked when you were reading. So how did you catch magic, then? Was it from sympathy? Was she likely to pass whatever this was on to Fierce because Fierce listened to her?

So this was magic, and she had to accept that. She'd never heard of any other way to take over someone's brain. Even hypnosis couldn't make you do stuff like that. Not outside of comic books and really dumb television.

Why didn't this make any sense? She word searched 'sympathy' and found that it didn't just mean caring about someone else, but also affinity. A relationship, a similarity.

So what did this mean? What did she know about alchemy? What did she know about magic?

In fairy tales, when someone got transformed, they turned into something like themselves. Prince Charming got turned into a beast. An ugly beast, but like the original prince. He never got turned into a statue of a duckling, or a flagstone.

Donna sank down in her chair. Voodoo dolls were supposed to look like the person, and didn't you have to put hair or a picture of the person on the doll before it was supposed to work? But what could she believe? What might actually work?

If magic spread sympathetically, like a disease, did the person doing this have to be like Donna? She imagined her long-lost twin in a tall pointy hat, and robes of darkest black, waving a wand. She sighed. That sounded a bit too cartoony.

In some ways, Donna was relieved that she was now sure that it wasn't her. She had no responsibility for the murders, any more than the shovel, the grill, or the baseball bat. Someone else was doing this to her. She was not a maniac.

Even so, she hated the thought of someone else in her body. It made her feel dirty, ashamed. She felt for the strangers she killed, but she mostly needed to stop the murders because she hated being someone's killer puppet.

Before she shut the computer down, she deleted the browser history.

A week after her last murder, Donna was prowling the athletics department at the local department store. Oakham had a shitty selection, but she'd been burned by online purchases on occasion. So she liked to check what she could touch before she went online. Thus far, the yoga pants were the same old cheap crap....

"Pardon me, can I get your opinion on something?"

Donna turned to see a man, tall and broad-shouldered. His hair was ordinary brown, slightly wavy, his eyes the same color. He looked about her age, maybe a little older, but his smile was boyish and sweet.

"Can I get you to tell me which one of these ties is better?"

Why should she? She didn't know this guy, and the implication that she was there just to advise him on his fashion choices rankled. He held up a pair of ties, neither of which looked remotely acceptable in front of his Franz Ferdinand T-shirt. Tell him to get stuffed? She looked at him, and his faltering smile.

"Hey, if you're busy..." he trailed off.

"What's the occasion?" She wondered why she said it.

"I've got a job interview and then I have to go to my grandmother's funeral."

"Same day?" At least Donna was sure she hadn't murdered granny.

He nodded.

"Double duty is always tricky. What color are you wearing?"

"Charcoal gray coat, black pants."

"Good choices." He swapped the two ties back and forth. "White shirt?"

"Cream, actually."

Donna considered. "The solid color will make you look more serious. I'd go with that."

"Thank you." He blushed. "Um, you're really nice."

"My boyfriend thinks so."

"Well, I didn't mean it that way, although I can see how he would."

He was sweet. She kind of liked him. She hadn't realized how lonely she felt. She didn't have any guy friends. Aside from

Jim. She wasn't throwing herself at this guy.

He stuck out a hand. "Nathan." They shook.

"Do people ever call you 'Nate'?"

"Not since fourth grade. I decided I wanted to try a new name, sort of redefine myself. Didn't work. I was still the same nerdy kid."

"I should let you get back to your tie choices."

"Hey, thank you. It was kind of awkward asking, and you were polite. I feel like I owe you a fruit smoothie or something."

"What would my very real boyfriend say?"

Nathan shrugged. "Whatever he likes, really. I'm not looking for anything. Just a way to say thank you."

What was the harm?

"As long as you pay for your tie."

He put back the checked tie, and bought the gray.

Stormee's Fruitee Smoothees was two storefronts down. Clouds were rolling in, so they sat inside.

"I don't think I got your name."

"I'm Donna. Nice to meet you, Nathan."

"Sorry about that tie thing. I'm a little flustered with the death of my grandmother. But if I get this job, I guess I'll move up here."

"Where are you from?"

"Hard Hittin' New Britain, Connecticut. Have you ever been?"

Donna felt a stab of wistfulness. She'd always wanted to go places. New Britain might as well have been the moon.

"What's it like?" She asked.

He shrugged. "Not as many trees. The people are rude. But the kielbasa is second to none if you know how to get it."

"Sounds nice."

"Of all the things I'd call New Britain, I don't think I've ever heard it called nice. It's a blue-collar burg, with a lot of immigrant enclaves that don't see eye to eye." He shrugged. "But you know, it's home. How about you? Where are you from?"

"Right here. Lived in Oakham all my life."

"Interesting. So what do you do?"

"Personal trainer."

"Do you have a card? If I get up here, I'm so taking you on to train me. You are amazingly fit."

"Thank you," Donna said, rummaging around in her purse. "Gotta walk the walk if I'm going to talk the talk. You aren't too shabby yourself. What's your exercise routine?"

He managed to look a little embarrassed.

"Lifting, running, and I'm a first Dan in Aikido. So if anyone ever tries to beat you up, call me."

"Good to know," Donna said, handing over her card.

"And I'll definitely come back to this place." He smiled. She liked his smile. It took over his face, made his eyes disappear.

Donna's straw hit the bottom of her smoothie.

"I've got a one-thirty appointment, so I should get going. But it was nice to meet you, Nathan. I hope you get that job."

"This looks like a nice and unexciting place to live. I think I could enjoy myself here."

Unexciting. Well, as long as you weren't Donna. Shit. She'd gone an entire conversation without thinking about her bloody spree.

"Donna, what a pleasant surprise."

"I haven't heard from you for a while, Auntie. So I thought I'd call you."

"This is wonderful. How have you been?"

"It's been kind of quiet," Donna said. In her case, this meant she hadn't killed anyone for more than ten days. "Jim's doing well. He's got some big project so he's spending a lot of time at work. Which is fine. It gives me more time to get my stuff done at home."

Tia Ana's laugh was short and harsh. "I know how that is."

"Is everything all right with you?"

"Carlos has been going through a rough patch, too. So much work, and they're not paying him overtime."

"I'm sorry. But what about you?"

"Enjoying my summer, but the gnawing feeling that I'm going to go back to students with the motivation of a bowl of oatmeal doesn't go away."

"I'm sorry. I thought you were teaching AP students."

"I am, and it doesn't seem to help. Urgh, each class has its own character, but this year's were miserably passive. I hope the next batch is a little more interested in school. But you didn't call to listen to me complain about my students. What's happening in Oakham?"

It's all blood and death and not being able to get the reek of charred flesh out of my nose, Donna didn't say. "Not a lot. I was just thinking about family."

"You know, Sylvia called me a few weeks ago." Ana let that hang in the air.

"Did she say anything?" The question was inane, but Donna could feel Ana not answering.

"She asked about you, if you'd called me." Donna realized that her aunt was torn between loyalty to her sister, Sylvia, Donna's mother, and Donna herself. Why? Sometimes they didn't talk to each other for a little while, but they didn't lie to each other. And they didn't set family against itself. "She said you'd been acting oddly."

"Anything specific?" Donna's heart was hammering in her chest as she asked.

"No, just that you might call me and say some weird things."

They both let that hang in the air for just a moment.

"And have I?" Donna ventured.

"No. I mean, I told her that you'd called, brought up your father for the first time that I can remember." What was her mother doing checking up on her? And the way she'd acted the last time Donna had called her. Was her mother in on this? The alchemy, the lies, the controlling her? Why? She'd never done anything strange. Donna had a normal childhood. Just… while she was taking classes to be a personal trainer, her mother had moved away for a new job. And Donna hadn't been able to follow her.

"Did you tell her about the picture?"

"I didn't."

"Have you sent it yet?"

"No. It's in my pile of things to do."

"Could you make sure you do that?"

"Donna, what's going on? This isn't like you. Or Sylvia."

Welcome to the new normal, Donna thought, *I'm lying to everyone.*

"Things have come up, and they're hard to explain." Which wasn't a lie. "I want to tell you, but it's all twisted up and messy." That was true, too.

"Are you pregnant? Is that the problem?"

"That's not it. Nothing like that."

"I'm disappointed that you won't talk to me about whatever this is."

"If I thought I could, I would. But this feels like something I have to do myself."

"You're never alone, Donna. Carlos and I love you a lot, we'd do anything for you."

And for that, Donna thanked her lucky stars. She might feel alone, and family might be out of reach, but they were there.

"I have to go," she said. "It's been great talking to you. I know what's happening is confusing, but you two are helping just by being there and being sane."

"You're not inspiring confidence by saying things like that."

"I know. But I don't want to lie to you."

"Donna, you know that I would never do anything to hurt you. What is this big mysterious problem of yours?"

She wanted to say. Wanted to shout the fear, the self-doubt, how it was all making her head explode. Why was this happening to her?

"I'll tell you when I can."

Donna listened to her aunt's exasperated sigh.

"Love you, I'll talk to you later," Donna said before slamming the phone down. She could feel the tears threatening to burst out of her. She couldn't do that. She'd sound insane.

CHAPTER 8

YOGA STRAP

Donna smelled the damp wetness of Oakham at night. Around her, the insects played their songs on leggy instruments, oblivious to her murderous intent. She was wearing jeans and work boots. The air was chill enough that she wished she was wearing more than a tank top, but she pushed ahead.

Another lawn. Another dark house. Donna would have closed her eyes if she could. It was too much to hope this was just a robbery. She'd killed someone every time she'd been out like this. She was about to kill again.

She wondered how she got there. Oakham was in the country, sprawled widely when away from its cute downtown. There was no way she could go to all these places on foot. And yet, when she came to herself, she was always walking. What happened when she wasn't aware? How did she get up and get dressed without waking Jim up?

Donna strode through the grass, up to the back door of the small house. Again, no neighbors were visible through the tall trees. Most of the murders she could recall were out of sight of nearby residents. Why? Cause, effect, or coincidence?

She tried the back door, only to find it locked. Donna could have cheered. Now, to go home, to get back in bed, go back to sleep. But her body had other ideas. She took off one of her boots, held it over a fist, and smashed a small pane of glass in the door. She swept the bottom of the pane with the boot's sole, then reached in, carefully, and unlocked the door.

She had to come up with a name for it. "My Possessor"

sounded too much like something she'd read in a slave narrative. She didn't know if it was a male, female, or whatever. Was it an alien, a ghost, a demon, unborn psychic twin, something worse? What else could take someone over?

While she was thinking, her body had put her boot back on, and had slipped into the house. Inside, she could barely see anything. She was in the kitchen, and a blazing green glow over the range said 3:34.

Her phone chirped. She'd received a text. Why the fuck was she carrying her phone? Why the hell was someone calling her at this time of night? But her hands were pulling out the phone. On the small screen, a text popped up.

"Concentration is key."

She stared. She wondered what Not-She was thinking. Why would she be carrying her phone, on, while she broke into someone's house to kill them? What kind of idiot was running her damn body?

Apparently, the other her couldn't believe it either, because she just stared at her phone. Was her other self illiterate?

After what seemed like ten minutes, another text arrived, unknown sender.

"The opposite of meditation. Instead of emptying your mind, focus on a single thing."

Huh. Her other self turned off the phone and put it away. But Donna was already thinking. The message, from her Magical Mentor. Who she was just going to assume was a guy, because she knew him through Peter and Rich. Did he know what she was doing? The only other pair of messages had appeared during the day, while she was talking with Fierce. 3:30 AM was a really strange time to be sending texts. Did he know she was awake? Was he keeping tabs on her? Why was nothing in her life not creepy right now?

After putting her phone away, she looked around the kitchen. Many implements of destruction here, the range, the knife block, a blender, plenty of glass. But she passed by.

She could barely see. She shuffled, keeping her boot soles close to the ground, so she wouldn't kick anything, or trip. She saw the table just soon enough to avoid it. She laid her hand on the smooth surface, tracing its edge as she passed by. From there a hallway, on the left side, a staircase. Quiet as a ghost, she crept up the stairs.

From the landing, she heard the sound of someone shifting in their sleep. That must be the one. The door was open, and she stepped in. Her boot kicked something soft on the floor. Something cloth. She knelt, put her hands on it. A gym bag. She slowly opened it, felt around inside. Clothing, antiperspirant, a yoga strap. She paused, then brought out the strap. She wrapped one end around her right hand, leaving the rest to dangle. She knew where this was going.

She stood, quiet as the grave, fumbled at the wall, then turned on the light.

He lay in bed, rubbing his eyes. Black hair with a white streak above his left eye. He sat up in bed, then dropped his hands, and a shock of recognition ran through her. Barry Reeder. He'd taken a couple of her classes, then moved on to something lower impact.

He looked up at her.

"Donna? Donna, I'm so sorry about this."

Her body stood still, as if it were as shocked as she was. He must have been, too. He reached over to his nightstand and drained a shot glass.

"I know what you are here for," Barry said.

"The Key of Aros the Philosopher." Aros. Donna realized she'd been looking for the wrong word. Aros, not Eros.

Barry's bark of laughter was brief. "Well, you won't get it. It's not something that should just be told. The fact that you have brought Donna into this demonstrates that you are unready for it. I don't think you would use it in a safe or responsible manner."

In two strides, Donna had crossed to him, her fist hammering down across his face. He fell back and lay on the coverlet, his fingers touching the side of his face. After a moment, he sat back up.

"Feel better after your little tantrum? You don't have the patience to read or understand the glosses on Aros' commentary, let alone the text. It doesn't help that you have murdered eight of my friends and associates, and have left a child an orphan."

"On the other hand, I got rid of that dog-fighting bastard," Donna heard herself snort. "You take the high ground, but you were an associate of his."

Barry's smile was weary.

"He was not our best. Still I'm not going to thank you. Of us all, he was the most like you. Scared, and desperate."

"I'm not desperate."

"No? You're out for a stroll in someone else's body. I thought you had enough money to have people do these things for you, or is this a case of if you want it done right, do it yourself?"

"You have it all wrong," Donna started to say. Barry cut her off.

"Alchemy is the art of subtlety. Very small things make great changes. The art of poison, for example, is intensely persnickety."

Donna felt her eyes go wide. She looked at her hand. No gloves. Trapped inside herself, she raged at her violator, whatever was possessing her.

Barry laughed, held up the glass. "Subtle. It's what has allowed us to have this civilized conversation. Even if you decided to torture me, I figured I could last six minutes."

"Where is the antidote?"

Barry's smile twitched. "You're right, there is one. But you don't even know what form it's in. It could be a small gel to be held under the tongue, a pill, a clear liquid. So many possibilities, so many items in the room. Of course, if you were any real kind of alchemist, you would have some idea what I might have taken, just by my symptoms."

He coughed. "And then you could deduce the cure, and what form it would have to take."

He laughed, but it stopped as a hiccup. They stared at each other. Barry seemed unable to hold his head still. It trembled, his eyes began to droop.

"Stay awake," Donna snapped. The inside her was horrified. She unwound the yoga strap, let it fall to the floor.

Barry's trembling was more intense. He brought his shaking gaze up to meet Donna's. He couldn't hold it. His eyes slid away, independent of each other. He managed a quavering smile, defiant.

"Well, it seems a bit late now." He slurred, his tongue slower than the words he was forming. "Sheemsh like goodbye."

His eyes rolled up in his head, and his head pulled back as he fell onto the bed. His arms came up, his hands clenched tight, as if he were about to box someone. Curled into fetal position, his head began to shake, twitched against the bedspread, breathing hitching, sometimes falling silent. Foam gathered at the corners of his mouth.

Donna just stood and watched. She had assumed that his poison would be easy, that he had concocted something that would kill him painlessly. His tongue protruded as he tried to gasp in more air. She only watched as he struggled, back arching, neck straining to reach his heels, lips fixed in a rictus, showing his teeth. And then it stopped. Barry was still lying in his tortured position, but he wasn't shaking anymore. Donna watched for his breathing, but his chest was still. No motion. The all-too-familiar stillness of death.

Donna wondered what she was going to do now. She could feel the tension in her arms. Fuck the bastard, whoever was making her do this, killing other people or driving them to suicide! What kind of asshole did this sort of thing?

She marched back down the stairs, turning on lights as she went. She searched from room to room, and found a set of three glassed-in bookshelves. She looked for a moment, then pulled the books off the shelf. This time, she didn't find any to her satisfaction, and left a pile of them in the middle of the floor. She pulled a box of matches from her pocket, struck one, then laid it on the books. The corner of one page, took instantly, the flames licking up, turning the black-printed words to ash. The tall flame caught another book, and another, and Donna turned her back and walked out of the house.

It didn't explode as she walked away, like it would have in a movie. She didn't look back, and felt herself beginning to fade. She fought. She wanted to see what happened next. How did she get home? Her body stumbled. Well, she'd done something. She could feel darkness crowding her, pushed back against it, trying to keep herself, her awareness. She stumbled and went to her knees, hands pressed against her temples.

"No. You. Don't," her mouth grated out. Donna shrieked in the silence of nowhere, shoving at the darkness that swarmed over her like goo. She swiped at the encroaching unconsciousness, kicking, screaming, anything to stay awake. Her limbs became cold and sluggish, she moved slower and slower. Until she couldn't move, and the oily blackness of oblivion engulfed her.

Donna woke up in her bed, next to Jim. She stared at him for a minute.

"Fuck." She said it loud enough that she woke him up. Jim stretched and yawned, opened his eyes. It was still a bit early.

"What's up, babe?"

"I went to sleep in the *tub*, Jim. When did I get here?"

Was that alarm in his eyes? Or just surprise?

"Around one in the morning. You cuddled up to me."

"One? How did I get out?"

"How should I know? I was asleep. I don't know what's going on when I'm asleep."

Was he? If he was involved, was he somehow coordinating this takeover, the murders? Jim seemed... well too dumb to be that guy. He was kind and a good guy. She shouldn't be thinking these things about him.

"OK, I'm sorry," Donna said. "I woke up confused. It couldn't have been you, I wasn't thinking straight."

Jim hunched in the blankets, clearly glad he was no longer on the spot. She didn't like lying to him, but she couldn't stand him watching her go to pieces. He couldn't be the violator. Whatever was doing this to her was confident and strong. Jim's strength came from momentum. He was great when things were going well, but he wasn't good at making difficult decisions. His hands fell onto her shoulders, and Donna felt herself stiffen.

"What's wrong?" He asked. "Did you have another one of those dreams? You can say really hurtful things after one of them."

Donna bit her lip and looked away.

"You're right, I can be mean after... after I dream bad stuff."

She wasn't calling them dreams anymore, and Jim's inability to accept them as anything else irritated her. "It's not you, you understand?"

"It's just that you're acting—"

"Crazy?" Donna's voice was hard as flint. "Go on say it, Jim. I'm acting crazy."

"I was going to say not yourself. You haven't been yourself."

She didn't like the sound of that. Not at all. Dammit, why couldn't anything in her life be simple? Why couldn't she have normal things like a good boyfriend, an easy job? Not being taken over and murdering people at night?

"I think I'm being very reasonable in some very unreasonable circumstances," Donna said.

"It doesn't feel like it." Jim was sulking.

"I'm *trying* to be reasonable, then."

"You could try a little harder."

Donna sucked in a breath and let it hiss out. What was she trying to do here? *Keep the peace with Jim, try not to explode.* Priorities. She let out another breath. She could sit on her feelings a bit longer.

"It's upsetting, and I'm not getting as much sleep as I should. Neither of us is a morning person, so I think we both need to back off just a little."

Jim mulled that over, subsiding. "I don't understand why you lash out." He turned to her, and she could see the hurt in his eyes. "We're good together. We have fun, we support each other, we were meant for each other. I want to keep this going."

Jim talking about his feelings made Donna uncomfortable. He lived in such a small world.

"You seem like you're pushing me away," He said. "I'm trying to be supportive, and I get that I'm only so good at it, but it seems like you aren't interested in keeping this relationship going. And it might just be me, but I want you to feel like you could just tell me it's not working. I want this relationship, I want time together. I want us, like we were."

The good old days. How long ago had that been, months? It seemed so much longer.

Jim, uncharacteristically, was waiting for her reply.

"I want that, too." She looked at him. "But we aren't those people anymore, and our relationship has more history now. I'm having a bad time, and we can't just wish that away. And you've been there for me," *mostly*, "and we've looked for an answer together. For that, I'm grateful. I want you to understand that I'm under a lot of stress that I don't understand, and you're crowding me. I've had a bad night. Let me get myself together, then we can talk."

"I just want to be there for you." He had that sad puppy look again, and Donna felt her heart going out to him. He meant well, didn't he? The creepiness was just a coincidence. Jim wasn't malicious, he wasn't out to get her. He wasn't all jagged edges that sought to tear at others, the way Danny had been. She put her arm across his shoulders.

"I'm sorting some stuff out. It's hard, and I don't know what I'm doing. If I knew what was causing these dreams," she trailed off, resenting that she couldn't tell him what she thought.

"I'm trying to make sense of it, I really am." Jim got a determined look in his eye. "Whatever it is, it's hurting you. It's pushing you, making you miserable, making you seem like someone else. It's coming between me and the Donna I love."

Donna's traitor heart wanted to fall into his arms, cry, and promise to be better. She ground her teeth, wouldn't let it happen. Not until she knew what the hell was up with him. She stared at him for a moment, then did hug him. He hugged her back. She could feel the nagging tension, wondered if he could, too.

Donna gazed into the black depths of her monstrous coffee. She was tired already. The night excursion, followed by her emotional roller coaster with Jim, made her feel like she hadn't slept in a week. Kickboxing class this morning, aerobics in the afternoon, and two half-hour massages, with an hour-long that began at six. She was raking in the money, but she was going to be exhausted by the time the sun went down.

Fierce was looking dragged herself. She stirred listlessly at her Middleweight.

"Why do they even offer a Bantam," she asked Donna. "Who

needs coffee, but only needs a thimble full?"

"Someone who isn't me," Donna said. "Someone who isn't anyone I know."

Fierce took a long drink.

"You aren't looking so good, Donna."

"Bad things again, not being myself." Donna looked around Café Gitan. The morning bustle was quiet, people lining up for and receiving the benediction of coffee. Those in line were subdued. Most people who had their prize walked straight out. No one paid them any attention. "Was in a guy's house, but I didn't kill him."

"That's good, right?"

"He killed himself. I was right there. He drank something toxic, and he died." Donna moved in closer, barely daring to speak the next words out loud. "I knew him."

Her face was a mask of horror. "Oh shit, Donna. Oh my God. How can you live with this?"

Donna hunched her shoulders, shrugged. "I don't know. I just am. One foot in front of the other."

Fierce stared at her. "We've got to do something. Now."

"What? *What*? Do you have a priest or some sort of magical protection in that purse of yours?"

"*Donna.*" Fierce's voice cracked like a whip, and Donna realized how hysterical she'd sounded.

"First, we're in a coffee shop," Fierce kept her voice low and calm. Donna clung to that. "I don't know a good place to talk about whatever the hell is making you do these things, but this is not ideal. Second, we need to figure out what is causing your trouble."

"How do we do that?" Donna fought to keep her voice from rising. "I haven't been able to. The last guy, Barry, he *knew*. And he knew I could hear him. But he didn't say anything helpful."

"But what do you think it might be? What kind of thing possesses people, and makes them kill? Could it be the ghost of a serial killer? Did you ever eat a sugar skull on Dia de las Muertos that you shouldn't have, anything like that?"

"Borderline racist, Fierce."

"I can be racist. My best friend is Mexican."

Fierce laughed, and Donna sighed, too worked up to join in.

"How weird are you thinking?" Fierce asked.

"I don't know. I can't even think of what this might be. Hit me with some ideas, we'll see if they fit."

Fierce was quiet for a moment. "What if it's aliens?"

"Aliens that can only collect the endorphins from a murderous rush? That was a movie. Why would aliens be killing people and going through their books? The book search doesn't fit. Maybe we should try to keep this to occult, rather than science fiction. I don't even want to think about some machine that swaps peoples' brains."

"OK. OK. Weird, but not comic-book or *Gilligan's Island* stuff." Fierce thought for a moment. "Possessed by the ghost of a serial killer."

It felt odd. Nevertheless, Donna pulled out her phone and did a quick search for Massachusetts serial killers.

"Kristen Gilbert… but she's still alive. And she did it by injections. Hm. The New Bedford Highway Killer is a candidate. Never found, but he only killed women. Charles Pierce, Jesus, only killed kids. The Boston Strangler was only into strangling. None of these feel right."

"What about Lizzie Borden?" Fierce asked. "She's pretty famous hereabouts."

Lizzie Borden took an ax/She gave her mother forty whacks/ After she saw what she had done/She gave her father forty-one/ Lizzie Borden got away /For her crime she did not pay. Donna hunched her shoulders. That seemed like the brutality level she'd been experiencing. She didn't like it, simply because it was so famous. Everyone knew about Lizzie Borden and her ax. There'd been movies about Borden. It was like saying that you were the reincarnation of Cleopatra. She was famous and cool, so everyone who was reincarnated had to be her. She tried to ignore the idea by flicking through the Wikipedia list of mass murderers in Massachusetts. And froze.

"What?" Fierce asked.

Donna didn't want to answer. Answering might make it more likely. She couldn't stop reading, although the information on the page was scant.

"What did you find, Donna?"

"Jesse Pomeroy. Oh shit."

Fierce let Donna continue her horrified reading.

"He was a brute," Donna said. "Tortured kids, killed some others, but he wasn't much more than a kid himself. Killed a four-year-old boy and a ten-year-old girl, both when he was fourteen, may have killed others. Died in 1932." Fierce went quiet. Donna couldn't stop staring at the illustration of Pomeroy. Baby-faced with dark hair, but something sinister in his eyes. Of course he'd been drawn that way.

"Salem witches?" Fierce ventured.

"Huh?" It came out with the grace of a belly-flop.

"The Salem witches. Didn't Salem change it's name to avoid the stigma?"

"That was Danvers, which is a lot closer to Boston," Donna said. Jesse Pomeroy had been from South Boston. Why discount one because of distance but not the other? For the same reason she didn't like Lizzie Borden. It sounded too much like a television show, something the occult investigator and the audience would know about. Donna had never gotten the impression that the Salem witches were witches at all. Just heavily-repressed Puritans who'd gone over the edge, a lesson on the explosive release religious fanaticism engendered.

"Not looking like that's getting any traction," Fierce said.

"Yeah, I get the murdering people, dead witches looking for revenge. What about going through the books? If they're dead, what are they going to need with something out of a book?"

"Maybe how to get out of their eternal torment?" Fierce's face was earnest.

"So why me?" Donna asked.

"You've got me there," Fierce said. "More importantly, if they've been around for three hundred years, why haven't we heard anything about it? I mean maybe there's a secret government agency dedicated to covering up the crimes of Salem witch ghosts?"

"See that breaks it," Donna said. "I have trouble believing in large conspiracies, especially large government ones. The US couldn't even keep the NSA's civilian wiretapping a secret, how am I supposed to believe that a state has an agency I've never heard about?"

Fierce frowned into her half-empty coffee. "I like conspiracy theories."

"But you don't actually believe in them, do you?"

Fierce thought for a moment. "What about an Indian shaman?"

Donna nearly choked on her coffee.

"You could have done something," Fierce continued. "I don't know what, to him. Or, come to think of it, could be a her. They have women shamans, right?"

"Fierce, why would someone like that focus on me? I'm Mexican, so I'm more closely related to them than virtually anyone else in this town." And then she remembered the text about magic obeying the laws of sympathy. Could a First Nation shaman have targeted her because she was closer, genetically, than most of the white people around her? But what about the Aros the Philosopher business? Sure people could be whatever they wanted, but alchemy seemed very European.

"How about the Dover Demon?" Fierce asked.

"What about alchemists," Donna countered. Rich had brought up alchemy, too.

"Are you back on them?" Fierce shrugged. "I don't know anything more than I did. I kind of thought you weren't serious about the alchemy thing. I mean, it's weirdly specific."

"Why should being precise be any sort of problem?"

"Because you'll just know when you hit the right answer."

"Why? Who's going to tell me?" This was unexpected, especially from Fierce. She was usually practical. Hard-headed. If anyone would be resistant to the madness that had taken over Donna's life, it should be Fierce.

"I don't know," Fierce said. "But if you're going to have any sort of chance, you have to be able to figure this out."

"But who's going to tell me? Rich and Peter ran away screaming. They seemed to know what was going on."

"So maybe you should put some pressure on them. You're running around, playing Blind Man's Bluff. People are dying, Donna. I think they owe you a little more than that if they know anything."

"It's dangerous, Fierce. They don't want to step into it."

"Listen to yourself a second. They don't want to get involved, but people are getting killed. If you were able to go to the police—"

"Which I can't."

"Which I know you can't, they would be liable for withholding information. But even if you can't make them legally responsible, they are morally. And they can't get out of that."

Donna considered that. Was the best way to go and beat them over the head with their moral responsibility?

"Let me think about that."

"Don't take too long," Fierce said.

They finished their coffee in silence. But when she left, Donna realized she was chanting 'Lizzie Borden took an ax/ Gave her father forty whacks' to herself. *Great.*

The Crowing Rooster was no Silver Bistro, but Donna appreciated that Jim was at least making an effort. They couldn't go to the Silver Bistro every time they went out.

"Donna, I've been wondering if there's some way we can get you professional help." He shoveled some delicate goat-cheese and walnut risotto into his mouth. "You seem to be having a hard time lately, and I've been worried about you."

"Worried?" Donna echoed. "Professional help sounds expensive." She sure as hell didn't want to go to any sort of therapist Jim recommended. "I'm still building my presence, and that will be a major drain on our resources." She'd almost said her resources. But Jim would have pounced on that, magnanimously offering to pay for it himself.

"We've got a fair amount of money to play with. I understand it's worrying, but it's hard to watch you get so upset after you have one of those dreams. You going through this is killing me."

Donna wondered if he could have made it more about him, how much he was being inconvenienced.

"The thing is, Jim, Oakham is a small town."

"If you could leave town…."

"Not an option," she said with finality. "And you know that."

"I've never understood that. Why can't you leave Oakham?"

Donna speared her Cajun blackened chicken with her fork, one of the tines scratching across the plate.

"I wish I understood it, too," she said. "But I don't. I also don't understand why you think I need therapy. That doesn't speak well of our relationship."

"I'm trying to show you I care," Jim did not look at her, but concentrated on cutting his steak. "Sometimes we have to do things we don't want to."

"Which makes you the hard man making the hard decision. Reducing me to the subject of that decision. Thanks for letting me make my own choices."

"All right, I'm sorry I brought it up. I thought I was doing something for you, trying to help you get back on an even keel."

Should she tell him how fucking high-handed his approach was? She closed her eyes. Relationships only worked if both sides were working at it. She wasn't holding up her end. Was it right to punish Jim by forcing him to do all the work? Was it right to stay in the relationship?

She wondered if she could move in with Fierce.

"Hey." Donna nearly jumped when Jim touched her hand. "I'm sorry. I see you going through something I don't understand, and it tears me up. I feel like I have to do something, even if it's the wrong thing. It's killing me, *killing me*, to see you freak out in the morning. I never know when it's going to hit, and I don't know how you're going to react. But there's clearly something wrong, and it's driving you crazy, and that drives me crazy. I want to help. I'm going to screw up because this is uncharted territory. It would be easier to leave you alone to face whatever demons you're wrestling with, but I care too much to do that."

Donna put her hands on his. He might be misguided, but he said the right things. His heart was in the right place. He wasn't perfect, he sometimes acted like a control freak, but he had a gentle soul. He liked to white knight, be the guy who rescued and protected her.

"It's OK," she said. "Neither of us knows what's going on, and I should have realized how frustrating it is because you don't have direct experience with what's happening. You're a good guy, Jim, and I know this has been hard." Her mother always said difficult times brought out the real person. Jim swung between being supportive and totally tone-deaf to her needs, but he got it right sometimes. Like right now.

She smiled at him, and wondered how long it had been since she'd done so.

They went home and had sex because he expected it. On her knees, face pressed into the pillow with Jim thrusting into her, Donna surprised herself by thinking about Nathan.

She had just come home from a massage when she discovered a cardboard envelope from her Tia Ana. She checked to make sure she was alone, then wondered why she'd done so. Then she tore off the strip and eased out the photo.

Her mother, without a doubt, in a summer dress, in the sunshine, some sort of outdoor picnic. She was standing next to a guy Donna had never seen before. Without a shirt, he was lean, athletic, but not broad-shouldered the way a body-builder would be. In his early twenties, trying to grow a mustache and failing, his hair blond at the tips, clearly showing brown roots. Who had hair like that? She brought the photo closer, trying to suck all the visual detail out of it. She should scan it, enhance the image.

That guy was her father? She sat down. She'd never known what her father looked like, except for her own differences from her mother. Lighter skin, a more prominent nose she'd hated when she was a teen, and a different jawline. She couldn't tell if they were all hers. In fact, if her aunt hadn't told her this was her father, she wouldn't have picked him out of a crowd.

She felt strange handling the picture. She'd gotten over her obsession of figuring out who her father was years ago, but she'd never stopped wondering. Had he been such a terrible person? Her mother had completely expunged him from her life, and from Donna's, too. She wondered if he'd ever tried to make contact.

Were her fingers tingling? So strange to suddenly have a piece that fit a void in her life. She wanted more, though, as if this little piece just made her crave answers now that she had something, rather than nothing.

Why now? With everything else going on, what was it that had made her mother bring up her father? So much was happening.

Where to put it? Jim would ask about the picture, and she didn't want to lie to him about it. Not if she could avoid it. She didn't want to talk to him about it. Not until she knew more. Not yet.

She looked at it once more, wondering who he was, where he was now. Did he have another family? Was he even alive? She went to the bedroom and tucked it under her jewelry.

As always, Donna was a little nervous when meeting a new massage client. She had her routine down, explaining the parameters and boundaries, what was expected of her, what was expected of the customer. Today's customer was middle-aged, not taking care of himself as much as he ought. He was confident, had an easy smile, and Donna relaxed.

"Before we get started. Do you have any questions?" she asked.

"You are very beautiful," he said.

Her smile froze.

"And I really mean that," he continued. "I mean drop-dead gorgeous. And I was sort of wondering if there was any possibility of, you know, maybe a happy ending?"

She should take out the hammer, let him see it before she smashed his head into a bloody ruin. Donna shot him a look straight in his eye, let out just a hint of that murderous desire.

"No." She said it with absolute, final calm.

"Well, I, huh..."

"I'm going to step outside," she said, careful and deliberate as a death notice. "Tell me when you are ready."

The door closed, and Donna ground her teeth, then let out a breath. She wouldn't let him shake her, no matter how much she wanted to cut his throat and watch his life spurt out into a bucket. She was a professional. She'd give him a good massage. She was stronger than this.

"I'm ready," came his voice. Donna hesitated. What if he

wasn't under the towel, or stroking himself on her table? Well, then fucking useless police would have to clean up after her.

With a breath to brace herself, she opened the door.

The Horn was busy, the customers cheerfully intoxicated. Donna stroked the smooth stem of her Manhattan. A perfect drink, and she'd had a few by now. She was waiting for the bar to get a little quieter before she confronted Peter. She respected that they didn't want to get involved, but she had to have some answers.

"You look like you're waiting for something." Peter hadn't just magically appeared, but he was damned sneaky when he tried to be.

"The right moment," she said.

"For me? Donna, am I in trouble?" She swam in Peter's brilliantly blue eyes. She wanted to tell him all about it, to rage at him.

"No," she forced herself to say. "I had a real asshole in for a massage today. It's damn difficult to work on someone who just asked you if you would jerk him off. Fucking degenerate." She looked at Peter. "Why are men like that?"

He gave her a sad look, then reached under the bar and pulled out the drink mixer. Without a word, he shook and poured her another Manhattan. She took a sip, then set it down, letting her silence exert pressure on him.

"I don't have *the* answer," he said. "But I do have *an* answer, if you want to hear it."

"I'm all ears," Donna said, downing the rest of her drink.

"Guys can spend a lot of time in their own heads. I think we talk to ourselves a lot more than women do. You have friends you can talk to, and there's a lot of guys who, without trying to be, are old-fashioned enough that they don't talk about their feelings. So what goes through guys' heads doesn't get a lot of air time. Or feedback."

Donna gave her empty glass a significant look, and Peter refilled it.

"Sometimes, a guy will come out with something that sounded perfectly reasonable in his own head, but is in fact a terrible idea. And he'll try it out on you, and you're the first person to hear it. He, of course, has all the lead-up that makes it all sound reasonable, but he hasn't told you that. You just get the end product with no idea how they got there."

That made sense to Donna. "It must be awful, spending so much time in your own head." She would have gone nuts without Fierce and Tia Ana and… Donna thought a moment. And Peter and Rich. And, she supposed, Jim. When had her social circle gotten so small? What had happened to Janet, Tammy, and Erica? When had she stopped hanging out with Erick and Jon? Where had her friends gone? And it wasn't because of the murders. They'd fallen away before all that started. Had she withdrawn, or had they?

"That looks like it was a pretty heavy thought," Peter said.

"Yeeeah, sorry, just realized my life has gone to shit in more ways than I had originally thought." She sighed, and remembered her original purpose in coming here.

"Peter, you and I need to talk about alchemy."

Peter frowned.

"Donna, we really can't get involved…."

"You and Rich already are involved. You can't weasel out of it. There's a lot going on here that I don't get, and you two know something, which is more than I do. I need your help."

"No." Peter's rejection was more a sigh than a statement. He looked up and down the bar, but nobody seemed to need his attention at that moment. "It's dangerous, and I think you appreciate that."

"Fine." Donna turned away from Peter, raised her glass. "Hey folks," she shouted into the semi-full bar. "Did you know Peter and Rich are into a lot more than drinks and guy sex?" She trailed off as Peter grabbed her wrist and pulled her back to the bar.

"Some things we don't tell just anybody," he growled.

"People are getting killed. You know something, and there's a lot you aren't telling me. So cut the bullshit or I will tell everyone who can listen *everything* I know about you two."

"You're threatening us. That's a fascinating way to ask for help."

"I'm done begging. I'm doing terrible shit to people and I need to stop and if that means I have to stomp on your delicate toes to get some results, you're going to end up with some very sore feet." She leaned in until they were practically nose to nose. "I feel less guilty with each one."

Peter looked at her, a mixture of pity and resignation on his face. Holding her gaze for a moment, he looked down the bar.

"I have a couple of customers waiting. Can I leave you here for a couple of minutes?"

"Sure. I know where you work." Donna's sense of victory was heady. She was getting somewhere.

She contemplated the bottles reflected in the mirror behind the bar, lined up like soldiers at attention. She felt the first twinges of regret. She liked Peter and Rich. They were good people, and while she didn't want to drag them into this, they clearly knew more about alchemists and maybe why she was murdering people. She shuddered.

"Donna." Rich was suddenly standing next to her.

"I didn't think you were working tonight," Donna said.

"I'm not. But we apparently need to talk."

"And this way Peter can get on with the bar. Don't you want him to be part of the conversation?"

Rich looked at his hands. "We trust each other. So let's go in the back. There's only so much I want the patrons to hear."

She stood, and he walked behind the bar and grabbed a half-full bottle of Bushmills and a couple of glasses.

"Not really my drink," Donna said, trying not to sound pushy.

Rich flashed her a brief smile. "It's not all for you."

He led Donna through the small kitchen, waving briefly to the short order cook on the way by. After a turn, he and Donna were in a small room whose main features were a table and eight chairs. The walls were rich, dark paneling, the light came from a small but ornate ceiling lamp. She found it surprisingly inviting. Rich pulled a chair out, invited Donna to sit.

When she had, Rich closed the door. Without saying anything, he filled his shot glass with dark amber Irish whiskey, and knocked half of it back. Donna remained quiet.

"I knew this day was going to come, and I'm still not ready for it," he said. "You are in a bad situation, and there's a good chance that you are going to pull down anyone who tries to give you a helping hand."

"So, I should just give up now?" Donna couldn't hide her bitterness. "How fucked am I? Rich, I don't even know."

He sighed, looked at the bottle, but didn't reach for it.

"You're up against someone who is, magically speaking, very powerful. Taking over someone's body is very complex and demanding, so they are by necessity good at it. You're going rounds with Muhammad Ali."

"So I can't win, is that what you're telling me?"

"Not without some sort of trick up your sleeve. You're inexperienced where your opponents know what they're doing, and they're throwing considerable weight against you."

"So this is a person. An alchemist."

Rich's look was thoughtful. "I think so. I can't imagine anything else out there being able to take you over." He looked like he wanted to add something else.

"What are you thinking?" Donna asked.

"Just that alchemists work in terms of physical items; potions, magical concoctions, metals, that sort of thing. So I'm wondering what you got. If there's a ring you wear that they have magicked up, or maybe you drank one of their weird brews and didn't know it. How did they get to you, Donna Otálora?"

Her? What had she done? No, what had been done to her? How? She thought of the handmade jewelry she had bought. Could that have been it? Her bracelets, maybe? That lovely ring with the purple gem?

"So what can I do?"

"Find how you've been contacted, figure out the conduit between them and you."

"Them?"

"Oakham is something of an alchemical haven, a college."

"Like an actual school?"

"Calling themselves a college makes them feel more official and institutional. It's more like a fraternity or a Rotary lodge."

"Fantastic. The Rotarians are making me murder people."

"No. So, OK, I haven't been clear. The college isn't your problem. I've met a couple of them, and they're overall peaceful, not the murdering sort. Or compelling someone else to murder sort. They're into enlightenment, self-knowledge. For some of them, the Great Art, which is what they call alchemy, is a road rather than a destination. Like yoga, inner enlightenment, that sort of thing. Only they can manifest some very powerful effects if they want."

"Was Barry Reeder one of them?"

"Your problem isn't the college. It's someone who is against the college. Possibly trying to destroy it."

Donna poured herself a drink, gulped it down. The Irish whiskey was harsh.

"Whoever it is keeps asking for the Key of Aros the Philosopher," she said. "Is that helpful?"

Rich shook his head. "I've met alchemists, but I don't know their art. They like their books, but I've never read any of the truly abstruse ones."

"You're not giving me a lot of love, here. Or a lot of hope. How do I figure out what they've done to me?"

Rich's face was grim. "There's no easy way to know. You could try smashing all the suspicious stuff you own, but if it turns out that it was something you drank, that could be in you for years."

Donna closed her eyes. Years. *Fuck.*

"Is there any way to arrange a meeting with any of them? Does the college have a campus or anything?"

"They're a secretive society currently under siege. I doubt they'll see anyone."

"Shit. So what can I do? What do I do? I'm drowning here, and people are getting their heads smashed open, roasted on their own grills. Do you have anything that I can fucking use?"

Rich shook his head. "I don't. And in fact, I have something worse to tell you."

"Lay it on me. Doesn't matter if the water is ten feet or a mile deep. It's still over my head."

"Magic isn't the only power in the universe, Donna. Watch out for any other sort of trick your guy may have up his sleeve."

Donna held her head in her hand. "This has been informative, if a bit short on solutions. I wish you had something more concrete that I could work with."

Rich poured himself another, drank it all in a smooth swallow.

"I do, too."

CHAPTER 9

BROKEN GLASS

Donna came to herself in the dark. She was walking on asphalt, her boots the only sound besides the songs of the summer insects. Why did Oakham have so many out-of-the-way houses? She cursed the omnipresent trees, the lack of streetlights that allowed her to walk in the dark. Why didn't Oakham care that people were being murdered?

Concentrate. She had to concentrate. If she could just shut everything else out, she might get somewhere. Her feet still moved, mindlessly striding through the grass in the dark. Once again, she was approaching a house. This would all be easier if she could close her eyes, somehow ignore the outside. But nothing about this situation was easy.

Donna tried to clear her mind. She had to focus.

Her hand came up, and she knocked on the door. That simple. She shifted from foot to foot, waiting. What was she going to do if the homeowner had a gun? Did she hear footsteps approaching? She did.

The door opened just a crack. She saw a lean face, mid-thirties, with immaculate hair, even at this late hour. A hint of stubble peppered his chin.

Her hand shot out, grabbing him by the windpipe. He wrenched himself back, and Donna surged through the door. She had the impression of a neat, well-ordered mudroom in cream and wood only for a moment. The world spun as his fist impacted her face. She staggered, came back with a counterpunch that rocked him. They stood, each watching the other for a moment, before she feinted with her right and then slammed her left fist into his collarbone.

He fell back, stumbling through the open doorway. She followed, reaching. His foot caught and he went over onto the flagstone floor. They were in a kitchen, but Donna didn't have much time to look for weapons. Her boot smacked into his ribs, and he curled around the blow, grunting. She kicked a second time, and Donna heard something crack, like a twig snapping. She pulled back for a third kick, but he rolled away.

He was on his feet, in a crouch, favoring his left side. She wondered who he was. Mid-thirties, his shoulders were narrow in his off-white button-down. Where he'd turned the cuffs up on his shirt, his arms were slender. He needed to work out.

He came at her, and she met him, savagery for savagery. Donna was only using her fists, as if she'd never been to her own kickboxing class. When they separated, she'd managed to bloody his nose and split his lip. Donna wiped her mouth on her wrist, and it came away bloody. She hurt from bruises that went right down to the bone.

The kitchen was well-appointed, with wood cabinets that had glass fronts. No veneer on them. The countertops were a complex rust red and off-white. Too bad she'd come here to kill this guy. He had excellent taste.

She'd backed him into a corner of his kitchen, sink to his left, counters and cabinets to his right. Donna looked out for his knife block but didn't see one. Where did he keep his knives?

He shoved his right hand into a drawer, and Donna snapped a kick into it. The wood splintered around his wrist. He pulled his hand out, thumb bent badly, fingers stiff.

"Do I have your attention?" Donna asked. "We can dance this dance, or we can…"

She ducked the first tumbler he flung at her. The second smashed into her wrist, numbing it, showering her with shards. Keeping her hand in front of her face, Donna rushed him. A juice glass deflected off her hand, and then she was on him, and they went down in a tangle of flailing limbs. She felt rather than saw the pint glass smash over her head. She rammed an elbow into his face, heard his skull *crack* on the floor.

She got to her feet, grabbed him by the hair, dragged him across the floor to a large, six-paned window that looked out to the side yard. He grabbed her hand and shouted something, but he couldn't get enough purchase to stop her. She stepped around him, spun him on his ass to face the window, her hand still full of his hair.

"The Key of Aros," she grated. "One of you shitbirds has to have it."

His laugh was harsh.

"Do you not get it?" Donna shouted down at him. "You know I'll kill you."

"How many of us have you killed so far? Eight, I think? And nothing to show for it?" He twisted his head around, glared at her. "Maybe you're going about this the wrong way?"

"What the hell is with you idiots?" Donna grated. She shoved him forward, smashing his face through the window. She held him there, head dangerously over a great shard of glass.

He started to scream, but Donna leaned her weight on his head, and he had to put everything he had into keeping his neck away from the sharp edges of the glass. He ended up with a single hand on the windowsill, trying to resist her.

"What do I have to do to get you to take me seriously?" Her voice rose.

"You. Clearly don't. Understand us." He gasped between words as she increased the pressure on his head. "Looks. Like. You. Never will."

"If you don't want to die, why resist? Why fight me?"

She couldn't see his face. Was he smiling, praying? She lurched forward as he suddenly went limp. She heard a sickening noise like a knife slicing through ham, then a bubbling sound. Blood cascaded down the window glass in a river.

What the hell, crazy asshole who was running her body? Why can't you figure your enemies out? This was the second one to kill himself, or give up the fight, while you were trying to intimidate them. Figure it out, you stupid asshole, this isn't working. But you apparently can't hear my thoughts, so I'm going to have to uselessly murder more people.

Donna had stepped back, and stared at the body. Blood still

streamed down the glass, gory as a slasher film, running down the sill and puddling on the floor.

Donna woke up aching. She was wearing the sports bra and panties she'd gone to bed in, but her ribs, her knuckles, her head, everything ached. She shuffled out of bed like an old woman, teeth gritted against the aches and pains, she came to the bathroom mirror and fought down a shriek.

A huge bruise had bloomed on her right cheek. Blood crusted her knuckles, her torso was a map of bruises. She looked like she'd been through a boxing match. Any doubts she'd had that these were dreams were now gone.

"Jim," she said.

Jim woke slowly, sat up and ran his hands through his hair, even sniffed himself, before he looked at her.

"Holy shit. Shit, Donna, what the hell happened to you?"

"It wasn't a dream," she said.

His eyes were big, looking at her collection of bruises and cuts.

"Oh my God, Donna."

"And you know nothing about it?"

"I slept through the night. Never woke up." His eyes were huge, imploring. "Oh God what's been happening to you? What have I let happen to you?"

He gently touched the bruise on her face, brushed the places her ribs had been kicked. She flinched.

"So you believe me," she said. "Finally. After all this, you believe me."

"I do. I have to. Oh God, that looks so painful." At least he took his hands away.

"We have to do something," he said. "This isn't right. You don't deserve this. No one does. Oh my God, I have to do something."

"Yes, so you've said." Donna didn't mean to snap. She was in pain. She grabbed a washcloth and shoved it at him. "Put some ice in this, would you?"

Jim walked out, and Donna had some time to think. She looked at herself in the mirror. Haggard and bruised, it was the face of someone at a women's shelter. She could only stare at that face, wondering who it was, until Jim came back with the cold washcloth.

The cool was soothing on her abused flesh. When it started to hurt, she moved it to her other injuries.

"We should get those looked at," Jim said.

"They're just bruises," she said, shaking him off. Much as she wanted to go to a doctor and make sure everything was OK, she couldn't. "I wouldn't be able to explain these, would I? Medical professionals are required to report anyone who looks like they've been beaten. And that's what this looks like."

"But I never…"

"I know that, of course you didn't. But I can't explain that I got taken over by… well, and kicked the crap out of someone? They'd think I was crazy. They'd think I was covering for you."

"That's crazy."

Donna shivered. She didn't know any battered women, but she'd heard stories. Friends of friends who made up all kinds of excuses. They walked into doorknobs, they fell down the stairs, or they got mugged more than everyone else in town combined. Donna shuddered. The fear with which they relayed the stories, knowing that but for the grace of God, that could be them.

Jim, of course, never had to think about it. She was protecting him.

"I don't want to talk to the police, OK?"

"What about the gym?"

"People will talk, but we don't have to report it. So there's going to be a little chatter, but I'm going to heal up, and we will be fine." Until another mind invasion left her a bloody mess again.

She couldn't read Jim's expression for a moment. For a second, he looked happy. What did he have to be happy about? Had she really seen it? Let it go, she told herself. She wasn't on very stable ground.

She shifted the ice pack to the bruise on her thigh.

"Hey, what's with the fist?" Jim asked. "You pissed at me or something?"

Donna wondered what he was talking about, then looked

down and discovered that her left hand was a fist. She opened her fingers, making sure she could.

"It's not you." She wasn't sure, though. She was pissed off at the asshole that was taking her over. And yeah, she was a little angry that Jim hadn't noticed she was getting out of bed at night. And that he hadn't just taken her word for it all. She found her hand in a fist again, looked at it, and then back to Jim. She wanted to punch him in his stupid fucking face. It would be so easy.

With an effort, she unclenched her hand again. Hitting Jim wasn't the solution. It would just make her feel better, and she wasn't even sure that was entirely true. That was her helplessness talking. She didn't want to take it out on Jim. Did she?

"Can you get me a drink of water?" She wasn't thirsty, but it got him away from her.

"Sure thing." But his face was closed. Still, he left.

Donna turned back to the mirror, looking at her battered reflection. It was going to be a heavy foundation day.

Donna held onto her Big Bruiser at the Café Gitan like a lifeline. The caffeine and sugar pop had breathed life back into her sore, aching bones. The heat of the coffee soothed her hands. She'd stretched and warmed up, but she felt like she could go right back to sleep. Today was light; luckily she was on break from kickboxing class.

The rain didn't put a damper on her. The bruises had done that all by themselves.

"Sorry I'm late," Fierce bustled up, dripping wet. "Idiots don't know how to drive in the rain."

Donna sighed in agreement, took another swallow of her coffee.

"Not looking so good, Donna. And you layered on the makeup today. It's not a flattering look for you."

"It's not foundation, Fierce, it's cover-up."

Fierce's face went slack in horror, and she grabbed Donna's wrist. "If he laid a fucking finger on you I will…."

"Chill. It wasn't Jim."

"Did you get mugged?" Fierce was searching Donna's face to find other bruises.

"I had a dream that fought back."

Fierce stared at Donna's face for a full minute.

"Quit it, someone is going to notice," Donna hissed.

"You're sure it wasn't Jim," Fierce asked.

Something about her earnestness melted Donna a little. She never had to worry with Fierce. She always had Donna's back.

"Totally wasn't. Couldn't have been." *Could it?*

"Ladies."

Donna looked up to see Nathan's kind face. His shirt was spotted with rain, but he was wearing the tie she'd selected for him.

"I got the job," he said with a smile.

"That's great. Congratulations."

Nate had a big, handsomely boyish face, and it lit up when he smiled.

"Thank you." He turned to Fierce. "I'm sorry, I didn't catch your name."

"Ah. Nate, this is Mildred Davies, nickname 'Fierce'."

Nate chuckled, "Mildred Fierce. I like it."

"Something I…" Donna started.

"Not a lot of people get that," Fierce cut in. "So you're new in town. Why don't you sit down next to me and tell me about yourself." She gave the seat next to her a dainty pat.

Nate sat down, gave Fierce another smile, and a quick wink toward Donna.

"I'm Nate Jardine, I just got a job up at the college as an assistant to the registrar."

"Jardine sounds French Canadian," Fierce cooed.

"A couple of generations back, sure. I was raised in Connecticut, though."

"That would explain your quite lumberjacky physique," Fierce winked at Donna.

"Down girl," Donna said. She told herself she wasn't irritated by Fierce's infatuation. Because Nate wasn't her guy. She'd barely spoken to him for fifteen minutes. Donna wasn't territorial like that.

"No harm in talking to the man," Fierce said. "He knows I'm not on the prowl."

"I just got out of a relationship, and I'm not looking for anything right now, so I'm sorry to disappoint," Nate said generally, rather than straight to Fierce. "Besides, Fierce, I was admiring your wedding ring. Are those real emeralds?"

"Diamond chips around a pair of half-karat emeralds," Fierce said as she stuck out her hand to let Nate look at the ring.

"He must love you a great deal." Nate's statement was gentle.

"He does, he certainly does," Fierce said.

"Well, it's good to know where all the cool kids get their coffee." Nate looked down at his Middleweight. "I've had bad experiences with the stuff you get at the office, and it's nice to get out to the local businesses. Wonderful to have met you, Fierce, and of course good to run into you again, Donna." Was there interest in his eyes, or was he just being friendly? Donna couldn't tell.

"See you around," Donna waved. He broke into a winning smile, saluted them with his coffee, and wandered out of the cafe.

"He looks large," Fierce said. "All of him. Tall, large hands, large feet..."

"And about half your age," Donna shot back. Why was she being so defensive about him?

"Donna, there's never any harm in looking. Nate seems like a nice guy, and maybe I'll think about him a bit, and maybe while Carl is doing his thing. But I do that with everyone. Even you once or twice."

Donna choked on her coffee.

"You what?"

"Come on. With that perfect skin, your slender hips, strong, toned body..." Fierce trailed off.

"I'm not sure how I feel about that," Donna said.

"Take it as a compliment," Fierce said with a shrug. "I mean, I've thought about a lot, and I mean a *lot* of people."

"How many have you told?"

"You can't just run around telling people that you fantasize about them. They get all uncomfortable."

Donna digested this. "So why tell me?"

"Because you can handle it and won't take it the wrong way."

Donna knew Carl. He was thickset, bulky without being fat. She found him unappealing. She could understand why Fierce had such an active fantasy life. Donna immediately regretted the uncharitable thought. Carl was a good man, Fierce loved him. Hadn't Fierce said that they'd had some trouble? Maybe she could get some advice on how to work it out with Jim.

Donna saw the worried look on Fierce's face.

"I haven't just ruined our friendship, have I? Was that too personal?"

"No, you're fine." Donna smiled. "But you know how you and Carl had some trouble, and you patched it up? How did you do that?"

Fierce tilted her head. "That kind of came out of nowhere."

"Jim and I aren't seeing eye to eye about a lot of stuff, and I don't know how to reach out. How did you put a relationship back together?"

"It's work," Fierce sighed. "A lot of work, and a lot of being honest with yourself."

She held out her hand. "This ring is a lot nicer than my first ring. Because Carl could afford it, and because he wanted to make this one bigger, make it more of a commitment."

"How did you put it all back together?" Donna paused. "You don't have to if you don't want to."

"We stopped lying to each other. Mostly. I mean, I sometimes gloss over unimportant stuff, but we're a lot more truthful with each other. And it's work, because sometimes I'd really rather not tell him stuff. But when it counts, we're honest."

"So, be honest with him?" Donna had spent a lot of time lying to Jim, brushing him off. Was she ready to stop that? Did she still feel threatened by him? She needed stability in her life. She needed Jim.

"It'll only work if he's being honest with you. You both have to want to make it better, or there's just going to be one of you doing all the work." Fierce paused. "Are you sure Jim is as committed as you are to keeping everything together?"

"Probably more than I am," Donna said.

"A ringing endorsement if I've ever heard one. Make sure you're both on the same page, that you both want the relationship and that you both want to work on it. One is not necessarily the other."

"Jim wants this. He wants us to stay together." Donna hoped repetition would make it true.

"Then you have nothing to worry about." Fierce took a pull from her coffee. "You don't have to convince me, Donna."

"I feel so bad because this weird shit is happening to me, and I'm dragging him down with me. I'd understand if he wanted to break up. I'm such a mess."

"If he won't stand with you when things are tough, he's not worth your time." Fierce's declaration was soft, but forceful.

Donna checked the time on her phone. "Urgh. Gotta go. I signed up for a weightlifting class."

"Wait, you're bodybuilding, now?"

Donna frowned. "If this shitwad alchemist is going to make me do dangerous shit, I need to strengthen up." Donna could feel her face tightening. "I hate this," she whispered.

"Keep going," Fierce said. "One foot in front of the other. It'll get better. It has to."

Donna wasn't sure.

Four days later, Donna was taking a rare Saturday off. She'd shaken some of the fear. Jim was at some company meeting, and Donna was enjoying the luxury of being alone in the apartment. But she rattled around too much. She needed some air. A walk, some time to think.

Their apartment was a mile and a half from Oakham's commercial district. The sun was out, the trees sighed in the low wind. It was absurdly pleasant. She breathed in the air, felt the warm sun on her skin. The fear, the helplessness, it all seemed so far away. She could feel the muscles in her back, so tight for so long, begin to unclench. Her aches faded. She should walk places more often, on beautiful days.

"Donna? Are you Donna?"

She turned to see a police officer. He'd gotten out of his car, and was standing on the sidewalk, fifteen feet behind her.

"Donna Otálora, right? You're Donna?"

"Officer Kutsenko, right?" He was just a little too far away for her to read his badge, but she remembered the bald head, the crooked teeth. "Was I doing anything wrong?"

"I just wanted to check and see if you remembered me," he said. Which sounded like only half the story.

"Yeah, I do. I didn't get a chance to thank you for being kind to me that day. I was pretty distraught, and you were very professional."

Kutsenko wrinkled up his mouth. Donna waited.

"Some stuff still bothers me about that day. You're under no obligation, of course, since this is unofficial, but I'd like to be able to talk to you about it."

Donna considered. He was older, probably fifty, so he probably wasn't hitting on her. And she had a lot of questions about that day at the police station, too.

"What were you thinking?" She asked.

"I dunno, maybe some time at the park on a bench, or maybe grab a doughnut or something."

"Did you really say you wanted a doughnut?"

Kutsenko smiled. "A little humor at my own expense helps to set people at ease."

"So, did you want to talk, like, now, or in a couple of days?"

"I'm off-shift at four, so today would be fine. If not, here's my card."

"Four sounds good. Dunkin' Donuts?"

His smile was crooked. "See you at a quarter past four, then." He got back in his blue and white cop car, and drove off. Donna watched him go. She wasn't even upset. Her beautiful day had been touched by the darkness that was encroaching on her life, but Kutsenko had seemed honest. She couldn't imagine some enlightenment-seeking alchemist taking a police job. Did they have potions to make themselves bulletproof?

What to do until then? The sun warmed her face, the air was fresh. Maybe an aimless stroll…

Four fifteen rolled around, and Donna was at Dunkin' Donuts. She hadn't been in one for years. It smelled of grease and sweet, with an undertone of sweat and desperation, the decor similarly plastic and soulless. She took a small, two-seat table in the minuscule seating area, and waited. She wasn't interested in the coffee, and really not hungry for one of the donuts.

Kutsenko wore a collared green polo shirt and jeans, and walked like he felt uncomfortable not wearing his cop belt. He didn't know where to rest his hands.

"So, what do I call you? Out of uniform, calling you Officer Kutsenko feels a little weird."

"Jerry is fine. And I want to repeat that this is unofficial. I'm here because I want to know a little more about what happened. Can I get you something to eat? Some coffee?"

"Thanks, I'm fine."

Jerry. Donna forced herself to think of him as Jerry, walked off and came back with a doughnut.

"It's a terrible thing to be a cop who likes these. You just never hear the end of it."

"You don't look like you eat a lot of them," Donna said. And he didn't. Kutsenko—*Jerry*—was around fifty. He was getting a little fat around his waist, but he wasn't the stereotypical fat cop. He was fit and clearly had been more trim than he was now.

"Everyone deserves a little vice," he said. "The key is not indulging it too often." He looked her up and down without lingering. "But you look like you know that already."

Well, he could make small talk, and be polite. Donna wondered how complicit he was in the whole thing at the police station. The Chief had just swooped in and basically thrown her out. Was Kutsenko just another part of the theater?

"The day you came to the station was... very strange," he said, looking at his hands, rather than her. "I mean, the Chief has never pulled me, or anyone else that I know, out of an interrogation."

Donna didn't say anything.

"Now, you were talking about some serious stuff." He glanced around. "And I get that it would be difficult to talk about, especially to a police officer. I'm only interested in what you were saying in as far as it related to Chief Schenck's actions."

Donna nodded.

"Pretend that I have no idea what police procedure is," she said.

"That's sort of beside the point. It feels like the Chief is covering something he doesn't want people to know about. And somehow, you figure into that."

"If I'm in collusion with him, you've just tipped your hand," Donna said.

Kutsenko's mouth was rueful, and he finished off his strawberry-frosted donut.

"That is a possibility, I suppose. But you didn't seem all that pleased with his intervention, either."

He had her there.

"My supposition," he continued. "Is that something in your confession involves him."

He let that hang for a moment.

"I wanted to talk with you here because it's public. Nobody wants to talk to a cop, or a stranger, without potential witnesses. That said, I'm required to begin an investigation on any illegal actions that you tell me about. I don't think I remember what you were talking about when you came into the station, so you should remind me what that was all about."

Donna shook her head. "It doesn't seem to matter. I tell people and they don't believe me. No one is paying attention. The paper doesn't cover it, the cops don't care. It's like being invisible." She shuddered.

"OK. I'm listening now."

Could she? She looked at him. He was still the fucking asshole who had thrown her out of the police station.

"It's hard," she started. "Look, no offense, I'm sure you're a nice guy, but you're also a cop." Her gaze landed on the plain, gold ring on his left hand. "Tell me about your wife."

His face froze. She tried to wait him out, but his scowl only deepened.

"Then you don't want it enough," she said. "You're just screwing around." She waited another moment, then started to get up.

"All right. All right. Sit down." He looked away from her for a moment. "Amanda died two and a half years ago."

Donna was mortified. "I'm so—"

He cut her off with a hard look. Well, she'd asked.

"We were high school sweethearts. She never had it easy. We got married just before I went off for the first Gulf War. I came back a different person. I tried to be the best man I could be for Amanda, but I wasn't the guy she'd fallen in love. But we worked on it. I joined the force, we had a family, and I was looking forward to some golden years once the kids were out of the house."

"Our youngest was in his third year of college. We'd started saving, and we were going to make a couple of trips. Go see London, maybe France, or Germany, where her family was from. And then…" he closed his eyes. "She started getting tired a lot. She had Leukemia. And she fought it. Every day, every hour, she fought. Four years. Four years is what we got, of hospital visits and doctors and procedures and drugs. We had some good weeks, even a few good months. But they didn't last. Now I come home to my empty house, and sometimes I still wake up and wonder where she is. Like she's been off for the weekend."

"So that's me," he said, his eyes tired.

Donna still hesitated. He'd certainly opened up, made himself vulnerable. She felt bad, making him talk about his dead wife. But bad enough to tell a policeman? At the same time, if she wasn't here to talk to him, why had she come anyway?

"I dream about… about hanging laundry," she said. "Not the usual sort of laundry, but stuff that has been viciously shredded. Laundry that has been burned so that it's impossible to recognize, charred until it's no longer recognizable as laundry. And it's always the laundry of men, and I'm always putting it up at night."

She let him digest that. He seemed interested, hadn't rejected what she was saying. Yet. Time to drop the bomb.

"I think I've got enough evidence that I'm not dreaming."

He thought about that for a moment.

"I think you realize that sounds pretty—" he started.

"Crazy?" she cut him off. "Go ahead, say it. You have no idea how much I wish I thought I was going crazy."

"I was going to say difficult to swallow."

"Well Officer, you stuck your nose into my business, and it's irritating for you to dismiss what I have to say."

"It's not what I was expecting, which I suppose is good because it isn't what I was afraid of, either."

"I've seen some things. Oakham is pretty well protected, far away from urban sprawl, away from the major drug highways, but we still get people who are off their nut." His gaze was appraising. "You're pretty together, if you don't mind me saying so. And you didn't lead off with the invisible goblins that are living under your bed."

Donna wasn't sure she hadn't just been insulted. On the other hand, he was at least listening.

"Was there a house fire in the middle of the night, about four weeks ago? Isolated house, suspicious circumstances?"

Kutsenko thought for a moment. "Yeah. We were supposed to keep an eye out for arsonists. The Chief is being really hands-on about it, handed us a list of likely suspects. So far, it hasn't come to anything."

And there it was.

"I dreamed I hung out some laundry in that house on the night it happened." She let that sink in. "How much power does Chief Schenck have? Enough to keep obituaries off the Oakham Advertiser website?"

"Why would he do that?" Kutsenko narrowed his eyes. "Are you saying he's got a vested interest in the, uh, laundry you are hanging?" Even as he stumbled, Donna had to give him points. He might not believe her, but he wasn't going to fuck up his chances by telling her so. It was oddly comforting. At least he wasn't going to call her a liar to her face.

"He threw me out of the police station when I started to tell you about this. He's taken over the investigation of the house that burned down after I hung laundry out behind it. It feels like he's involved."

"Won't go over in a court of law. Hell, not even really enough to start an official investigation."

"But you know something is wrong. Otherwise, you wouldn't be here."

Kutsenko, she just couldn't think of him as just Jerry, frowned, as if he'd been found out. She wondered how often he was involved in this sort of give and take. She figured he usually had the upper hand in any interrogation.

"Yeah, OK. But again, I don't have an inkling of something I could go looking for an indictment with."

"So how do we go about it?"

"We? There isn't a 'we' here. First of all, you're a civilian and more vulnerable than I am. Do not try to get into this. It will expose us both, and might get you hurt." Kutsenko paused. "Look, you've given me a lot to think about. I'm not sure I can say I'm going to swallow all of it. But I do feel like there's something going on. If I nose around and take on the elephant one bite at a time, it'll come clear."

"So I'm supposed to just sit on my ass and let you do all the work? I'm the one that's getting fucked by this deal."

"I'm not hanging you out to dry. I'm going to do what I can, within the law, to figure out what's going on. And maybe it's going to be a little tough on you, but you don't want to see what happens if I take my shot and miss."

Donna considered that.

"Is there anything you can offer me? Any sort of protection, in case the Chief gets suspicious?"

Kutenko spread his hands. "Not officially. I can give you my number, but I think it would be best if you didn't contact me unless it's an emergency. If Schenck twigs onto us talking, we may lose our opportunity. And possibly more than that."

"So I've helped you, but you've got nothing for me."

He couldn't meet her eyes, and instead stared at his hands.

"In the short term, no. I'm hoping you can be patient enough to hang on while I get what I need. I don't know how long that will be, and I know it's hard. But you're in no worse shape than you were when we started this conversation."

"My situation is intolerable. Some time in the next two weeks, I'm going to… hang out someone else's bloody sheets. I'm going to do it. And that's pretty damn hard to live with, so I hope you're ready for it."

She stood up, glaring at him. How could he do so damn little for her? What did she care if he caught Schenck a month, three months, a year from now?

He was standing, reached out to grab her shoulder. She

glared at him, and he thought better of it.

"I will figure out what's going on. I promise you that." He said it low, to keep the other patrons from hearing.

"Do it soon," was all Donna said before turning and leaving.

CHAPTER 10

FEMININE WILES

Jim had made some sort of killing at work, and came home all smiles. He insisted on taking her out to dinner, excited as a nine-year-old after eating a pound of Halloween candy.

It had been days since Donna had spoken with Kutsenko. She didn't know exactly how many. Donna's sense of time had gone to shit. She had started crossing days off her calendar with big "X"s, like those idiots on a sixties TV show. It helped her remember what day it was when she woke up. Her phone now displayed the day and date, and was scrupulously programmed to notify her of every appointment an hour in advance, then half an hour, then fifteen minutes. She hated it. Where had her brain gone?

"It's not like I made a lot of money for the company," Jim was enthusing as Donna eyed the bread. Why was their order taking so long? Was it just that Jim wouldn't shut the hell up?

"It's more like I found a way to remove a roadblock. There's this project we've been working on, very important, very long-term. We've run across several stumbling blocks, and there's been this one that's just been stumping everyone."

He continued, but Donna tuned him out. He could congratulate himself for hours, and Donna just wasn't up to being his mirror. It had been a week and a half since she'd forced the guy's head down onto a shard of glass. Another would be coming. She was going to murder someone else. Her bruises had faded, but it was hard to be supportive when she dreaded the looming inevitability. When would she kill? How horrible would it be? These questions chased each other around her head.

"Sometimes it's just a matter of taking a step back from what the actual problem is and sort of looking at it a different way. The problem is usually what everyone has taken for granted, and the answer is basically lying around, just waiting for the right person to realize it."

Donna clenched her jaw so he wouldn't see her yawn. She was being supportive. She was working to keep the relationship together.

He noticed anyway. "Yeah, sorry, I do natter on about myself a bit." His rueful grin was charming. "I know I don't deserve you. You're hotter than I am, smarter than I am, and more patient. And I don't always demonstrate my appreciation, but I want you to know how much you mean to me. My life wouldn't be half as good without you."

He brought out a jewelry box, turned it toward her and opened it. Small blue gems sparkled from a silver necklace set with intricate knot work. She was a little dizzy looking at it, and when she picked it up, it was cold in her hand. It was lovely, and with all the tiny symbols on the swooping curves, it had a hand-made look. But she didn't love it. She put a big, plastic grin on for Jim.

"Let me see it on you," he said. Standing behind her, he clipped it on. It was heavier than she had anticipated. It sat on her collar bones with a chill that wouldn't go away. She shuddered.

"You OK?"

"Yeah, just a little cold." She preened as best she could, and was rewarded with Jim's beaming smile.

"I'm glad you like it," he said. "I had it made specially for you. I think it brings out your eyes."

Was he being deliberately stupid? What the hell was wrong with Jim? "Awww, thank you," she said.

"I love it on you," he said.

"I don't know, it's so showy. Something for a night out, but I don't know about wearing it to the gym."

"Don't be ridiculous," he said. "I'm sure that'll stand up to every day wear."

"I would be so self-conscious about it, though. It's so lovely, and I'd worry that someone would steal it. The chain is short, so I can't wear it under anything."

It sat on the points of her collar, still cold, and surprisingly heavy. Was this thing made of uranium? She could ignore it for now. Maybe she could wear it over a turtleneck.

"It's fancy, I'll give you that, but I don't think anyone would want to steal it." Jim's face was a picture of concern. "Why would you even take it off?"

"Well, if I was taking a shower, for example. Things get left and picked up. I can't keep my eye on everything all the time."

"Right, right." Jim retreated, to her relief. She hated the sparring, hated his hidden agendas. Why wouldn't he tell her why he wanted her to wear it all the time? Why did it feel like a collar, Jim marking his territory?

"Well thank you, Jim. It'll always have a special place in my heart." She was lying again. Why couldn't she tell him the truth?

"You can think of it as a pre-engagement ring, sort of." Jim's smile was satisfied, as if he's just consumed the proverbial canary, and Donna wanted to punch him in his stupid fucking face. Go right across the table, hear the dinnerware and glasses smashing into the floor. Break his nose, see the spurt of blood as it flattened against his face. Hit him again and again as the skin tore, and blood seeped from rents so deep she could see the white bone of his skull. Hear the relentless meaty thwack of her fists bashing his face.

Donna pulled herself out of the vision, making sure there her plastic smile was still plastered to her face. The smell of his blood was still in her nostrils, tantalizing.

"You looked like you were miles away," he said.

"Not so far," Donna said.

With Jim at work and no appointments for the rest of the day, Donna cleared her mind. Like a blank screen at a theater, or a television tuned to a dead channel. Nothing. Blankness. Four white walls and a ceiling, nothing in the room. She breathed in, taking in good air, then breathed out, letting all the bad stuff go.

Donna shifted her position. Meditation fucking sucked.

Making her mind blank was hard. She could calm her thoughts, but there was always an undercurrent of her brain working. Yes, she should be able to clear her head, increase her mindfulness. To be able to shake off the intruder, she had to concentrate. She'd done it… twice. Both times when absolutely focused. She had to build on that, like building muscle.

She could do it when she was working out. Counting her reps was easy, with her thoughts right there, doing nothing else. But she was doing something, monitoring herself, had the sensations of her body. Sitting, meditating, not doing anything, was difficult. Not letting herself slip off into thoughts, plans and worries was hard. Usually, she enjoyed a challenge. But not today.

Today was her third day of finding a quiet moment, and sitting down to meditate. Maybe it would be easier with some sort of instructor, but she was afraid that someone would ask her questions. She hated keeping her violator's secrets, lying to Jim, having to talk around what was happening for Kutsenko's convenience. Why was this happening to her? Why would anyone single her out this way? What was so special about her?

When was it going to happen next? It had been a week and a half since the last murder. The anticipation, knowing that the next time she went to bed, she could wake up strangling the shit out of someone, ate at her. It might be someone she knew, again. She shuddered, grit her teeth, trying not to think about Barry.

Donna let out a breath and refocused herself. Meditation. She was emptying her mind. She would control herself, invader or not.

She took a deep breath and cleared her mind, visualizing an empty room. It was clear, clean, and free of dirt. In went the good air, and out went the bad. Why the hell was Jim so enamored with that necklace?

"Shit." The room echoed the word spoken aloud. She was never going to reach enlightenment at this rate.

Donna woke to find herself in front of The Horn. The sky was dark, the cars parked outside were few. How late was it? She never closed the place down. Was this what it looked like in the hours after midnight?

She hated to admit it to herself, but it was something of a relief. At least she wasn't waiting in anticipation, wondering about the next time she was going to kill someone. It was now.

She was in her slinkiest red dress, again. Her violator sure liked this dress. She wondered if she'd put on any makeup. She wasn't carrying anything, which meant she was going to improvise again. Find some horrible way to kill someone with what she found at hand. She hoped it wouldn't be The Horn. That would suck. Going somewhere she'd be recognized and then killing someone? She would have nowhere to go after that. Piece of shit alchemist, not satisfied with ruining parts of her life, he was ruining everything in her life.

Her feet took her into The Horn, and the scents washed over her; beer and wood and just a hint of manliness she assumed came from Rich or Peter. The Horn smelled good, never of puke or stale beer.

She bellied up to the bar, which had a few quiet patrons. The congenial atmosphere of the evenings had turned into a subdued, almost sulky quiet.

"Little late for you, isn't it, Donna?" Peter's thick neck, fierce beard and lovely blue eyes seldom failed to give Donna a little shiver of delight. He wore a tight shirt that showed off his muscular shoulders. Not bodybuilder sculpted, but strong, thick.

"Hey Peter, have I told you that you're my favorite bartender, like ever?" Her hand reached out to caress his. "Gimme a Gray Goose, on the rocks."

Peter cocked his head, blinked, and poured her a vodka. The drink burned down her throat as she took it all in one big gulp.

"Another?" he asked.

"I'll pass. I mean, I didn't come here to drink. I came to talk to you. You're always so good at your job."

"Kind of you to notice. Hey, I'll be back in a minute, I think I hear the sound of a tip being left."

Donna was left on her own. She watched Peter talk to one of the patrons, a droopy-looking man in a threadbare heavy metal T-shirt. What was she going to do? She was going to wait to find out, maybe find out something about the guy in her head's plan.

But the fucking instant he tried to do something, she was going to fight tooth and nail.

And just like that, Peter was back. Donna drew little nothings with her finger on the bar.

"Were you drinking somewhere else before you came here?" He asked.

"I'm entirely sober, Peter. But I just can't get you out of my head. How, you know, strong you look. How handsome, with those blue eyes of yours, and the broad shoulders. Those hands look like they're just made for running up and down a woman's body, if you catch my drift."

If she could have, Donna would have pissed herself laughing. She was trying to seduce Peter?

He put his elbow on the bar.

"I'm not sure what you're saying, Donna. We've known each other for a couple of years, but I don't think you've ever said anything like that. Is Mildred with you? You're usually together when you're getting your serious drink on."

"No, I'm all on my own, looking for some company to spend the night with." She brushed her fingers over his naked head.

Was this a seduction? Or just getting him to lower his guard so she could bash his head in? What had changed? Hadn't she been going after alchemists? How did the bastard in her head know she'd talked to Rich? How could she fight something this absurdly stupid?

"What about Jim?"

Donna's giggle was high and movie-like. It felt practiced.

"Jim's really just a boy. And sometimes I get a hankering for someone a bit more manly." She traced imaginary patterns on his thick forearms.

"That seems nice, Donna. Yeah, closing up is always busy. I have to cash out the drawer, make sure those who can't move under their own power get safely on their way." He checked his watch. "We're going to close in about fifteen minutes, so why don't you stick around, and we'll have a little fun, just the two of us."

The implication stopped Donna cold. She was going to kill him. Murder Peter. Oh shit. How to tell him? She cleared her mind, concentrated. Concentrated on feeling her body, her mouth. Nothing. She felt her lips crinkle up in a cutesy little smile.

Fuck. Fuck fuck fuck fuck fuck fuck fuck! She raged impotently as she sat, watching the bar close around her. One by one, the patrons shuffled out, Peter making sure they got out all right, encouraging the single patron who didn't want to go.

All that time, Donna was trying to figure out how to stop this. She raged at her stillness, her inability to affect anything, her mouth, her hands, anything. And all the while, she sat watching Peter, unsuspecting, as he put away bottles, swept the floor, shut off the lights, and counted out the register. The deep and mysterious shadows made the bar feel more intimate.

Peter finally smiled at her over his beard. "That's everything. I wasn't sure you were going to hang around."

"Why wouldn't I?"

A grin crinkled all the way up to his eyes.

"Let's go out to the back," he said.

He hooked his arm in hers, and pressed close. He was warm, and smelled of musk, with just a hint of beer, in a masculine way. It was quite pleasant to be this close to him. But Donna knew what was coming. Donna tried to fight the footsteps that took her toward the back of the bar.

"Hang on, let me lock this door," Peter turned away, Donna looked at the new room.

Before she could take anything in, Peter's strong arms wrapped around her from behind, pinning her arms to her sides. He bent back, lifting her feet off the ground. She felt her feet flailing, but couldn't connect with anything.

"I don't know who's in there," he growled into her ear. "But you are clearly the world's biggest fucking idiot." Donna could have cried in relief. He knew. "Donna would never come on to me in such a clumsy fashion, and I know a thing or two about the sort of twisted shit that's going on in this town. This was a mistake."

"You're fucked is what you are you son of a whore," Donna scraped the words out. "Bastard child-magician. You don't know anything about true power."

"Possibly because power isn't something I'm interested in."

"What do you want, then? We can come to an arrangement. I can offer you so much more than you have. Money, power, a proper introduction to the Great Art."

"So I can go displacing my friends' souls to murder people? Gee, that sounds like a load of fun."

"Name what you want. Anything. We can get you so much."

"I'd like you to open an extension of the Harvard School of Bartending right here in Oakham, because I want to take their mixer course, but two hours travel is too much."

"We will drive you from this town, hedge wizard. We will crush you like the bug you are."

"And now you're a we? That doesn't sound very powerful. I'd be more impressed if you were just a lone nut job, but now that I know there's more than one of you, I'm seriously disappointed. You need to stop killing people, and leave Donna out of whatever goofy game you douche-cannons are playing. People are trying to live their lives, and don't need you or me killing them because they're inconvenient."

Donna felt her legs kick into the air behind her, Peter still had her hoisted off her feet.

"Put me down," she shouted.

Peter took a handful of her hair and slowly bent her neck back until her ear was right next to his mouth.

"The only reason I'm not breaking your neck right now is because I'm fond of Donna. You got that?"

She didn't respond, except maybe to kick harder. Somehow, she couldn't find his legs.

"I've got all evening, and it's going to be a while before I get tired," Peter said in her ear. "We can do this until you turn into a pumpkin, or we can try some sort of negotiation."

"Go to Hell. You're nothing but a boil on the ass of the Great Art. You aren't anything of consequence, and you never will be."

Peter laughed, and because he was holding her so close, Donna felt it right down to her bones. She liked it.

"What a twisted set of priorities you have." Peter said, still close to her ear. "Why don't you get out of here. I'd like to have a polite conversation with someone I like."

"You have just made the worst enemy you could imagine," Donna's mouth grated the words out. *And fuck you, shithead,* she thought in the confines of her own head.

Donna felt something stretch. Inside her head, as if her brain was made of pie dough. She could feel her face, felt the muscles go slack, and something rose from the back of her skull. She could feel the tremors in her limbs, like she was going to start convulsing. Her knees spasmed, kicking in the air. She felt a tearing, like a hole had been ripped in her scalp. Was she having a stroke? Her face didn't feel right, unresponsive, drooping. Was she going to drool? Peter put her on her feet, but she couldn't stand. She stretched out her arm to steady herself, and managed, somehow, to find Peter's shoulder.

"Donna?" Peter was supporting her, his hands warm and strong.

She raised her hand and touched her nose. Following that, she ran her hand across her hair, then looked at it. No blood. That fucker hadn't actually exploded out of her head.

"Uhhhngh," she managed to say. Peter remained where he was.

Donna pushed away from him. She lurched, and Peter reached out for her, but she waved him off.

"That sucks," she said. Her own thoughts, her own voice.

"And you really are Donna?"

"I know you and Rich are married, how about that?"

"Good enough." He held out his hand, but Donna didn't want help. She steadied herself on the wall.

"I think I prefer blacking out," she said. "That was awful." She touched her scalp, which still tingled. Still no blood.

"I suspect the blackouts are at least partially for your comfort."

"Why is he such an asshole?" Donna asked. "Why is he being such an asshole to me?"

"Because he can. He needs something, and you are apparently convenient," Peter said. "I kind of wonder if he's a local politician."

"Can't be. He's actually doing something."

Peter shook his head. "And you're already cracking jokes."

"I've just had a person extract themselves, painfully, out of my head." Peter opened his mouth, but Donna shushed him. "If I can make a joke, you can at least pretend it was funny. Humor me. I've had a shitty day."

Peter didn't smile.

"I've just been dragged into something I really didn't want to be," he said. "And I don't blame you, but this guy is really an asshole, and I expect he's going to go out of his way to make my life—*our lives*—miserable."

"And now you have some inkling of how I feel. I hate that you've been dragged into this, but not as much as I hate that I'm already involved. You know more about…" she waved her hands aimlessly, "magic than I do, but I can't help wonder if we might have solved this thing if you had gotten involved right at the beginning."

He gave her a hard look. "I have a business to run and a man I love. We aren't powerful, we're just like you, trying to get by. I hoped that if we stayed out of it, we wouldn't get pulled in. I'm still not sure we didn't get dragged in because we tried to help you. I have to go home and tell Rich to prepare for some load of shit, I don't know what, and I don't know when. But I'm pretty sure it's headed our way."

"You can grill hot dogs without flashing back to your hand pressing some guy's face against his own grill, face charring, eyeballs shrinking." Donna said it quietly, but Peter flinched. "I'm happy to finally have some sort of ally, but I really wish you had gotten involved sooner."

Peter sighed, looked at her, and then down at the floor.

"Let's go have a drink," he said.

With his hand on her shoulder, they walked to the dark bar. He mixed her a Manhattan, as much by feel as by sight.

"Why me?" she asked in a small voice.

"I don't know. I can't think of a reason. I don't even know what he's doing. Taking over someone's body is difficult and requires a lot of juice, so to speak. Why you? There's something special about you, Donna. Some connection that's being exploited." He poured himself a neat shot of gin, then drank it.

"Not to make light of your onrushing trouble," Donna said. "But whatever comes your way may give us an idea who's coming after you."

"I was thinking that myself. It might come to nothing. It's possible this guy is some sort of socially-maladjusted whackjob who still lives in his mother's basement. Of course, during high school, I fit that description pretty well."

Maybe it was the booze, but he was beginning to loosen up. She needed informed allies. Fierce was great for moral support, but she didn't know a damn thing about alchemists, chaos magic or whatever else.

He put his head in his hand, and with the other poured himself another gin. He sipped this one.

"Don't get too liquored up. I'm going to need a ride home."

He pushed the drink aside.

"How did you get here? How far away do you live?"

"Two miles."

"Not a convenient walk, then."

"Car. There's a car. I've heard it before."

They looked at each other, then raced to the front of the bar. Peter, in practical shoes, beat her to the window.

She had a momentary glimpse of a dark-colored car vanishing into the darkness. Then nothing.

"Was that waiting?" Had she arrived from that direction? She seemed to remember walking across the street to get to The Horn.

"I didn't get a good look. It was already moving by the time I saw it. Mass license plate, though. Didn't get the number."

Donna sighed, punched the wall. So close. But now she knew how she was getting around. All of it mattered, all of it helped. Something, anything, might provide the crack she needed to wedge this whole fucking mess open. Why did that always seem like it was just out of reach?

"Got anything else you need to tell me tonight? If not, then I'm going to need you to take me home."

Donna had to pound on her own door to wake Jim enough to let her in. It was humiliating, but in a moment she was in Jim's arms, and some of the fear began to melt away.

"What happened?"

"I don't know, I don't know. I sort of kicked him out of my head."

He thought about that for a little while.

"So, definitely a him?"

"What?"

"You feel like it's definitely some sort of him taking over your head. A masculine presence."

"What the hell are you on about?" It was past two, she'd been tired when she went to sleep, and now Jim was babbling all sorts of inane shit? "Why pick up on that?"

"OK, never mind. We should go to bed."

"No, I want you to tell me what the hell made you pick that up. Your girlfriend has just been brought home after being possessed, and your first reaction is to wonder about the gender of whoever's doing this to me? No, Jim, I'm fucking fine, not a problem at all, and yes I fucked a guy so I could get a ride home."

"You're tired…"

"No, I'm pissed off. What kind of priorities do you have? It's like you don't even care that I just got home, after my body was hijacked. You want to know if I think some guy is taking me over. It makes me wonder if you would care if I ever got roofied."

"That's not fair," Jim said.

"How so?"

"You know what, forget it. I can't talk to you when you're like this."

"What? Hurt? Frightened? Emotional?" She heard the words tumble out of her mouth, knew that this wasn't helping. She clenched her hands and then unclenched them again, just to make sure she was still running the show.

"Unreasonable," he shot back. "You're taking everything I say as an insult. I can't talk to you when you're this way."

"And what could possibly have set me off?"

"Maybe coming home at three in the morning with a lame-ass excuse," Jim said, glaring at her.

They were both shouting. Jim was steamed, and Donna forced herself not to shoot back at him. She could feel the tension in her jaws. She wasn't going to escalate this any further.

"Jim, I'm tired, I've just had a very frightening experience. Can we please let this wait until morning?"

"Fine." He was seething, his shoulders rigid. He turned and stalked back into the apartment. Donna wrapped her arms around herself, feeling cold and alone. She closed the door behind her, twisted the bolt. The *thunk* of the lock was loud in the silence of Jim's absence. Something wet dropped onto Donna's hand. A tear. She touched her cheek, and discovered she had been silently weeping. She clenched her hands, fought the tears. She wiped at her face, erasing her weakness. She looked up at the ceiling, eyes closed, breathing. She felt sick to her stomach. She wouldn't cry. She was going to stop crying immediately.

She was alone, her face hot, but the tears had stopped. She was going to work this out. She was going to vent her rage on whoever was shoving himself into her brain, the fucking alchemist. She was going to find him and kick his ass. And until that happened, she would not let him ruin her life. She had worked hard to get where she was, she was tough. She was capable, and she was not going to let this pile of shit break up her relationship with Jim. She wouldn't allow it.

Assuming Jim could stop being a selfish, oversensitive shit. Stress always made everything more difficult. She knew that. But if Jim wasn't going to be the one who put the stability into their relationship, then it fell to Donna.

She walked into the bedroom, took off her dress in the dark, and climbed under the covers. She had to be up and in class in three hours.

She'd missed morning coffee with Fierce in pursuit of more sleep, so she called and arranged lunch. The first day of her new kickboxing class was a mess, partially because Donna hadn't had her coffee. Donna wobbled on her feet, but even if her kicks and punches were less than convincing, she finished the class. She felt better afterward, her head more clear.

Now, what to do? She was no closer to finding out who was

doing this. Not until he moved against The Horn.

"Not looking so good Donna." Fierce didn't sugar-coat it.

"Spent a night not being myself. But I managed to get some results."

"That's good, right? Why aren't you happy about this?"

"Peter and Rich are now involved. And I feel kind of bad about it. I wanted to respect their privacy, but at the same time, they know something about how this all might be working."

Fierce fiddled with her napkin. "I know you like to be polite, but sometimes, people get forced into doing things they should be doing. You need allies. You need to stop the..." she looked around. "You need to stop the killing. And if Rich and Peter know something, they needed to be involved."

"Momma insisted on politeness." Donna felt stupid saying it.

"Some things she couldn't anticipate." Fierce's voice was sympathetic. Donna felt ground down. Like she'd failed last night, instead of won. Why didn't this feel like winning?

"I'm waiting for Peter and Rich to have some sort of misfortune. I threatened them, and I'm hoping that when the bad guy makes his move, I'll be able to figure out who they are. I feel bad about that, but on the other hand, I've got so few other options. TV cops always have a load of clues to look at. Why have I got so few?"

"Real world doesn't work like TV. For them, it's easy, interrupted by commercials every ten minutes, and all over in an hour. We live in a messier world." She wasn't scolding. For that Donna loved her.

She was saved from having to come up with a cogent reply by the arrival of lunch. Fierce had a salad with Cajun blackened chicken. Donna's order was a breakfast burrito, chorizo and eggs. Fierce was silent for a few minutes as Donna tore into her lunch.

"How do I act toward them?" Donna was mopping up a bit of green salsa with a scrap of tortilla.

"How do you mean?"

"I still kind of resent them for hanging back. And at the same time I'm sort of grateful that they got involved at all."

"Get rid of the resentment. Seriously, right now." Fierce leaned toward Donna. "They're reluctantly helping, and you don't want to give them any excuse to regret their decision, or worse, change their minds. So suck it up, Buttercup, and don't look back. You have help, now."

Donna felt a rueful smile spread over her face. "I think I've given that very pep talk to people in my classes."

"I'm just proving to you that I do listen when you talk," Fierce said.

Donna tried to smile, tried to laugh. It all died. She ended up staring at Fierce's salad, feeling her face fall.

"I can't do this, Fierce. There's just too much. Jim isn't being understanding. I mean, I totally didn't kill anyone, and I still feel like shit because I didn't do anything to stop it. It was all Peter."

"So you need to go talk to him and figure out what he did. Don't piss around with this, go and talk to him tonight and see what you can learn."

"Yes, mother."

"Don't be cute. And make sure you're home by ten. I know you like those boys, but they're up to no good."

Again, the attempt to smile failed. If even Fierce couldn't get her to smile, Donna realized, she was in a bad place. "And I've got Jim to talk to before I go out tonight. Not looking forward to that, either."

"I know you feel like you're going through Hell," Fierce said. "But keep pushing. You'll get somewhere better."

"That assumes Hell is essentially featureless, and that there aren't any better or worse locations," Donna said. "Not to sound bitter, but I've always hated that expression."

"On the other hand, you could sit down in the middle of a pit of coals, complaining about your dry skin, and feel sorry for yourself."

"I wouldn't be killing people."

"You will if you do nothing. Giving up isn't an option, Donna. Sitting in a pool of your own pity isn't an option, either."

"I need some time to get my head together, Fierce. Some time off, some sleep where I don't worry that I'm going to wake up beating some poor fucker's face in." She wanted a Manhattan. Any sort of drink, really.

"I wish I could give it to you. Is there anything else? Do you need, like a couple of days off, somewhere else to stay?"

Donna bristled at the suggestion. She wasn't some battered wife. And yet, somehow, her life had gotten away from her. She couldn't catch up, couldn't get her breath. Why was this happening to her? Why was it so warm in here? Donna was abruptly hot all over, her arms covered with sweat. She put a hand to her chest. Something was cutting off her air, like an invisible weight on her chest. She stood up, but her feet were clumsy. Was she having a heart attack?

She tried to stagger away, find the ladies' room, but her feet and hands were too remote to function properly. The room spun around her, and she heard the crash of plates, but didn't know where. She was on the ground again. Couldn't breathe. Somewhere, Fierce was saying something. But she was too far away to hear, Donna fought to drag in breath, but nothing was coming in.

"…a panic attack." Fierce was saying it from a mile away, somehow reaching for Donna with impossibly-long arms. She recognized the words, but they didn't mean anything. *Panic attack, panic attack, panic attack, why would anyone having a panic attack not be able to breathe? Why was everything so dark, and why was the room so hot?*

"…need…focus…something." Fierce was going in and out like a bad phone call. Donna just wanted to hug herself, get the crushing weight off her chest, breathe.

Fierce loomed over her, wiped the perspiration off Donna's head.

"Look at me," she said. Somewhere beyond Fierce, other faces peered down. "Focus on me," Fierce was still muffled, but somehow intelligible.

"Breathe in." Fierce said, and took a deep breath. Donna could only stare, aware that her own breath was as rapid as a dog panting.

"You're going to be fine," Fierce said. "Breathe in again." And she did it, and somehow, the intolerable pressure on Donna's heart began to ease off.

"Breathe, it's easy," Fierce was the only thing Donna could hold onto. Everything else just squirmed out of her mind.

Somewhere, other people were talking.

"Breathe in," Fierce said, and Donna did. The weight was going away, she could take in air.

After an eternity, the tightness in Donna's chest eased, although her head was buzzing. Fierce helped her sit up, carefully sat her in a chair. Her limbs were shaky, and she felt nauseous. Somewhere, Donna had pulled the tablecloth down. Dishes, thankfully unbroken, were scattered across the carpet. Fierce was picking them up. Donna moved to help, but got speared with a deadly look, and slumped back in her chair.

Then Donna noticed the people who were staring. Oh shit. She put her face in her hands, trying not to think about how many people had just seen her. How many people would be talking about this before the week was done?

Fierce was done with the plates in a moment, and was talking with someone in a waiter's outfit, and a guy in a suit. The manager.

Someone plunked a glass of water in front of her, and Donna gulped it down. It didn't settle her stomach, but it got rid of her cotton mouth. The room temperature had returned to normal, somehow. After some time, Fierce sat down. Her lunch was a mess that had clearly been dumped and then hastily put back on its plate.

"How are you feeling?" Fierce asked.

"Intensely embarrassed."

"Well, I think we both know you need to relax a bit. Have you ever had a panic attack before?"

Donna shook her head. "Never. I've never been nervous, never had trouble handling pressure." She'd had a terrifying moment when she thought that the alchemist might be taking her over. The thought made her shudder. She still had no idea how to tell if possession was coming. She clenched a fist.

"You need to chill," Fierce said. "You've just had a major stress indicator."

"And what? I roll over? Give up? Ease off until he figures out the next person he wants to murder?" Donna stood up. "Thanks for lunch, Fierce. I really needed this talk, but right now, I need to go work off some stress." *And maybe take a nap*, she added to herself.

Fierce's face was sad when Donna turned away. Maybe she'd save Fierce some grief if she cut her off. Maybe Peter and Rich had been right not to get involved. She walked out of the restaurant in silence, leaving Fierce to pay the check.

She made a special dinner for Jim. Carefully caramelized the onions, cooked the pork medallions, mixed it all together with a balsamic honey glaze. Garnished with sliced fingerling potatoes with dill, and buttered green beans on the side.

He walked in the door at five fifteen, the way he always did. You could set your watch by the time he got home. He never had to stay late. Sometimes it drove Donna fucking crazy, especially when she was running behind because an appointment hadn't shown up for half an hour.

"Hey, honey. Oooh, that smells good." He loved her pork and green beans. "What's the special occasion?"

"It's been a hard couple of weeks, and you've been supportive, and I wanted you to know that I appreciate it."

His look turned sly. "This is poisoned, isn't it?"

"I put a little poison in your breakfast every morning, then cook the antidote into your dinner at night." She'd seen that in a movie. She didn't remember which one.

"Soooo, you're saying I should never go out for McDonald's."

"I'm saying you would not like the consequences if you did."

"I guess I'd better eat up, then." And he did. With gusto. Whatever other troubles they had, Jim loved her cooking.

He was vocal about his appreciation, and that eased some of Donna's tension.

"Sorry I've been hard on you for the past week," she said, after the dishes had been cleared. "You know it's been kind of crazy with everything, and not being able to sleep without being afraid of waking up somewhere unfamiliar. And you really have been there for me."

Jim's smile took a moment to get started, but it bloomed into a full grin. He looked so good when he was smiling. Donna realized how much she had missed that.

"So, I'm not all that sure about what's been going on with you at night. I... I realize that you've told me before, but I have to confess that I wasn't paying as much attention as I should have been. So, first of all, I'm sorry for not taking you seriously. It was a lot to take in. But now I'm with you, so get me up to speed."

Donna could have broken down right there. He wanted to know. He'd done a full one hundred and eighty degrees from solidly not believing in her to being on her side. It was such a relief to not have to wonder where he stood.

"I haven't been able to find out that much. I mean, I wake up, walk up to someone's house, kill them gruesomely, and then blackout. I never know how I get there, I… I almost never know who I'm about to assault. It's really, I mean it's horrible, the things that I do, like these people are just objects that hold a secret. And if they don't do what, I, he, whoever, wants, he'll just take them the hell apart like they're nothing." She shuddered.

"Do they have any connection?" Jim was engaged. He wasn't just feigning interest.

"Maybe. Rich tells me they're all part—"

"Rich? What, the bartender at The Horn?"

"Yes." She felt like she was on less firm ground, now. "Rich and Peter are sort of magical. Chaos magicians, I think they called themselves."

"And you believe them?" She was losing him. Of course, what she was telling him sounded insane. She probably wouldn't have believed it, six months ago.

"Yeah, I do. But the thing is that they know things about what's going on. They say that the people that, that are getting murdered are all alchemists, from an organization."

"A secret group of alchemists? What, like the Illuminati?"

"I… I don't know. I mean, aren't the Illuminati supposed to be powerful and stuff? The alchemists seem to be just taking it, letting the murders happen. A couple have fought back, but if they had any sort of clout, you'd think they would have tried to find me. But they haven't. And a few of them were really Buddhist about the whole thing, and that was almost as creepy."

Jim was too fascinated to prompt her to go on, but she didn't need it.

"If they really were a cabal, wouldn't they have some sort of way to stop what's happening? They're being picked off, one by one. And they aren't doing anything about it. I mean, all I have is Peter's word for it. Maybe someone just needs to kill random people. They don't seem at all the same."

"When you say some of them were Buddhist, what did you mean by that?"

Donna couldn't look at him. "When you kick down someone's door, and they say they know you're coming to kill them, you'd expect a reaction, right? He didn't. And I knew him, Jim. He took one of my classes."

"Oh crap. And you have no idea why this person is doing this."

"At least he spared me from having to kill someone I knew. Not that it was a lot better, but still. His calm in the face of death was terrifying. He knew it was inevitable and went his own way, rather than let someone else dictate how he was going to die. Can you imagine that? Being that cool when someone is coming to murder you?"

Jim shook his head.

"Peter has given me a couple of pointers on what to do to fight the… I don't know, possession? And sometimes I get these Yoda texts. I don't know how much they help, though."

"Yoda texts? Holy crap, there's been a lot going on in your life that I had no idea about."

"What was there to say? It was hard enough to say I'm being possessed and murdering people at night. It sounds crazy in my own ears. But the rest of this stuff?" Donna could feel the tightness in her back easing. Talking to Fierce about the whole mess was one thing, but for Jim to be so open, so understanding, was an unspeakable relief. She lived with Jim. Carrying this secret, not letting him know, it had been killing her. How many months had she been trying to make him understand?

"I'm sorry. I really am. I can't begin to understand how much this has hurt you," he said.

"You know? Let's move on from that. Let's see what we can do together, and maybe figure this out," Donna said.

He tilted his head. "How could I possibly help?" The question was slow.

"You know people I don't. You've got White Guys Club. Maybe you could talk to them, see if anything is going on, have they noticed anything weird? Maybe they know some of the people that were killed?" She hesitated. "You don't know anyone who used to go to dogfights, do you?"

"Ew, God no. Yuck. We don't do anything illegal. We're just a small group of business guys who like to hang out on the occasional Friday. Like Masons, without the mumbo-jumbo, and maybe a bit more drinking."

"Well, maybe the more people know about this the better. Someone has to know something about these people. They don't even get obits on the Advertiser page."

"I don't know if it's all that weird. Who reads obituaries anymore? Oakham's a small town, and everyone knows everyone else. If you knew someone who died, you'd know before it got updated on the web page."

He had a point. Everyone knew everyone in Oakham.

"So why isn't everyone talking about this? Why isn't there this mass panic because, like twelve people have been murdered, and everyone is going about their daily lives like it's nothing. Why doesn't anyone know about this?"

Jim shook his head. "I don't know. I mean, are they having funerals? What kind of person is killed that no one cares about?"

"I don't know, but even if they're secret weirdos, they don't deserve this," Donna said. She shivered, remembering the man she'd burned to death in his own garage.

"But you have to admit there's something wrong with someone who dies and is unmourned."

"Different, maybe. Not wrong. Not bad. A person's life has its own value. I don't measure it by what other people think."

Jim held up his hands in surrender. "Hey, I think it's terrible, too. We're not fighting over that."

"We're not fighting over anything," Donna said. Which was a wonder, really.

"No, we're not." And he let that hang there. No twinkle in his eye, no point to make. Why did Donna feel so weird about the conversation?

CHAPTER 11

HEAVY BOOTS

Donna pushed the nagging distractions from her mind. Which unleashed a cascade of thoughts, most of them about not thinking. *Dammit.*

She let out a breath in a long sigh. She wasn't going to get it back today. Practice hadn't made perfect, but she was getting better. Maybe. Mediation was a process, and she wanted results... last month, really. She was still hesitant about sleeping, but what could she do? She needed to sleep.

She crossed her arms, felt the solid bulk of her shoulders. The weight-lifting class was paying off. Her arms were thicker, she was already lifting more than she had three weeks ago. But she didn't feel any safer. She wasn't secure.

Slow inhale, hold it, then slow exhale. Not meditation, but something to calm herself. She hated the helplessness of it all. How did you fight someone who took over your head? How could anyone do that?

This wasn't productive. She had to think, to move forward. How was she going to get through this, make sure everything she'd built up didn't collapse around her? She'd worked hard to make Oakham trust her, to show them that she was a good physical trainer, a good masseuse. If people found out that she was a serial murderer, and her defense was that someone had taken over her mind? She'd be locked away. Outside of Oakham. She closed her eyes, remembering the waves of nausea that had assaulted her when she'd tried to flee. If that didn't let up, prison was a death sentence. The agony, the dehydration from the constant vomiting. She wouldn't survive a week outside of Oakham.

How did she get herself so trapped? Why didn't other people get nauseous when they left their hometowns?

Peace. She needed peace. Peace of mind, security. This wasn't helping.

What she needed was to kick the fucker who was doing this in the face. Tell him to cut it the hell out. She punched her thigh. Which was part of the reason she was having trouble with meditation. She wasn't relaxing. Just thinking about that fucking bastard was enough to bring her blood to a boil. She sucked at meditation.

Donna stared down at the guy on the ground. She was holding his hand in a painful lock. How had this happened? She looked around. People. People from her class. Her class. She'd just finished a kickboxing class. She remembered that. They were staring at her. Everyone in the room was staring at her. Except the guy at her feet.

Art. Artie. Arthur. Took her class. He'd come up behind her, put his hand on her shoulder. She hadn't expected that. What had happened next? She'd put her hand on his. She remembered that. She'd turned. After twisting his hand so that he couldn't escape. She'd bent his wrist back, and his knees had buckled. And that was a good thing, because she'd held him at bay with his own stiff, unbending elbow.

And she'd hit him. Not gently. She could remember the feel of breaking cartilage under her fist.

Oh shit.

"Donna."

She let him go, and he crab-walked away from her.

"I'm sorry." It sounded lame and hollow. "I'm a little tightly wound these days." Wait, there wasn't any blood on his face. She hadn't broken his nose.

Her students had formed a circle around her, clearly afraid. She couldn't blame them.

"What's going on?" *Shit.* Tim was at the door. How was she going to explain this?

Brittney, a slip of a girl, shallow as only a seventeen year-old could be, stepped up, and turned on a big, bright smile.

"Donna was just showing us why you don't touch someone without permission." She turned to face Donna. "You weren't going to hurt Artie, right?"

"No." Donna said it quickly. "No, I was just startled." She clasped her hands in front of her to keep them from trembling. She'd thought Brittney was shallow and stupid. But there was something under that surface that Donna had never seen before. Some steel, the ability to think fast. Where had that come from?

"I hope I wasn't too rough on you, Art. But Brittney's right, you need to be careful about approaching people from behind."

"Sorry," Art flashed a sheepish grin. He raised his hand, and Donna took it, hauling him to his feet. Smiles all around, except for Tim, who knew something was up. The rest of her class was smiling because they didn't know what else to do.

"Well, I've got to go get changed," Brittney said. She hooked her arm around Donna's and half-dragged her into the dressing room. Once they were out of Tim's sight, Brittney turned on Donna.

"Tell me what's going on. Is Jim hitting you?"

"No, I'm fine," Donna said, too fast.

"Don't you give me that bullshit." Brittney waved a stiff finger in Donna's face. How the hell was she so fierce for someone so tiny? "Someone's got you scared. Believe me, I know the signs. Tell me it's not Jim again, and I'll believe you."

Donna hesitated. The whole necklace thing was still raw in her mind. She touched her throat. But that wasn't abuse. He wasn't hitting her. He wasn't stealing her money, didn't belittle her all the time. The sex wasn't gross. He wasn't Danny. She needed someone to hold on to. Until she figured this shit out, she needed people to cling to.

"It's not Jim."

"Do you have a stalker? What's got you so worked up?"

"It's just, I've got so much going on. So many balls in the air. And I'm not sleeping well," she smiled. "But thank you for looking out for me."

"Sometimes, friends are all we have." Something dark

passed across Brittney's face. But then it cleared. "If you have any trouble, just give me a call. You have my number, right?"

Who *was* this tiger? "I do. Thank you. I'm fine, but if I get in trouble, I'll make sure I call you."

They hugged, and Brittney left, her tiny perfect teenage ass bouncing. Why hadn't she seen this side of Brittney before? There was hardened steel in that tight little frame.

Despite Jim being weird and the dreams that weren't dreams, Donna was comforted. She wasn't alone.

The Horn was busy in the evening.

"Did you dodge the road work as you came in?" Rich asked.

"I came up Maple. Why? What are they fixing?"

Rich's smile was bitter. "Us."

"Wait, what?"

Rich shook her Manhattan, his smile fixed and bitter.

"I've seen it happen with other restaurants. Someone official gets a burr under their saddle, and there just happens to be a problem with the sewer down the road."

Donna sipped her Manhattan. "Okay. So?"

"Here's the clever part. About a week after they've thoroughly torn up the line, they're going to stage a surprise health inspection of our kitchen."

"Still not getting it."

"They have just invaded a rat haven with heavy equipment and a lot of noise. Where do you think the rats are going to go?"

"Ah." Donna finally got it. "Sounds like a pain in the ass."

"Oh, it will be. We'll trap them by the dozen, but they've probably made more than five hundred rats homeless." He sighed and shook his head. "The only good news is that we know your guy is in politics. It takes some serious pull to get this sort of bullshit happening."

"So it's the mayor?"

"Or someone Kirby listens to."

"I didn't think he listened to anybody."

"Nobody without money. You have to support him during his campaign to have any sort of access to him afterward. I don't think I need to tell you how that works."

Donna sighed into her drink. Politicians were politicians.

"That narrows it down," she said. "It tells us that we're dealing with someone wealthy and well-connected. Someone who had to leave a trail of contributions to our dearly-beloved mayor."

"That'll probably narrow it down to thirty of forty contributors." Rich's mouth was pursed and sour. "What do you think you might do with that?"

"Stop them from messing with The Horn? I don't know, I don't think I can do anything for you there." Donna could match Rich's mood. How many people had *he* killed?

"You do understand that this is our livelihood, right? We support ourselves with The Horn."

The right thing to do would be to sympathize. Yes, they were going to face a tough time.

"I'm sorry if people's deaths are interfering with your lifestyle, Rich. That must be really hard for you." She shouldn't be saying this, but the anger just poured out of her.

He leaned in, his mouth ugly. "You tracked your shit around on our floor, and now you're giving us shit for telling you so?"

Donna needed to back down, Rich and Peter were her only allies who knew anything about alchemy. She couldn't afford to alienate them. Instead, she jammed her finger in Rich's face.

"So long as people you don't know get murdered, you're happy to sit back and do nothing. When you knew more than I did about how it was getting done, you sat back and let me kill people. Fuck you and your bullshit, Rich. Tracking mud on your floor was the only way to get your attention, and I shouldn't have had to. You've done nothing but make this hard for me, dragging your damn feet, and now you're complaining about being inconvenienced?" Everyone was turning against her, as if it was somehow her fault. She slapped down everything in her wallet, close to a hundred bucks, and shoved it at Rich.

"Here. Hopefully this will salve your conscience."

"Donna," Rich called after her, but she kept on walking. Fuck them. They weren't getting murdered, they didn't care. Donna didn't need this.

She spent the rest of the evening drinking at home. Jim was...
somewhere, and the only way she could cool off her blazing
fury was by pouring alcohol on it. Television was crap, she
wanted the punch the faces of every single talking head on the
news, comedy or some damned cop drama. She hated them all.
Fuck Rich, *fuck* Peter, *fuck* Jim for being a passive-aggressive
dill hole about *everything*.

She shouldn't be drinking alone. She shouldn't be drinking
while angry. She poured herself another and downed it quickly.
She hadn't seen Fierce since that whole mess at the restaurant.
Rich and Peter were showing their cowardice. Why was it that
everyone abandoned her when the chips were down?

Her friends had been abandoning her for some time. How
fucked up was it that her time at Café Gitan and The Horn had
become her only social outlets? How had that happened?

She was too drunk to really nail it all down. She should
make a note to think about it later.

Donna woke to find herself on the streets again. Fog rolled across
the road, eerie, chill, and lending the night an appropriate,
gothic feel. Donna was once again walking down one of
Oakham's many deserted roads. Forested land was broken by
lawns, the houses set well back from the road. This was an
expensive part of Oakham, somewhere that you couldn't smell
the neighbor's cigarette smoke. Donna wondered how many
people she had killed around here.

Ahead, she saw a light. Donna gathered herself, afraid that
she might not be able to stop the intruder now. She was shit at
meditation. The Yoda texts had ceased after two, she had no
idea what to do next.

As she debated with herself mentally, her body strode
towards the only source of light. A garage, with the door
open, light flooding out of it. What was this? She smelled hot
metal. A scruffy man was working on a bench. As far as she
could tell, he was blowtorching something. A shelf of drawers
dominated the left-hand wall, a band saw stood to the right,
a fume hood above the bench proper. Everywhere was the
gleam of polished metal; bowls, ornate scrollwork, weather

vanes, and other items Donna couldn't identify.

He straddled a wooden bench, singed and stained from years of work, playing a blowtorch around on a bowl in front of him. Finished or not, the intricate enamel pattern was already beautiful. She wished she'd happened on his work before.

As she approached, he turned to her. Curly hair the color of worn copper sprang from his head and face, like he was a wiry, off-color dandelion. He was shorter than Donna. He took off his leather gloves, and shoved his protective goggles up on his forehead. He looked like some sort of demented tinker.

He extended a hand. "Dennis, pleased to meet you."

Normally, she had the element of surprise. But he'd seen her. Let her walk up to him, and his jewelry shop. *Now what, you ambushing piece of shit?*

She took his hand, they shook.

"You look kinda lost," he said.

"Uh, I kind of am."

"Well that's a relief," he said, putting the blowtorch down. "I was afraid you might be here to kill me."

Donna's body stiffened. Here it was, right in her face.

"You see, someone's going around killing my fellow alchemists, and I thought that might have been you." He looked her up and down. "How many people are likely to wander by at three in the morning, anyway? Oakham is pretty quiet after sundown."

"Do you know what I'm looking for?"

"Oh, it's something you can't be bothered to read. I can't imagine it's all that important. You seem to have a hammer."

Terrified as she was, Donna laughed in her head. *What are you going to do now, you mother fucker?*

"At a loss for words?" Dennis picked up a hammer and flipped it in his hand. "You've killed a few of my friends without burning their houses down. You seem to like the bludgeon and fire, although you've been creative with a couple of them." He snatched up the still-burning blowtorch. He extended both hands toward her.

"Take your pick."

"So, you aren't the namby-pamby that so many of your

fellow collegians are," Donna sneered.

Dennis snickered. Donna reached for the hammer, but he moved it up, out of her reach.

"Sorry, that was rude." He was baiting her. She was now closer than she had been. He extended the hammer again. "Try again?"

The confidence of the man frightened her. He knew how to distract someone. He was dangerous.

She reached out again, and he jerked it up high. This time, he shifted his feet, caught her behind the knee, sending her sprawling backwards.

"You're not very good at this," he said. "I totally understand how you could have smashed Thomas's face in with a shovel. But how did you manage to overpower Ross? Did you get him drunk first?"

Donna focused all her energy on pushing away the blackness. She had no breath to center her. Only her own thoughts to distract her. She centered herself. And pushed, expanding her consciousness, sweeping everything that was not *her* out of her mind.

She felt her body convulse. Her head began to explode by short stages. Donna didn't let that distract her. She pushed, focused only on throwing her violator out. The darkness clawed at her, cloying and sticky.

The headache increased to a screaming migraine. Had she hit her head on a rock? Was she bleeding? Concussed?

She let the questions go, concentrated, pushed her will against the black, boiling it away. The pain from her head grew to agony.

She felt a nearly-audible pop that echoed through her head. She could feel the clammy wet fog, the asphalt beneath her. Her head was a blazing ball of pain, but it was *her* blazing ball of pain.

"Holy fuck, I did it." She stared up at the black sky, taking deep breaths into her lungs.

Dennis strode over to her, hammer and blowtorch in each hand.

"I threw him out," she gasped. "I'm not him anymore."

"Sure."

The headache screamed at her now, as if her brain had swollen and was trying to break out of her skull. How could anything hurt so much?

He crouched over her, hammer and blowtorch at the ready.

"Careful, you fucking idiot."

"No offense, but I'm not sure I believe you."

Oh this was all she needed. The headache was receding. She still felt like she'd been scalped, but it was tolerable. Donna stood, a little unsteady on her feet.

"Dennis, you need to back the fuck off with that blowtorch."

Her kick caught him right below the ribs. The breath huffed out of him, and he was on his knees, gasping for breath. The hammer clattered to the asphalt, the blowtorch rolling slowly away. Donna followed up by kicking him in the face, knocking him backwards.

He struggled to get up, but Donna put her boot on his neck, forcing him back to the ground.

"The difference between me and the jackass who just departed is that I'm not going to burn your face until I can see the inside of your skull," she said. "I will not, however, take your shit. You're going to walk away, assuming you don't do anything idiotic. I want you to tell the rest of your little college buds…" What? What did she want to tell them? "That any help you could send me would be greatly appreciated. My name is Donna Otálora, and I want this to be done. Whoever is doing this is looking for the Key of Aros the Philosopher, so if someone could figure out how to have your internecine slap-fight in a way that doesn't involve me, that would be just peachy."

Dennis looked up at her. Donna took her boot off his throat, reached down to help him up. He looked at her warily as he stood.

"Aros the Philosopher, you say?" He rubbed his neck. "Do you know what he wants it for?"

Donna threw up her hands. "Do I have to do fucking *everything* for you? You guys are magic, can't you figure out who is attacking you?"

He shook his head. "It doesn't work like that."

Of course it didn't. "Then get on the damn stick and figure something out. How many of you have to be murdered before you fight back, do something?"

"There are ethical considerations," Dennis said.

"What about me? Aren't you all supposed to be on the road to enlightenment? I'm utterly not involved in this, and you bastards haven't lifted a finger to do anything about it. Shouldn't you be doing *something*?"

"Of course we regret your involvement. But that's the responsibility of the person who is doing it, not us."

"There's nothing you can do. Fine. Whatever. Is there anything *I* can do?"

"There's nothing that I can suggest that you would understand," he said. Donna could feel her forearms aching with the tightness of her fists. After all this, after learning to throw him out of her head, all the College could give her was condescension?

"You are damn lucky I don't grab that torch that's burning a hole in the street and burn down your goddam house."

"I know it sounds unfair…" he started, but he stopped when Donna raised her fists.

"Don't. Just don't. Whatever you say is just going to make me sympathize with the person that's killing you patronizing shitheads." Donna turned and walked away. His silence was all the confirmation she needed. She didn't matter to either side in this conflict. She was invisible, expendable. Enlightened, her ass.

Donna staggered back to the apartment, exhausted, disgusted. She unlocked the door, then tried to tiptoe inside.

"Donna?" Jim turned on a light and Donna nearly smashed into a side table.

"Jesus fucking Christ, Jim. Don't do that to me." She was fighting the painful after-effects of throwing that bastard out of her head, and that walk hadn't burned off the anger.

"You left the apartment in a pretty bad state," Jim said. "When I got home, I thought we'd been robbed."

"No, just me on a tear."

"Naturally, I ran to your jewelry box. I wanted to make sure your necklace..."

"Of course the necklace. Jesus, Jim, weren't you even a little worried that I was out wandering the streets at three in the morning."

"I just don't understand why you won't wear it." Jim's voice was rising. "Is there something wrong with it? I bought it for you."

"Oh stop, you fucking simpering little *shit*. I hate your fucking necklace, it's ugly, and I've just come back from kicking the shit out of a guy, and you're wondering why I'm not wearing your favorite piece of jewelry. What the *fuck* is wrong with you?"

"You've been using this weird delusion of yours to browbeat me for months," Jim yelled back. "I'm not having it. I refuse to let you run roughshod over me because you say you're having strange dreams."

"Yes, that's it, I have to be delusional or manipulative. I couldn't possibly be having my own pain. Please tell me all about the way I'm acting and how you totally understand it." Donna knew this was a bad direction, but she just couldn't keep her rage and frustration dammed.

"I can't believe you're bringing this up *again*. Of course you can't possibly be wrong, and Jesus bless anyone who even thinks about offering you advice, because you will rip them a new one. Don't try to advise Donna. Not perfect Donna who knows everything."

"Says the man who has no *fucking* clue what I'm going through. Who told me I wasn't killing people. I had to rub your face in the shit shower my life has become."

"Says the uptight ice queen. You know I bet if you unclenched enough to actually enjoy sex, this might not—"

And then it was quiet. And Jim was sprawled on the floor. Donna looked down and saw her hand was a fist.

Well, shit. She shouldn't have done that. Holy shit, she really shouldn't have done that. She was losing control. She'd cold-cocked Jim.

She had to leave. Where could she go? Fierce's place? No. She couldn't go to anyone. She couldn't face anyone. She'd hit

Jim. He was being a dick and totally needed it, but that wasn't something civilized people did. Even in the middle of an argument with a complete fucking asshole.

Where should she go? The question buzzed around her brain like a hyperactive fly. She had to get out. Where to go? Where could she go that he couldn't find her? A motel? There weren't that many in Oakham. And it wouldn't take long for Jim to track her down. Fuck. Fuck *fuck* fuck *fuck*.

What Oakham did have was plenty of forested space. She could camp out. Just for a couple of days. Just until she got her head together.

She looked at her cell phone. She wouldn't be able to take it. The temptation to call someone, even Jim, would be too much. And it was just going to be for a couple of days.

She pulled out the small, two-person tent from the closet, went to her bedroom and pulled her stash of emergency cash out of her underwear drawer. After a moment, she pulled a hoodie and two changes of clothing, stuffed them in a backpack, and fled.

CHAPTER 12

BULLET

After three days, Donna thoroughly missed civilized life. She wanted a shower. She didn't need bubble bath, or anything like that, but she really needed to get the stink off her. Dunking her head into the river wasn't nearly as workable.

She missed coffee. She missed coffee more than clean underwear, or television.

She was afraid. What would people think of her? She couldn't face Fierce, couldn't face Jim. Couldn't face anyone. She'd sucker-punched Jim, of her own volition. Goddammit, she was out of control. She had to get some of her life back before she tried to interact with people again. If ever.

She wasn't punishing herself. She swore to herself that she wasn't. The days were long and excruciatingly dull, she was living off canned food that she bought on the occasional late-night trip to a 24-hour market. She felt like a Neanderthal, scavenging on the fringes of society. No phone, nothing to read, nothing to do but sit and think, try to figure out where everything had gone wrong.

She still had the gym key. Thank God for small favors. She so wanted to get clean, even if she knew it wouldn't last long.

The promise of cleanliness was a balm, and she obsessed about it all day. How she would luxuriate in the hot spray, with a roof over her head. The feel of soap running away the grunge, untangling her increasingly messy hair. The trappings of civilization, the glorious luxuries she had taken for granted.

The sun went down, and she walked over to the gym. She

watched from the tree line. She could see the parking lot, but couldn't be seen. They would close around nine… and then Donna would get her shower. The wait was almost unendurable. Minutes crawled past.

She wondered how people were reacting to her disappearance. What was Jim telling people? How was Fierce? She regretted biting Fierce's head off. She regretted a lot of things.

She watched people, regular people, people who didn't have to hide from their mind-violators, go out to their cars. Some walked alone, some chatted. She knew some of them. She wanted to talk to them.

And finally, they had gone. The lights went out, and a few minutes later, Tim walked to his car and drove off. And she was alone. She could feel the tears running down her face, to be so close to them, and at the same time, so far away.

The plan worked, though. The shower was a miracle, a reminder of what normal was. The delight of scraping the filth off her body, the hot rush of water over her skin. She didn't have to be afraid. Didn't have to watch her back, look over her shoulder. It was heaven.

She toweled off, looked in a mirror, and adjusted her hair. It was, she supposed, a stupid thing to worry about. She hadn't shaved her legs, either. She didn't think she was going to need to impress anyone soon. Being clean somehow let her think better, now that she wasn't worried that shit was crawling in her hair.

The night was dark and still as she left. She felt good.

A hand clamped over her forearm.

"You need to come with me."

She looked from the hand to the man. Sandy hair, short cut, cold eyes, wearing a suit, of all things.

"No," she said. "Let me go."

"I'm taking you to someone you've been working with. Someone important." His grip tightened. His smile was cold, his eyes dead. He probably outweighed her by forty pounds.

"Tell me who," she said.

"Can't until we're there."

She yanked her arm back, which shifted him forward. She

brought her right shin crashing into the side of his knee. With a wet pop, he fell, screaming. She stared for a moment at the man on the ground, his leg at an unnatural angle.

Donna ran. She didn't stop to see if he was permanently crippled, she just ran. She'd hurt someone, probably critically. She crashed through the brush, sounding like an elephant in her own ears.

She was blind in the night. She crossed roads, trying to avoid street lights. After some time, she realized she was completely lost. Did it matter? She found herself a small open patch, leaned against a tree trunk. She was too frightened, her heart pounding too hard.

Who had he been? Who was looking for her? Someone she'd been working with? What the hell did that mean?

And… and she'd just hurt someone. Badly. Nobody walked away from a dislocated knee like that without surgery. And she'd done it. She'd really fucked him up. It hadn't been like that with Artie, when she hadn't known she was doing it. She'd knowingly fucked that guy up.

So why didn't she feel bad about it? Was she a sociopath? Had constant exposure to the murders her body was committing damaged her so badly that hurting people didn't bother her? It was a frightening feeling. She put her head in her hands, fully expecting to bawl her eyes out. But she didn't. Her life was so disrupted, was it really any wonder she didn't feel any remorse? Could she feel anything?

The questions bounced off each other, neither in focus nor going away. Then, the exhaustion and the fear of the day overtook her, and she nodded off against the tree's trunk.

Donna woke with a start. The sun wasn't up, but there was enough pre-dawn light. She didn't know where she was, but she stood, dusted off her jeans, and headed out. She stepped out into the sidewalk, just to get her bearings. She recognized the neighborhood instantly, not too far from the gym. She hadn't run as far as she thought she had, last night.

She had to get off the streets before dawn. She didn't want to be visible in Oakham during the day. She was safely back in her little camp by the time the sun was fully up. Despite everything, she was glad to see it. She had so little, even her little scrub location was something to hold onto.

Who was that guy? The question had buzzed around her head since she had met him, and now it came out in force. What did she know?

He'd been waiting for her. Someone knew that she still had keys to the gym. And was waiting for her. Shit. That was creepy.

He hadn't even tried to bring her peacefully. He'd just grabbed her. He'd been wearing a suit. Had he been the guy making her kill people?

Donna woke in the night. Something moved, not in the leaves around her little tent, but somewhere else. She heard a whine, like a mosquito or a far-off dentist drilling a tooth. She shook her head, but it didn't change. What the hell? It expanded, began filling her head. She covered her ears, but the sound, the feeling, only grew.

It was him. She closed her eyes, and summoning everything she was, pressed. She did not shove violently, but threw force at him in a constant flow, like a hose. The shrill whine lessened. She set her teeth, kept her focus sharp. She could feel the point of the drill between her eyes, boring at her. She stayed tense, keeping it away, not letting it gain traction. She controlled her breath, burned her pent-up frustration at the intruder. She would not murder someone. Somewhere distant, she felt sweat break on her face, knew that her teeth were clenched. No. She thought of nothing but negation, she would not let it happen. Her filthy nails dug into her palms, and she used that pain to keep herself strong.

The sound dimmed, the annoyance eased off, then faded to nothing. She kept the denial up until she was certain it was gone.

She was sweating as if she had just taught an entire class. She swiped a hand across her face, feeling the slickness. It was still her hand, and she controlled it. She laughed, listening to her half-mad self, alone in the woods. Why hadn't she been able to feel him coming before? Was it something in the woods? The quiet?

Who cared? This was a victory. He had come for her, and he hadn't gotten her. She wanted to get up and dance, but her legs were too cramped. She crawled out of her sitting position. She needed to stretch. She wanted another shower. She wanted to go home.

Even if she felt like celebrating, she had no one to talk with.

Why didn't this feel like victory anymore? And what was she going to do? He had driven her into the woods. He'd sent someone after her. How was she going to deal with this?

Around her, the insects sang, ignoring her. She couldn't, she realized, just wait for something to happen. She had to make it happen.

How?

Thoughts churned in her head, but eventually, the insects lulled her back to sleep.

Donna finished her morning exercise routine, using tree branches as bars. She wished she could go back to the gym. Everything was so much more convenient there. She shook the thought off. She'd had enough time to soak in self-pity, but it wouldn't get her anywhere.

Homelessness was all about time. Enormous amounts of time. She wished she had a book, but then again, she wished she had a pile of books. She should buy some of those shitty books the 24-hour market kept in a dark corner. Anything was better than the long nothing of boredom. Without a daily grind of things to do, time weighed heavily on her. There had been so many distractions in her daily life. So many things that needed doing, so much time preparing. With all that gone, with her friends gone, she was alone, awash in all the time she needed, with so little to fill it.

How long was she going to stay out here? Weeks? Months? Fall was coming, and she didn't want to be out in freezing weather with only her tent. She had to figure things out.

She woke to hear someone blundering through the undergrowth. She was out of her tent in a flash, creeping away as quietly as she could. The sun was down, the last light lingering on the cloudy horizon. Dim, but not yet dark. The approach sounded like an elephant, someone clearly unused to walking over dried leaves and bracken.

Donna hunkered down, a tree between her and the approaching noise, and remained as still as she could. The crunching, smashing, and occasionally swearing approached, and out of the dim light appeared a large man in a dark suit. What the hell was he doing out here? Suits were for classy people, not thugs blundering around in the woods like drunken buffalo. Her little encampment was miles from the road, a good distance from the Massaquott River. This was, she knew, not a coincidence.

He nearly stumbled on her tent before he stopped.

"Hey." He said it in a low voice, as if afraid he was going to wake her up. What the hell?

"Donna," he said. He knew her name. Frozen fear ran up her spine. He'd been sent to find her. The insects filled the air with liquid, pervasive noise. What to do?

His boss murdered people. He was the only person who had the sort of power to send people against her. The Police Chief would just send cops, right? She was relieved that these guys weren't cops. She would feel terrible if she fucked up a cop, like Kutsenko. What was he doing right now?

"Hey, look, I don't want to get violent. But I've got orders, and I want you to come peacefully. OK?"

If she said anything, she'd give away her position.

"Look, we've got a real comfortable room for you, a shower, a nice soft bed. It's better than out here, let me tell you."

All she had to do was give in. Be their instrument. She controlled her breathing, stayed motionless.

"Are you even in there? Goddammit, I'm going to be pissed if I just made that speech to an empty tent."

He started in for her tent. Her first instinct was to go after him right then. She had so little of her own anymore, and this asshole was intruding on it. She felt the muscles bunching in her forearms as he approached the front of the tent. He unzipped the front of the tent, poked his head inside, as Donna crept up behind him. Then, at the worst possible moment, he turned around.

His face was a blank look of surprise when she smashed him across the head with a tree branch. He was down, but still conscious as he tried to scramble away from her. She brought the branch down on his leg. He turned, fumbling in his jacket, but she was on top of him, pressing the branch into his neck. He could reach for the gun, or he could breathe. He chose to breathe.

"Now, since you're so friendly, let's have a chat," she said.

"All right," he said. Probably just for time.

"Who do you work for?"

"Can't tell you that," he said. "Sorry, but it's dangerous."

"Dangerous to who?"

"Everyone."

He couldn't have intrigued her more if he'd tried.

She leaned in. "How dangerous?"

He tried to shift her, but she was ready. The end of the stick hit the dirt. She smashed her forehead down on his nose. The wet crunch filled her skull. When she brought her face back up, blood was flowing down his face from his flattened nose.

With her left hand, she reached into his jacket, feeling around for the pistol she knew was there. He tried to fend her off, but she smashed her forearm onto his nose. He yelled and tried to curl up in pain, but she was still on top of him. She pulled the pistol out.

"I'm trying to keep this civil, but you're the one who showed up with the gun." She pointed it at him. He stopped struggling. Chairman Mao was right. Power did grow from the barrel of a gun.

He was bleeding from the side of his head where she'd whacked him. And from his nose. Not a good day to be him.

"I'm being hunted," she said. "I don't want to hurt you, I think we can agree that I will."

He shook his head in agreement, not taking his eyes off the gun. She found it intoxicating. She had his complete attention.

"If you won't tell me who you working for, at least tell me he how many goons he has."

"Goons?"

She extended the gun.

"There's ten of us. Not including the guy you crippled a few days back."

Ten. That was going to be tough. The gun was heavy in her hand. They would all have guns. She might get lucky with a couple of them, but they were armed. She wouldn't be able to take even half of them out. She was no commando.

She didn't want to. She didn't want to kill them, cripple them, or anything else. But her frustration grew as they stared at each other. She wouldn't be able to keep him there forever. What could she do with him? Any promise was likely as temporary as his fear. Once out of sight, he would tell them where she was. Even if she moved her campsite, they would know she was camping.

Holding him prisoner wasn't an option. Feeding him, wiping his ass, gagging him, all too much work.

She squeezed the trigger. The bullet punched through his skull, a shower of gore and brains came out the back. His head snapped backwards, then the rest of his body followed as he collapsed in a heap. She stared as his chest spasmed, drew a breath, let it out, and then was still.

She should feel something. She'd just murdered someone. Took away his future. His mother would mourn him. Did he have someone who loved him? A wife? A husband? Kids? She had expected crippling remorse for killing the man. Some sort of regret, letting her know that what she had done was bad, that murder was wrong. She felt nothing but a strange emptiness. What the hell was wrong with her?

She'd deal with that later. She looked at the body again. She wasn't going to bury him. That was a lot of effort and it would take her all day.

Wait, what else was she planning on doing? She had nothing but time on her hands.

She went through his pockets. He had a wallet, keys, and a cell phone. She stared at the keys for a moment before realizing what they meant. And her evening went from nothing to do all the way to a full day in less than fifteen minutes.

She packed her tent, moved a mile up the river, and set it up again. Tomorrow morning, she would take time to bring down branches and camouflage it. She didn't want to be found again.

His driver's license was from Massachusetts, his address in Bolton, a few towns over. His name had been Jacob Stein. She didn't find a picture of a wife or kids. But she did find an ATM card, a platinum Visa, a AAA card, and a gym membership to a place she didn't recognize. The broken pieces of a life she had ended. And eighty-two dollars in cash.

While the sun was still down, she headed for the nearest road. Few cars were parked so far from the town center, so the Ford Mustang wasn't that difficult to locate. She sat in the car. Now what? She had to move it, make sure whoever found the car would look around somewhere else for the former owner.

She drove a few miles, to an extension road with a few widely-spaced houses, and left the car there. She pocketed the insurance information and had a four-mile bushwhack back to the body in the dark.

The sun was rising before she was back to Jacob's corpse. The flies had already found him.

She started digging. An hour later, she had come to the conclusion that Stein wasn't getting a proper six-foot deep burial. Maybe four. She was sheened with sweat, smeared with dirt, and thinking about dumping his dead ass in the Massaquott River. She'd built a two foot tall pile of stones she'd pulled out of the notoriously rocky Massachusetts soil. But something, maybe regret, maybe the desire to not leave a job unfinished, maybe the desire not to be prosecuted for murder, kept her digging.

It was close to noon by the time she'd finished, packing down the dirt over his body as best she could. It still looked obvious to her, but maybe it would go unnoticed.

She crawled back into her tent and indulged in a nap. It had been a long day already.

She woke to the cooling sunset. The sun wasn't down, but the trees were throwing long shadows.

Donna hadn't intended to become some sort of creepy Oakham stalker. But she was a lot less nervous about moving around in the dark.

She took out Stein's phone. She figured she had one call

before they figured out that he wasn't using it. Who to call? Jim? Fierce? She shook her head. She couldn't justify herself to either of them. What would she say? Her mother? Auntie Ana? Jesus, what a conversation that would be. She stared at the phone.

She still had Officer Kutsenko's number, she realized. What was the point of that, though? He hadn't done anything to help her. She was about to dismiss the thought when she realized he was also the only person she knew who might know her legal status. And she didn't know him as well as she knew Fierce. She might be able to face him without feeling utterly ashamed of herself.

She put the phone away, watched the sun lower until it vanished behind the Western hills. It was peaceful, but deadly boring.

She took out the phone, her one lifeline to the normal world she was so excluded from, and dialed Kutsenko.

Two hours later, she was hiding in the undergrowth just off Oak Street. She'd left her gun up a tree, where it wasn't likely to be found. Shooting Kutsenko was not an option, and considering the violence she'd committed recently she didn't want the option. She watched, from her concealed position, as cars passed. None of them slowed. None of them cared.

She thought she recognized Kutsenko's police car as it slowed down and stopped. She couldn't see in, though. Who was waiting in the car? Schenck? She should have brought the gun. But the driver turned the car off, and Kutsenko stepped out of the car.

"Officer Kutsenko," she said.

"Donna?" he played his flashlight into the trees, but Donna was already behind the trunk of a particularly thick one.

"Promise you're not going to try to apprehend me."

He was silent for a minute.

"Donna, you and I need to talk."

"We can't talk unless I know that you aren't going to try to haul me in."

"That's not my intention. But I do have my duty as an officer."

She waited, silent. The searching beam of his flashlight

searched for her. She remained as still as she could, praying he didn't find her. The beam touched her, and she wanted to scream, but it moved on, and she could breathe again.

"Stop looking for me. Please," she said.

The questing beam winked out, and the night was dark and quiet.

"You sure kicked the wasps' nest," he said, facing to her right. "You're wanted on charges of domestic assault."

"I may have overreacted," she said, hanging her head. "Have you seen the victim? Is Jim OK?"

"I haven't seen the alleged victim," Kutsenko said.

Why was this care for Jim squirming inside her? He'd probably already sold all her shit. Dammit, she hadn't thought about him for days.

"Where are you staying?" Kutsenko asked it gently.

"Not going to tell you that."

"I can't help you if you leave me out in the cold," he said. "I want to help."

"You made helpful noises before, but I'm out of my apartment, and on the wanted list. You're going to have to do a bit more than just talk."

Kutsenko folded his arms over his chest.

"Your conspiracy is frankly difficult to believe. The fact that you are now on the list doesn't make that any more believable."

Of course it didn't. People lied to the police all the time. She had lied to him, by omission. She was doing so again, by not telling him she'd shot a man dead and buried his body. She shivered.

"Have you discovered anything since we last spoke?" she asked.

"Precious little." There was a scream in her, building slowly. She wanted to shout at him, tell him that she's killed someone. She'd shot a hole in Jacob Stein's face, watched his brains get blown out the back of his head. She was a murderer, and this time, it was entirely her. No one had forced her to do it.

"Has there been an influx of assholes in suits?" She asked.

He was too good to give anything away.

"Maybe. What does that have to do with your current situation?"

"They're hunting me. They've all got on dark suits like they're the Secret Service."

Kutsenko was quiet.

"Donna, you're starting to sound paranoid." He said it quietly. "Are you sure these things are happening? Because being pursued by men in suits is something someone off their meds tends to think."

Donna could feel the desire to punch his stupid fucking face welling up from her spine. The night had been comfortable, but now she was suddenly hot, her heart pounding.

"One of them laid hands on me, Jerry. I was forced to hurt him. A lot."

"If it was self-defense then you're fine. You have a legal right to protect yourself."

"To be determined by a jury. Which will come down to he-said, she-said. Do you really think I beat the shit out of some innocent bastard because I'm out of my skull? You think I can't tell the difference between reality and fantasy?"

"I'm having some trouble with what you're saying, Donna. I want to believe that you are in your right mind, and that someone, somehow, is forcing you to… do things. But the more I think about it, the more off the reservation it gets."

"Have you noticed guys in suits running around town?" Returning to her earlier question seemed like more stable ground.

He was quiet for a moment.

"There have been some incidents involving the police and some guys in suits over the last couple of days."

He'd been winding her up. Fucking bastard.

"Can I ask where?" She could hear the brittleness in her own voice.

"You don't want to mess with these people," he said.

"No, they don't want to mess with me. It might take a little effort to convince them of this, however."

"Donna, I'm worried about you. How far you might take this."

"Did I mention that I have a pistol? That a suit guy jumped me wearing a gun?" She let the implication hang in the air.

"Let me repeat that I haven't taken this anywhere. I have been pushed."

He sighed. He looked tired.

"I didn't bring the pistol," she said. "I realize that means I can't back up what I've said."

"No, that's OK. I don't anticipate there being a rash of gunshot deaths in Oakham." He left it there. So many things he couldn't say. So many things she couldn't tell him. The dance was tiring for her, too.

"But you should know that the guys with suits are new in town. I wouldn't immediately draw the conclusion that they are the individuals you are having trouble with, congregating around Thurmond Corey's place."

Thurmond Corey. Some sort of uncle or distant cousin of Jim's. The rich recluse of Oakham, lived in some mansion that occupied an entire block. Didn't Fierce do his taxes?

"I'm sure that it's nothing," she said. "Probably a coincidence that they've been seen at his place."

Kutsenko danced the dance well. Everything he'd said could salve his conscience and be plausibly deniable if this went to court. Was this any reason to trust him? She was having a lot of trust problems recently.

"How's the chief?" She asked.

"Busy. He's doing a lot of covering, excusing and quashing. Unofficially, of course."

Donna grunted. He nodded, in his own way acknowledging they had the same enemy. And now she had a name. But she couldn't work with Kutsenko. Not with what she had done, what she might have to do. Not openly. He had the luxury of thinking the system wasn't rigged.

"Anything else I might want to know before I continue my patrol?"

"You might want to take a vacation."

He shook his head, his mouth in a cynical twist. "That would leave you in the lion's den without anyone who might understand. Chief Schenck's got everyone on edge."

"Wait, so you sort of do believe me? What the Hell, Kutsenko?"

He crossed his arms over his chest. "There's a lot of weird stuff going on in Oakham. I just can't afford to dismiss you as crazy, because what you say isn't the maddest stuff I've heard. Nor the worst."

"I'm sorry," she said. "It must be really bad if I'm making sense."

He looked tired. "I'm just trying to be a good cop, look out for people, keep Oakham safe. I don't want to get into politics, and I don't want to work for a corrupt bastard."

"We all have our burdens to bear," Donna said, thinking about Stein.

Donna slept fitfully that night, expecting to hear more feet approaching. Every sigh of the wind or unexpected animal noise snapped her awake. But the feared retribution didn't materialize. She faced the morning, bone-weary but determined. She had a name. Thurmond Corey. He was sending out the guys in suits, sent Stein to his death. So what did that mean? They were looking for her. Since she'd started to deny herself to him, he'd started with another tactic. Probably. It wasn't damning proof, but it was certainly worth looking into.

How to move around Oakham without getting noticed? She was already beginning to look rough around the edges. Maybe it would be best to wait until nightfall.

She napped on and off through the day, in between washing in the Massaquott, her improvised workout, and planning. By the time the sun was down, she was itching to get something done.

Donna didn't feel right, walking from the nearly-abandoned side road of Oakham toward the town center.

The Corey mansion was a gigantic Italianate monstrosity completely at odds with the more traditional New England rest of the town. Money could buy it, but it apparently couldn't buy taste. It didn't look like a fortified compound but the more Donna watched it, the more she was convinced that it was. The low brick wall that separated the estate from the sidewalk was backed up by bushes. The gate and U-shaped driveway were

the only ways to get onto the property without making a hell of
a lot of noise.

From her vantage point across the street, leaning casually
against a neighbor's tree, she caught glimpses inside the wall.
The grass was manicured to within an inch of its life. Gray
sedans brought men in dark suits into and out of the gated
driveway. The walk-up gate wasn't locked, but even Girl Scouts
couldn't get through it without talking to one or two suits. She
was going to need an in.

No delivery got through without being inspected. The guys
all seemed to know each other, and there weren't any women
among them. So there went the easy stuff.

It frustrated her that she couldn't keep a 24-hour watch on
the place, but that was probably for the best. If she skulked that
much, someone was going to notice her. She watched mostly at
night, when the darkness made it easier for her to hide, but the
lit-up yard was easy to watch.

They kept regular hours. They kept a pair of twelve-hour
shifts, changing at six. Fierce was probably having fits running
up their overtime. God, she missed Fierce. She wanted a break,
time away, the ability to sleep without keeping a fearful ear out
for someone sneaking up on her. Would she ever have anything
resembling a normal life again? She missed the many things
she had taken for granted. Sometimes she counted the things
she missed, but stopped when it started to make her crazy.

The suit-guys didn't sleep at the Corey House. They all left
when they were done with their shifts. That, Donna realized,
would be her key to get one alone.

Most of them drove off, and she couldn't follow them. One,
though, kept an apartment about two blocks from the Corey
house. He'd get off-shift, head straight for his apartment, which
was the ground floor of a charming Queen Anne. Among its
graces were a huge wrap-around porch, a turret, a mature
maple in the front yard, and best of all, a for-rent sign for the
upstairs apartment.

Night in residential Oakham was quiet. The foot traffic
was almost exclusively dog-walkers, who were all too happy to
ignore the homeless woman. The streets, never busy to begin

with, took on the low pulse of a coma patient.

Donna stalked her victim for two nights. The first, he got off punctually at six PM, and drove straight back to his apartment. He parked in the driveway, and took to the count of eleven Mississippi to get to the stairs, had his keys in the lock four counts later, and the door slammed closed three after that. Not a lot of time.

Donna huddled in the shadow of the house, waiting. She didn't have a phone to check the time on, but she was sure he was late. Fuck. Were they on to her? Had he moved? She gripped the gun in the back of her waistband and waited.

When she finally heard him pull up, she held her breath, trying to hear everything she could. The sound of one car door slamming, then another opened? Was he with someone? Now he was taking forever to get to the front steps, and Donna's hands were claws from tension. The timing was completely out the window. Should she abort the plan?

His foot landed on the first step, and she was in motion. She rounded the corner and he was struggling under the weight of some grocery bags. She poured on the speed, and he saw her, dropped the groceries, and sprinted for the door. She caught up with him just as he got his back to the door, hands reaching for his pistol. She brought her gun up, and he froze.

CHAPTER 13

TERRIBLE THINGS

Donna shoved the guy through the door. He turned, his arms still up. She felt for the door behind her, then closed it. Fumbling without looking, she slid the bolt and the deadbolt home. Let the food rot on the porch.

At a quick glance, the apartment seemed uninhabited. No pictures on the bland white walls, and precious little furniture. She backed him away from the entrance.

"You realize if you shoot me, you'll have a shitload of people down on you."

"Won't be much help. You'll be dead." They were in some sort of dining room/living room combination. With a couch, a small table, and a gigantic television. Of course. Guys. Through one door, she could see a small kitchen. She didn't want to turn her head long enough to look through the other.

"To the bedroom," she said, gesturing with the pistol.

To her surprise, he had a nice bed, with a wooden frame, rather tasteful in a modern arts and crafts sort of way. Where had it come from? It had a good slatted headboard. Good. She only had one set of handcuffs.

She cuffed his arms over his head, wrists through the slats. He was muscular, so he might be able to break one slat, but she doubted he'd be able to break two.

Only when he was secured did she sit on the small chair, and point the gun at the floor.

"OK, look, you've got me where you want me. Can we talk this out? I mean, you really don't want to shoot me, do you?"

"Why don't you ask your co-worker, Mr. Stein."

"Stein quit," he said, too quickly.

"He's dead. I shot him," she said it with matter-of-fact flatness.

"Bullshit," he said.

"I don't care if you believe me or not," she said. It was so good to have someone to talk to. "So we're going to have a chat."

"And then what?"

"That'll depend on how the chat ends."

"I'm not scared of you."

"You should be," Donna said "The problem is I can't let you go. I had the same problem with Stein. You could promise not to go back to Thurmond, and then go straight to him. You could promise to leave town the instant I let you go, but you could phone him later. I'd really prefer not to kill you. I would. But right now, I don't see any way around it."

He took in a deep shuddering sigh.

"I can't talk you out of it?"

She shrugged. "You appear to have taken a job in which you were ordered to kidnap a woman. I'm sure you don't deserve death, but you took a pretty bad job in which you expected to do horrible things."

"I have a wife and kids," he said.

"What are their names?"

He hesitated.

"Kind of what I thought. Look, I don't think you're scum, and if it gives you any comfort, I'll make it as painless as possible. But you're not getting out of this room."

His look was blank. She whipped out the napkin she had been hiding, and gagged him, tying it tight behind his head. He glared at her, grunting.

She pulled the gun, pointed it at his left eye. "The louder you are, the shorter you have to live."

She sat again. "I'm hoping that I can figure some way out of this. I don't want to kill you, but I can't afford to have you running around." She looked at him. "I also need to intimidate some people. Your people. The ones who kept looking for me even after I crippled one of your guys and made another one disappear. Do you know how much this sucks? How far I've been pushed? I don't want to kill anyone, but there doesn't seem to be any other way to survive. Letting one of you guys drag me somewhere doesn't seem like a long-term survival strategy."

"I'm tired. I'm tired of having to deal with this bullshit. I want to have my life back. I want a warm meal, something not out of a can. I want my apartment back, I want to do my job. Do you have any idea how fucking infuriating it is to have people hunting you? To have to run out of your own home and hide?" She leaned in on him. "It makes me fucking crazy."

He stared at her, his terrified eyes wide. "What I want is to get information about the other people Thurmond has hired, about his security measures. But I've got no way of knowing how much you're going to lie." He struggled against the handcuffs, and got nowhere.

What to do with him? He tried to say something through his gag. Donna didn't really care what it was. The sad truth was that she no longer had any reason to keep him alive.

She grabbed a pillow and headed for the kitchen. For a guy who had no sofa, he had an impressively filled knife block. She pulled out a long, thin knife, looked at her dirty reflection in the shiny blade. The rage came flooding back.

She put the pillow on the back side of the knife, and returned to the bedroom. He didn't have time to react before she'd put the knife to his throat, pushed the pillow down, and drew the knife out. She heard a hiss as his blood soaked into the soft cloth and he convulsed. In less than a minute, even the quivering had stopped. She had murdered again. Why wasn't it bothering her? She'd crossed a line, something she'd been told she should never do all her life. Because it was so easy?

She tossed the sopping wet pillow to another part of the bed where it landed with a squishy thump. She looked down at the face. Hard to believe she'd been speaking with him less than five minutes ago. His face was waxy where it wasn't smeared with blood. She should feel sad, looking down at his dead features.

After a moment, Donna realized she had only solved one problem. He was dead. How could she make whoever found him take notice? Castrating him felt childish, the act of someone with a sexual grudge. What could she cut that made a point about his job? His eyes? His face? Torso? What would make the mutilation intimidating?

Cut out his heart like an Aztec sacrifice? If they thought of her by her heritage, maybe that would work. She could be some sort of terrifying Mexican.

She went into his kitchen to look for a sturdy knife she could use to open his chest. Sawing through bone would be no joke. The kitchen was neat, and well-stocked. He had a good set of cast iron pans, a fancy set of knives in a block, and a small stove. He'd obviously spent a lot of time here. The fridge was stocked with fresh lettuce, onions, radishes. He'd been a big fan of the Oakham farmer's market. The thought of fresh vegetables made her stomach rumble.

She wanted a meal that wasn't cold, hadn't come out of a can. Something filling. Fresh meat, a burger. She opened the freezer, and sure enough, he had a load of frozen meat. She didn't have time to defrost something.

She thought about him. The dead man in the bedroom. He was muscular.

Could she? Was she really considering cannibalism? Well, it would scare the shit out of Thurmond and his fucking assholes. And she was so hungry.

She pulled some onions and a jar of green salsa out of the fridge, chose a knife from the block, and cut up the onions. It was a good, sharp knife. She held it out in front of her, staring at the edge. Was she willing to go through with this? To make this whole mess as hideous as possible? Was she really dedicated to making this worse for the people who were after her than they had made it for her? Could she go through with it?

She was already doubly a murderer, had crippled a man. And still they were coming after her. She had to do this. She had to make them fear her. Her grip on the knife tightened until her knuckles turned white.

She stalked back to the bedroom. The air was close, hotter than the kitchen, and loaded with the stink of blood. The body lay in the bed, the sheets stained with red.

She slit his pants up from the ankle. He'd been more of a

body-builder than a runner. His thighs were solid, meaty even. His skin seemed waxy, pale. Probably because he was lying in a bed soaked with his blood. She made two false starts. She couldn't cut the skin. It was like stabbing someone, causing them pain. She squared her jaw, set her teeth, lifted the knife, and brought it down on his thigh.

The knife tip pierced it, the feel was like any other piece of meat. And now the knife was half-way into the inside of his thigh. She sawed upward, toward his crotch, until she had a significant flap of meat. Blood oozed out of the cut. Grabbing one end of the flap, she sawed down towards his knee.

She ended up with a fillet about the size of her hand. Separated from the body, the cut looked like one of those pork shoulders with the skin still on. Only she couldn't trick herself into thinking that it was. She knew what it was: human meat.

She took it to the kitchen. On a cutting board, she scraped the fat and skin off, leaving a chunk of muscle. Dice it? No, there would be more impact if it were whole. She'd only eat some of it. Her stomach rumbled at the thought.

She cooked it like a pork chop. It was greasier than store-bought pork, and she had to pour a bit of the melted fat down the drain. It wasn't her sink, what did she care? The onions went in when it was close to done, and then a bit of green salsa. She smiled as the waft of delicious food enveloped her. Maybe it would keep people from smelling the body in the bedroom.

She plated the cut. She looked at it. She was hungry. She looked at the meat, human meat. Did she really want to go through with this? Would it be enough to just kill and slice the meat off him? No. They had to know. They had to see. They had to fear.

Determined, she cut a tiny piece off and put it in her mouth. Delicious. She'd prepared it just right. The meat was tender, the onions and salsa giving it savor. Oh God, it was good. Without thinking she cut off a larger piece, stuffed it greedily into her mouth. Just chewing was a delight. She slumped back in her chair, loving every moment of the warm meat that filled her belly mouthful by mouthful. She had intended to leave some, so that the police would know what she had done. But the taste was so good, her belly so happy, that she ate the whole thing.

She stood up, knowing the word cannibal would haunt her for the rest of her days. Even if she got out of this alive, even if she never told anyone, she would always know.

She wouldn't go back for a second cut. She stood, wiped her mouth on her sleeve, and took a minute to look around the apartment. Had she left anything? She discovered the gun on the chair next to the bed. Wouldn't want to leave that. She re-wrapped it in her towel, tucked the bundle under her arm. She wanted to take a shower, but she didn't have the time. And the vulnerability of nakedness… no.

She grabbed the doorknob, listened. She didn't hear anyone in the hall outside. Straightening up, like she was supposed to be there, she opened the door, locked the knob from the inside, and closed it behind her. She was confronted with the dropped groceries scattered on the porch. She could only pick up some, and she resolved to drop them at the first sign of pursuit. But a bundle of bananas and some cucumbers would be welcome.

It was close to full dark by the time she got back to her camp. She was jumpy and paranoid, stopping at irregular times, listening for anyone that might be following her. No one. Brushing aside the leafy branches she had left for camouflage, she crawled into her tent. She closed her eyes, but all she could think of was the line she had crossed. Cannibal. Jeffrey Dahmer, José Luis Calva, the Donner Party. She was one of them, despicable people who ate other human beings. She'd enjoyed having a full stomach. What did that make her? Was that really the best way to deal with the people… the people who had shit all over her life? The people who were hunting her. The people who had forced her to kill over and over and over.

Hatred welled up in her in a black tide. They pushed and they pushed, and now she had to do awful things. How else was she going to stop them? How was she going to live with herself? She would figure that out later.

She was still too worked up to sleep, so she lay, staring at the darkness that was the top of her tent, planning.

The buzzing woke her. The drone of something unnatural tickling at the back of her head.

"Aw fuck shit shit."

She could feel an insubstantial drill pressing against her head. She did not wait for it, but pushed her *rage* and *frustration* up as a bulwark. *Focus.* She focused her *hate* on the intruder. It wasn't enough to block him, she wanted to hurt him. She wanted hammers smashing that precision drill, ruining his ability to come at her.

It felt good to be on the attack. She concentrated on the interloper, bludgeoned him with her anger, letting him get a taste of her hate.

Incredibly, she won. The painful whine of the probe withdrew, leaving only the quiet of the Oakham night. Had she gotten that strong? Had her attacker become that much weaker?

Had cannibalism made her so repugnant that even he didn't want to use her anymore? Had it supercharged her, mystically? One thing was for sure, she wasn't going to get any sleep.

She crept out of her tent, listened. The night insects were loud. Somewhere an owl hooted. But nothing shifted, no branches crackled in the darkness. She looked up at the bright stars, remote and uncaring. She needed to talk with someone. The Horn would be open.

She was used to sauntering down the darkened streets, avoiding the pools of light. She settled into a shadow where she could watch the rear entrance of the bar. And waited.

Another watcher arrived. He drove a sporty car alongside the curb, shut off the car, and waited. Did he see her? Should she leave? Should she have brought the gun?

Donna's belly burned, her hands shook. Would nothing stop them? Rage bloomed in her, and she fought to control it. They had guns. Every one of them she had ever faced had a shoulder holster. She didn't.

She kicked a rock, which skittered into a larger one. She scooped the larger one up. It felt good in her hand. She turned and walked in the opposite direction of the car. She walked around the block in order to creep up behind the car. She'd hoped that her fury would somehow subside by the time she got to the car, but she found herself walking stiff-legged, her hand cramping from gripping the rock.

She didn't care if he saw her as she stalked up to the car. He saw her in the rear-view mirror, and was turning around when she swung the rock and shattered the window. It didn't collapse as she had hoped, so she slammed the rock into it again, showering him with tiny squares of glass. Not giving him any more time to react, she thrust her face towards him, snapping her teeth like a determined shark. His face blank with panic, he twisted the ignition and roared off.

Donna watched him go, bitter laughter bubbling up from some unknown place inside her. She doubled over, sides aching, and eventually fell to her knees, the laughter feeling like it was being wrung out of her. She didn't know how long she was there before she was looking up into Peter's eyes.

"Oh Christ, Peter." Her sides ached, and her voice was raw, but she'd finally stopped laughing.

"What the hell, Donna? I heard you all the way inside The Horn."

"You need to get back inside," she said. "We should meet when you get off work, but not here. I scared off one of those assholes in suits, but I expect he'll be back when he recovers his nerve.

He helped her up. She started to turn away but he held onto her.

"I have to ask…" he started.

"It's true." She said. She saw the revulsion in his eyes, just like she'd been afraid of. "If you want to talk anyway, I'll be at the alley behind the fish fry for a couple of hours." She turned and walked off, her sides still aching.

The alley behind the fish fry was perfect. Dark in the center, well lit at both ends, with the expected amount of loose gravel and broken glass at the ends. No one would be able to approach either end without Donna knowing about it.

Peter came alone. "That's a hell of a thing you did."

She shook her head. "I had to. These guys won't quit.

Thurmond Corey is apparently paying them enough that they don't care that I've crippled one of them, shot another. And they still keep coming for me. So I thought I'd rattle their cages. And it seems to have worked.

"Holy shit, Donna."

"Holy shit." She said it without inflection, numbed by her own actions. "I really freaked that guy out." She tried to stop the grin that crept over her face.

"Thurmond Corey? Really?"

"Sounds crazy, doesn't it? I mean, he's been sort of reclusive for the past couple of years, but yeah, I was creeped out recognizing the name."

"It gives us a name, but not much else, unfortunately," Peter said. "We probably know where to find him, but, I don't know. I mean, I had no idea he was any sort of alchemist. Although being able to turn lead into gold might explain his wealth. I always thought he'd been a hedge fund manager who invested well, and retired here to be in a small community."

"That could still be true. It's just that now he's got other interests."

"How does that help us, though?"

"Now we're an *us*?" Donna kept her anger at his cowardice leashed. "Great."

"Remember when I said I didn't want you tracking your troubles into The Horn? Since they've been digging up the sewer lines, the rats have come into the kitchen in droves. And, surprise, we had a health inspection two days ago. We're on probation with sixteen things to be fixed by the end of the month. Which will be expensive and disruptive."

"Corey's got some reach, then. Not everyone can order roadwork, or an inspection. If he can reach into politics, I wonder if he's got Schenck under his thumb, too."

"The police chief? Well, that would explain a lot," Peter said. "And would be pretty disturbing. I mean, if Corey's got the cops in his pocket, there isn't a lot he can't do."

"Yeah, but he isn't running all the cops. There's at least one, and I suspect a couple others, who think this town smells. But there's always a few bad ones willing to do whatever they're told. Without knowing which is which, though, I think we can't count on the PD." They looked at each other. "Not that I was counting on them," Donna said.

"Which leaves us fighting shadows. I'm not thrilled about challenging someone who has shown themselves to be so ruthless and magically potent."

"Of course not," Donna didn't bother to keep the disappointment out of her voice. "Can you at least get a message to someone?"

"Fierce?"

"Yes." Donna closed her eyes. She missed Fierce so much.

"I'll see what I can do. Just because Corey's got this town swarming with guys in suits bent on kidnapping you doesn't mean he doesn't have other rats running around."

She wanted to hit him hard enough to shatter her own knuckles. Couldn't he find any sort of spine at all?

"Thank you, Peter. I know this has been hard on you."

She turned to him, and for the first time, she could see how tired he was. The purple shadows under his eyes, the sag in his posture. Even his beard seemed limp and lifeless. She wondered how she looked, bathing in the river, skimping on her soap. She probably looked like a fucking urban cave woman. Somewhere, she felt the stirrings of sympathy for Peter and his cowardice, his unwillingness to get involved. But at the same time, he hadn't been hunted by men with guns.

"Thanks," she said again, and walked out of the alley, deep in thought. She let her feet take their own hard stride as she wondered what to do. Political influence and a hold over the cops… if half of what she'd heard about Thurmond Corey was true, he could afford to bribe a lot of the town. And he seemed to be the sort who aimed for the head, rather than the body.

Her vision filled with stars, and she heard a thump. The ground tilted, and her knees couldn't hold her up. Shaking her head, she struggled to get to her feet, and couldn't.

"Well, you weren't so tough after all." The words washed over her. What did they mean? Hands gripped her, and she heard the click of metal. She raised her hand to the back of her head and felt like a trickle of blood. Her other hand came with it. She saw the handcuffs, wondered briefly why she wasn't in the bathtub.

She shook her head, trying to clear the fog. She couldn't figure out what was going on, why she couldn't stand properly. Hard hands were on her again, and she was herded into the back seat of a car. *Oh Fuck.*

CHAPTER 14

TEETH

The world blurred around Donna, swirling. She was being pushed into a car. Somehow, her hands were handcuffed. She had to get out of this. She had to figure a way out of this now. She pushed herself to focus. Someone was leaning over her.

She smashed forward with her forehead, caught him on the side of the head. She brought up her legs and kicked out, but he had already moved away.

Who was she fighting? She couldn't tell, except that he was bulky and moved fast. He was out of the car, out of her reach. She clambered out of the car and took off at a run, not looking where she was going. Her foot caught, and she went sprawling on the pavement. He was on top of her, her cuffed hands trapped beneath her. She screamed and kicked, but he was heavy and strong. Gripping her neck and her shoulder, he hauled her to her feet. Everything was blurry, but she could see his dark hair, the pale complexion. She didn't know him. She shook her head, and ground her teeth. Her head was still ringing, and her head throbbed. No time for that, now.

"Not as tough as you thought you were," he said. She hated his gravelly voice, his meaty hands. He wasn't tall, but he was blocky. Her heart was hammering, she was ready to beat the fuck out of him if that was what it took. But she had to wait for the right opportunity.

He backhanded her heavily, and she staggered. She forced herself to stand upright.

"Fuck you, you fucking weak piece of shit."

That got her another slap, this one sending jagged pain across her face. She felt blood ooze down her chin.

"Shut the fuck up. You have been a major pain in our asses, but that's over."

She stared at him.

"Do you know what they want me for?"

"I don't care," he said with a shrug. "I do my job, I get paid, I go home at night and I sleep soundly."

They looked at each other. He was loose, waiting for her to try something. She tried to kick him in the crotch. He avoided it, then shoved her while she was still on one leg.

She went down on her hip, hard. Pain shot up her side, and she let out a wail. She let it scream through her for a moment, then pushed herself to her feet. He just watched her, too far away. She tried anyway, but he caught her short with a blow to her gut. She doubled over, unable to breathe. She struggled to bring in air, and for a terrifying eternity, couldn't. At last, she gasped a tiny amount of air in, the tears of pain and effort streaming down her face.

"Try that shit again, and I will fuck you up. We can't shoot you, or kill you, but we've got some free reign outside of that." He said it without emotion, as if he were a snake that had somehow found a human skin to walk around in.

She was still doubled over, breathing painfully. He knelt down next to her, grabbed her by the hair.

"You fucked up a decent guy," he said. "Paul was—"

She lunged. Surprised, he fell, and she landed on top of him, face to face. She shoved her mouth into his eye socket, closed her teeth on his eyelid. Donna kept her jaw clenched tight and let him push her off. The lid tore as she landed on her back, bloody lid still clenched in her teeth. He half-sat up, hand covering his bloody eye. She grinned, then spit the flap of skin onto the asphalt next to her.

She struggled to her feet, and he stood, also. She edged toward him, arms, still cuffed, up defensively. He uncovered his bloody, lidless eye and settled into a defensive stance. She tried to circle towards his injury, but he pivoted, always keeping his eye toward her. Shit. But the longer she stalled, the worse shape his eye would be in.

That didn't help her now. Not much. He came at her with a straight-on punch that she took on the shoulder. The impact rocked her. She couldn't take a lot of those. She ducked the next swing, and lunged straight into him. They went down in a tangled heap again. She went for his face, and he snapped back hard enough to bang his own head on the pavement.

His sweaty hands grabbed at her hoodie, but she had grabbed onto his neck and was pulling herself up toward his face. He was trying to roll and get her under him, but every time he tried, she'd get a knee or a shin into his crotch. With a long rip, the seam of her hoodie let go, and she shoved herself up until they were face to face again.

His mutilated eye was huge and blood-covered, and his good eye wide with fear. He grabbed her by the hair, pulled her head back. Her hands found his thick neck and began to squeeze. He pulled her back far enough that she began to lose purchase. But as her hands slipped, she dragged her nails across his neck, found his windpipe, and crushed it from the sides with her cuffed hands.

He gagged, letting her go, and she was on him again. She latched onto his bloody eye and sucked at the socket like it was the bottom of a milkshake. The eye bulged into her mouth. He shoved her from below, and she bit down, the olive-like eye popping out of its socket and into her mouth. He screamed, and she felt the string-like optic nerve between her lips, still attached.

She bit down hard, the string snapped, and the eye in her mouth exploded like a juicy grape. He shoved her off, bellowing in pain and rage. She spat the tough skin of the eye into the gutter.

He went for his pistol, but Donna bulled into him, taking advantage of his eyeless side. She smashed her cuffed fists into the side of his face. He stumbled, fumbling with the half-drawn pistol. She elbowed him in the throat, slammed a knee into his ribs, keeping on him, not letting him recover. Her arms ached, but she didn't let up, battering him, never allowing him the chance to swing back. When he dropped his hand from his socket, she laid into it, relentlessly pounding his blind side.

When he fell, she looked back and realized she'd driven him completely across the street. Somewhere behind her, he'd dropped his pistol. Adrenaline pounded through her, but she knew she was going to pay for it in just a few minutes. She had to finish this soon.

She stood over him, breathing heavily. He held out a hand to ward her off, the other hand still ineffectively trying to stem the tide of blood that covered the side of his face.

"Just so you know, your eye really hit the spot," she said. With a supreme effort, she turned her back on him and walked away. She saw his gun on the pavement and picked it up. She was building up quite a collection.

She walked with stiff quiet until she turned the corner of a building. Once she was out of his line of sight, she ran, heedless of the aches in her head, her hip, her shoulders, her face. Everything hurt, but she had to get away from him as fast as she could. She was still handcuffed, but she would figure that one out later. Every step jarred her bones, and the pain started to sink in. Soon she was loping in blind agony, slowing down to a walk. Oakham was still dark, and she was limping past quiet houses.

No sound of pursuit. She needed to get off the road as quickly as possible. Her gait was little more than a drunken stagger. With the adrenaline gone, her head was a furious ball of agony, her vision swam in and out of focus.

She didn't see him until she stumbled into him. She hit something as unforgiving as a fence post and went down. Where was the gun? She scrabbled around for it before hands landed on her shoulders. She lashed out with her shackled fists, but didn't make contact. Through the fog, a boyish face appeared.

"That was either the best party I've ever missed, or you're in a shitload of trouble."

She wanted to scream at him. She had a busted lip, was carrying a gun, handcuffed, and he was making jokes? Nathan?

"Come on, Donna, let's get you off the street."

She pulled away. Her headache was screaming agony,

but she had to know it was really Nathan. She looked at him, squinted. When had the sky gotten so light? She couldn't focus. She swayed on her feet, fell against him.

"Donna, it's me. Nathan. You helped me buy a tie. You're clearly in a lot of trouble, and it would be best if we got off the street."

She couldn't seem to let him go. They had a sort of three-legged walk, him supporting her. Was this safe? What did she know about him? She was too weak to fight him. She'd figure something out later.

They got to his apartment, and Donna thanked all sorts of saints that he had a first-floor apartment. He lowered her down on the couch, then walked out of the room. What was he doing? Was he calling Thurmond? Her headache had faded a bit, but the aches in her face and legs hadn't. She doubted she'd be able to walk.

Nathan came back into the room, knelt in front of her. He unlocked the cuffs, one after the other.

"You have handcuff keys?"

"Don't you?" he asked.

Even a weak smile made her lips sting.

"Where's the gun?" She asked in a hoarse whisper.

"I was hoping to get you some first aid." He looked at her. "Your pupils aren't different sizes, so that's good."

"The gun."

From somewhere beyond her focused attention, he produced some gauze and ointment. He started to dab at her lip, the pain of it screeching through her tired brain. She batted his hand away.

"The gun. Where is the gun?"

He stopped dabbing, looked at her.

"I picked it up, assuming it was yours. I don't like them lying around the house, so I stuck it in my safe."

It seemed so sensible.

"Just tell me that you aren't going to sell me out or call your boss about me."

"I'm not going to sell you out, but I did call my boss to tell him that I was taking a sick day today."

That made sense. She nodded her assent. He handed her a bag of frozen peas, which she put on the growing lump on her head. He went back to dabbing at her face. She was so tired. Nathan worked patiently, cleaning the blood off her face. She didn't think she was bleeding anywhere else. Bruised, yes. Her face was starting to throb. She probably looked like she'd been through a boxing match.

Nathan's touch was tender, soothing. Millimeter by millimeter, she felt herself unhitching, letting herself believe she'd gotten away, that he wasn't just another guy who was hunting her. She slumped onto the couch.

"Hey, can't have you going to sleep quite yet," he said. "I need you to stay awake for a couple of hours."

"Well shit," she said as he took more crusted blood off her cheek. It hurt every time he did it, but she felt cleaner.

"I have to admit, you were not what I was expecting when I went out jogging this morning."

She might have smiled.

"Not to pry, but can I ask what happened?"

It seemed like a reasonable request, but where the hell should she start? All the way back with the guys who were hunting her? The alchemists?

"This guy was trying to shove me into his car."

"Holy shit. Is he still out there?" He started to get up, but she grabbed his arm.

"I've got reason to believe he's associated with the police." Which was sort of a stretch. She suspected Thurmond and Schenk were tied together, but nothing solid.

He looked at her, studying her face. With a sigh, he ran his fingers through his hair, sat down next to her on the couch.

"I thought I was moving to a quiet town, away from city craziness," he said.

"We've got our own special kind of crazy," she said.

"Did you know the guy? What do you think he wanted?"

"I didn't know him, but his boss has it in for me."

"Has it in for you." Nathan gave her a look. "Did you exercise him too hard? Make him look like a tool by lifting more than he could? How the hell could he be so pissed off that he would send someone to beat you up?"

"It's complicated," she said.

"Is that his gun?"

She nodded.

"He handcuffed you, had a gun, and you managed to get away from him. You're pretty hardcore."

She decided not to tell him about the eyeball. She really needed to brush her teeth. She shifted the bag of peas. Her head still hurt, and now the cold was adding another layer of discomfort.

"You're taking this awfully well. Should I be worried?"

"I don't think so. I mean, I'm not in the habit of picking up strays. But we know each other, and you looked you needed some help."

Why was she getting a creepy vibe? So far he'd been nothing but polite.

"If you don't mind, I think a hot bath would help," she said.

"Yeeeah, give me like five minutes to make it presentable."

"Doesn't look like I'll be going far," she said with a deliberately wan smile. He smiled back, his boyish puppy-dog smile at odds with talk of guns and handcuffs.

While he cleaned his bathroom, Donna looked around her. The room was Spartan. Aside from the couch, there was a huge television on the wall, a small plastic shelf with books, and a few knickknacks on top. She stood, carefully, and kept one hand on the couch as she moved around it to the bookshelf. No alchemical texts, but he read a mishmash of mysteries and thrillers, with a fair amount of space dedicated to Iain Banks, Patricia Highsmith, and Archer Mayor. Interesting.

On top of the shelf, the small pile of junk turned out to be small plastic Godzilla figures. Eight of them, all different in their oddly pudgy way.

"Don't judge." She jumped and turned to see Nathan, looking a little sheepish. "But a guy loves what a guy loves. Anyway, the bathroom is now pretty clean. The door doesn't lock from the inside, but I hope that doesn't bother you too much."

She shrugged and shifted the frozen peas again.

Alone in the bathroom, Donna took a moment to look at

herself naked. She looked like shit. Her hair was matted, her face bruised and swelling. Those haunted, hunted eyes couldn't be hers.

She was developing a wicked-looking bruise on her hip, her shins were black and blue. She couldn't account for several of the fist-sized bruises across her ribs, but she could guess where she'd picked them up.

The bath water was hot, and Donna slid into it only by inches. So many parts hurt. She hissed through her teeth as the hot water seemed to grow hotter around her injuries. When she was finally all in, the hot soak was at once painful and soothing. And for the first time in what seemed like years, Donna started to relax.

"Hey," Donna jumped, but Nathan was talking through the door. "I'm going to talk to you a little. I want to make sure you don't blackout in the tub."

"Sure. What do you want to talk about?"

"I was going to make breakfast, and I figured I'd offer you some. "Are you a vegetarian or anything? Do you eat eggs?"

"Eggs are fine."

"That's a relief. I don't cook a lot of things well, but my omelets aren't bad."

"You don't have to, you know."

"I don't have to do a lot of things. But you're probably hungry, so I thought I'd whip up, well, the only thing I know how to cook well."

The combination of the hot bath and his eagerness to please made her smile. Painfully, and she was sure she'd just torn the scab that was forming on her lip. Food sounded good. Not food from a can. Not something that had been a person. Something normal.

"That would be nice. Three eggs, if you would." She tried not to think of eyes.

It was quiet after that, but she could hear the clank of dishes. After a few minutes, the smell of cooking eggs wafted its way to her. Her stomach rumbled. She felt like less of a shambles. With a sigh of disappointment, she left the bath's comforting embrace, toweled off, and put her clothes back on.

She opened the door, and Nathan was sitting at his small table, reading, two steaming plates of eggs in front of him.

"You look better," he said. He pushed a plate towards her, and started eating his own. She sat, consciously ate in small bites so she wouldn't just shove her face into the plate and hammer those eggs down. Eating at a table, when did that become something to appreciate?

"I can't stay long," she said when she was done. "I don't want to bring trouble into your... uh… apartment."

"You're a mess, Donna. Someone just tried to kidnap you this morning. Where are you sleeping these days? I keep hearing rumors about some homeless murderer, but it's all hearsay. And since homeless people don't tend to have cars, and the way you look, I'm kind of assuming that's you." He looked at her. "I don't think you're in trouble, I think you're in a whole heap of shit."

"I am, and I'd prefer not to bring it down on you."

"Fair enough. Can I get you to tell me about the whole thing?"

He'd been more than kind. She had few friends right now. But to tell him the whole thing might make her slip and talk about the cannibalism. How would he react to that?

"There's not a lot to tell. Shadowy cabal of people trying to get me to do things I don't want to do."

"Why don't you just leave? Running isn't the bravest thing to do, but it'll get you out of the situation."

Donna's smile was wan. "Tried it. Still here."

"Why do I get the feeling there's a lot you aren't telling me?"

"Because there is a lot I'm not telling you. I don't want to get you hurt."

He considered her. "Fair enough. So you can crash here for two days, because that's all the sick leave I've built up. No offense to you, but I'm not comfortable leaving you in the apartment alone."

"Fair enough. Look, I'm tired. Do you mind if I crash out?"

He shrugged. "Not a problem. I'll get you a couple of blankets for the couch."

Sleep was difficult. She had to constantly squirm around to find a position that wasn't painful. How was she ever going to sleep? The sofa was just uncomfortable, she was too warm under even the light blanket Nathan had provided, and somehow everything was scratchy. She was never—

Donna woke, and immediately saw that it was dark out. Oh shit, how long had she slept? The pressure in her bladder told her a long time.

She struggled to get up. She ached all over. Her head was sore, as if she'd been hit with a ball-peen hammer, and various other parts were not happy about anything. She levered herself up and limped to the bathroom.

Coming out, Nathan was again in the kitchen.

"You were tired," he said.

"Guess so," she said. Despite her aches, she felt alert, awake, and safe for the first time in... how long had it been? Before she'd left the house. Before she'd punched Jim. Before the violator had invaded her mind. A long time. She felt safe. Nathan hadn't creeped on her, didn't seem like he was going to take advantage of her.

"I should probably get going," she said.

"If you want to. Like I said, I've got another day of sick leave, and I'm happy to give you a roof for another day so you're stronger before you head back out into the wild."

"I'm not sure..."

"You just slept for fourteen hours," Nathan said. "You look better than you did, but I bet you couldn't fight off a kitten."

"Good thing you don't have one." Donna didn't feel normal, but the curdle of fear that had become her constant companion had eased. She was safe here.

He cooked. She ate with gusto, knowing she was going back to cans soon. She was too tired to do much after the meal, and slept through the rest of the night.

"I hope you don't mind if I stay the rest of the day and leave tonight," Donna said over a big plate of spaghetti with sauce from a jar. Nathan was running out of large meals to serve her.

"You are welcome to spend the night again."

"I think it would be best if I sneaked out tonight."

"Is there any way I can help you?"

"You've done more than enough. This has been the best two days I've had in a long time."

He blushed a bit.

"I would like to know what kind of shit might be headed my way," he said.

Dammit. He had a point.

"Have you been to The Horn?"

"Not really. I know where it is, though."

"Peter and Rich, the guys who own it, have helped me out a time or two." She was vague about it. "Now, there's been some sewer work up on their road, and they've had a sudden health inspection, just when all the rats disturbed by the road work have discovered their kitchen."

"That's kind of far-reaching and serious," he said.

"I can leave now," much as she didn't want to.

"Just for you. These people are crazy. What do they want with you?"

"They want me to kill for them."

He dropped his fork. "Holy shit."

"Yeah."

"Are you like some sort of spy, then?"

"I wish." She almost laughed. "If I was a spy or an assassin, I'd have the skills to get the job done. And I'd probably know who was pulling my strings. It's taken me months to figure out who's behind all this, and he's really stepping up his efforts." She closed her eyes and sighed. She wasn't going to go into anything. She couldn't stand it if she started talking about cannibalism.

"Do you have a plan?"

"I'd rather not tell you. Anything you know can be told to someone else."

"I would never…"

"You need to think about the kind of people this involves." She hated bursting his bubble. "I'm not afraid you're going to go out, get drunk, and blab to the wrong person. I'm afraid someone is going to hurt you. And I hope that if it comes to that, they'll hurt you less if you have nothing to give them." She shivered.

It was his turn to be silent.

"You're really afraid that someone's going to kidnap and torture me?"

"Someone has already tried to kidnap me, and they weren't gentle about it." For emphasis, she touched her lip.

"It's just so incongruous," he said. "Small-town America. This is the sort of stuff you hear about happening in Russia, or Somalia."

Donna shrugged. "And since the police are doing jack shit, I have to take care of this myself."

Nathan nodded. "I see what you're getting at. And I guess I have to just acknowledge that the situation sucks. But if I can do anything else that you think might not kill me, don't hesitate."

She smiled, reached out, and caressed his cheek. "Thank you. I don't know if I'll be able to, but knowing you are willing makes me feel a lot less alone."

He smiled, touched her hand. "You don't owe me anything. Just doing what any decent person would have."

"A lot of people would have just kept on going." She could feel a hunger building in her, a desire for contact.

"Might as well not look at me that way," Nathan said. "I've got a personal policy against sleeping with women who have had a recent trauma."

She pulled back. She should be furious. At the same time, it was sweet of him. She didn't have the energy to hide her disappointed smile, but what else could she do?

"I'm all kinds of complimented," he said. "You have a great fashion sense, you were kind to a guy who was new in town, and even after you've been homeless, you are hopelessly out of my league. But we're both in the sort of situation that leads to bad relationships. And I want to give us a fair shot." He paused. "When this is all over, and we're standing in the smoking ruins of whatever super villain's base, let's give this another try."

Donna sat back, feeling the hot prickle of embarrassment creep up her face. How long had it been since she'd received a compliment like that? Too long, clearly.

Rather than say anything, she dug into her spaghetti. But she couldn't hide her smile. All this time, she'd been living for the moment when her problem was over. Now, there was something on the other side of the tunnel.

Donna left his apartment after dark. Her last request had been to borrow the phone, and set up a meeting with Fierce that night. Her body still ached, but at least the headache came and went. She could walk, rather than hobble, and her skin was a patchwork of bruises.

Her route was circuitous, and she checked often to make sure she hadn't been followed. When she left the road, she followed a meandering path back to her camp. To her relief, nothing had been disturbed.

Donna lurked in the tree line, waiting for Fierce. There were things she couldn't tell her, not about the meat, not about the eye. But they needed to talk. Maybe get a piece of her old life back. To know she wasn't alone.

She saw Fierce's car on the approach. She squinted, not ready to trust. Was that actually her in the car? Something was wrong. The head looked too bulky to be Fierce. But as she turned the car off, and opened the door, Donna saw the bone-white of a neck brace, and the black patch that covered one eye.

"Holy shit, Fierce!" Donna was charging down toward her, but stopped herself short of trying to hug Fierce.

Fierce looked at her with one eye.

"Some people came to talk to me, asked me questions about you." Donna's heart froze.

"Oh fuck, Fierce." She clenched her fists so tightly her ragged nails bit into her palms. She couldn't even look at her, she was so ashamed. It wasn't her fault, but those fucking bastards had hurt Fierce. They'd ruined her life, and now they were using other people to get to her. She was going to kill them. She was going to flay the fucking skin off their backs with burning sticks. She turned away, blind to everything but her fury, but Fierce grabbed her by the shoulders.

"You can't go off half-cocked," Fierce said. "We need to plan this carefully."

Donna stood, seething, still unable to look Fierce in the eye. She was furious beyond weeping. She started to shake.

"I. Fucking. *Hate*. Them."

"I know. This wasn't you. This was them." Fierce waited, to let that sink it. "It's not your fault."

"If it weren't for me…" Donna started, more miserable than furious now.

"Beating yourself up doesn't get shit done, Donna. Pull yourself together."

Donna was paralyzed. All the horrible shit. Everything that had happened to her, and somehow, she thought they were going to throw softballs at her friends. The Horn was crawling with rats, but that wasn't anything physical. What a fool she'd been. Corey'd had her murder people. She was damn lucky Fierce was still breathing.

"If we're going after this shit stain, I need you to pull your head out of your asshole and start figuring out reality," Fierce was relentless. "I can't do shit, you have to be my hands."

Donna got the courage to look Fierce in the eye. She didn't see much bruising, but Fierce's one visible eye glared with a startling rage.

"You're looking pretty rough, yourself," Fierce's voice was surprisingly mild.

"They never were very delicate. I'm on the receiving end, this time. It could be worse, I've slammed faces into hot grills."

Fierce set her mouth. "Then we need to give better than we get."

She was right. Of course she was right.

"It's Thurmond Corey, by the way. He's the bastard that's been doing all of this."

Fierce's eye narrowed.

"He hired all the suits running around Oakham," Donna said. "The ones that keep coming after me." The ones she kept killing.

Fierce grabbed her elbow, her fingers sinking in.

"Are you sure? Thurmond Corey."

"Yes," Donna didn't hesitate.

"He's got crazy security, motion detectors and infrared

cameras that he turns on when the sun goes down. But it's always off during the day. "

Donna wondered how much that would apply now that he had his goons crawling all over the place. Of course this wouldn't be simple.

"His mobility isn't what it used to be. He's been…"

Donna yelled as the all-too-familiar intrusive drill began its work on her head. Dammit, she couldn't afford to let him catch even a glimpse of Fierce.

She fought. Pressed against the probe, blunting the attack. Either she was getting much stronger, or he was getting weaker. Fending off the attacks was easy. They didn't hurt anymore, either.

Why stop there? She reached out and encompassed the drill, smothering it with her strength. There, in her mind's eye, she saw the long tether that connected them. She ran along it, into a churning ethereal nothingness, like the inside of a cloud. Always she kept a sense of where that cord was. When in the distance she saw what it was attached to, and jumped into it with both feet.

Donna heard the beep of medical equipment. With an effort, she opened unfamiliar eyes. Jim was standing in front of her.

Jim? The shock snapped her concentration, and she was back in herself, on her knees, next to Fierce.

"Donna, are you still Donna?" Fierce was shaking her shoulder, as if trying to wake her up. Donna swung around, and saw Fierce's bulky phone was in her other hand.

"Woah, Fierce, I'm me again. He didn't get through." Donna got to her feet, but Fierce gestured with her phone.

"Tell me something only you would know," Fierce said. Did she have a stun gun in her phone case?

"You fantasize about me sexually, and it makes me a little uncomfortable?"

Fierce put her phone in a holster.

"Is that a weapon?" Donna asked.

"I've just had a very bad experience, and I'm not going to be caught out again."

They looked at each other for a moment. Tell her about seeing Jim?

"How do I get into Corey's House?"

Fierce's smile was a thin scar, like a knife wound.

"That'll be easier than you think."

CHAPTER 15

KNIFE

Jim had always denied there was any connection between himself and the reclusive Thurmond. Donna was going to put that mess on hold until she had taken care of this problem. Then she was going to settle his fucking hash.

The sun was just past noon, warm but not too hot. Clouds were gathering on the horizon, though. Donna had done her best to wash herself, put on a clean top and pants. She said a silent goodbye to her little camp. No matter how this came out, she wouldn't be coming back here. She stuck a pistol in the back of her jeans, and walked through the front gate of the Corey mansion.

No one stopped her. The front door was large and ornate, intended to be imposing. Donna leaned on the buzzer.

"Who is it?" the distorted voice asked.

"I'm Donna. I'm the woman your boss is looking for, and I want to come in."

She listened to the silence. Good, he was hesitating. She checked to make sure there was only one camera on her. She didn't want to give away the game too soon.

He buzzed her through. The door was as heavy as it looked, solid wood, and Donna had to muscle it open. Godamned intimidation attempt.

The man behind the desk was one of the Suit Goons, dark suit, pistol in hand, pointing at her. About fifteen feet separated them.

"Do you know who I am?" She asked.

"Donna. The woman we've been looking for."

"Then you know that you can't shoot me. Mr. Corey will be very upset if you do."

"Right now, I only give half a shit about Corey."

"Then you've heard about me," she said. "Know the things I have done to your co-workers."

He swallowed.

"Think about it," Donna continued. "I've killed a couple of you. It's going to be six months before one of you will walk again. And you can't put eyes back in sockets."

She took a step forward. "You, unfortunately, have one of two choices. You can shoot me, and I have no doubt you have the nerve to do so. We both know how easy that is." She took another step. "Or you could turn away and leave. Because if you don't, I'm going to fuck you up. You might win, you might even put a bullet in me, but if we fight, you aren't going to walk away unscathed." She took another step.

He looked at her, his lips pursed, gun still raised.

"It's only a job," she said. "You don't want to risk getting physical therapy just because of a job, right? Even worse, you might lose an eye, some teeth. And of course, you know about that little incident in the apartment a couple of blocks from here?" She licked her lips with a slow languid savor.

He didn't say anything. He didn't need to. She could see the sweat creeping out of his hairline.

"Are you sure you want to sacrifice that much for this job? An eye? Some teeth? Everything?" She gave her best confident, toothy grin. Her own heart was hammering away.

"I'm going to walk out of here," he said. "You're right. This job isn't worth that much to me." Keeping his gun trained on her, he stepped out from behind the desk. Donna stepped to the side, letting him pass.

"Have a good life," she said as he side-stepped past her. He holstered his gun as he got to the door, then darted out. Donna walked to the door and made sure it was locked behind him.

Now, where to find Thurmond Corey? She pulled out her pistol, in case the next Suit Goon wasn't as reasonable.

The mansion was well-appointed. Donna walked into a

fantastic dining room with a beautiful burl wood table, the grain a fiery swirl. Above it hung a chandelier dripping with red and white crystal, which had to take the staff hours to clean. The kitchen was quiet, but Donna could hear the faint medical beep in the distance.

Following the sound, Donna came to a room with a bed and a maze of medical machines. The man lying in the bed was little more than a skeleton, shrouded in a bed he clearly would never leave. On a table, beside the oxygen tank, the IV, and the monitoring equipment, was a table of strange bricolage. At first Donna thought it was chemistry equipment, but chemistry sets didn't include candles, knives, and bowls of odd-colored crystals.

"Hello Donna," his voice was raw, like a heavy smoker's.

So here it was. Finally, she was speaking with Thurmond Corey. She fought down the urge to pinch his mouth and nose closed without listening to him. She had a lot of questions.

"I suppose I should be flattered that you know my name."

"This will be one of the most important conversations of your life," the sickly thing in the bed said.

"And your last. Remember that with everything you say."

"You are here because of me," he raised his withered hand. "I gave you life. You owe me *everything*,"

"I was raised by my mother, alone. You abandoned me, you putrid old fuck."

She walked toward the bed. The smell of old man was cloying, the reek of despair mixed with an imperfectly-sealed catheter bag.

"Do not talk to me that way—" he started.

"Or you'll what? Give me a whipping? Raise your hand to me?"

Those eyes, deep in their shrunken sockets, blazed with anger. Donna stared right back at him. He raised a claw and pointed at her.

"Everything you are is because of me. Your strength, the fact that you got in here to find me, who you think is the source of your trouble. It's a pity you didn't learn more."

Donna turned away, so the rage didn't explode into action.

"The only thing you taught me was to murder."

She stepped around the bed, shifted the gun to her left hand, and picked up the knife. That might be useful later.

"So, this is how you've been taking me over."

"It was necessary."

"For what? Had they offended you? Did the college reject your application and hurt your delicate feelings?"

He said nothing, but his eyes remained on her.

"Now you clam up? I killed a lot of people, and I don't even know why. I did your shitwork, and you can't even be bothered to tell me why you needed the Key of Aros the Philosopher? Go ahead, tell me how tough you are, how necessary it was to kill them."

"A certain amount of intimidation is necessary, otherwise no one will take you seriously."

Donna felt a laugh burst out of her.

"I see that worked very well. I mean, you started killing people and then you had to keep on killing people. Man, if we could have just killed them a little harder, maybe that would have intimidated them. Do you have any concept of how you turned my life into shit? I had a business, I had a boyfriend, I had a life. I was well-adjusted. And you had to go shit all over that because of some piece of esoteric bullshit. You drove me out of my home, destroyed my fucking life. You owe me an explanation."

"You have no position from which to negotiate. What will you do? You are pathetic."

"Every time you do not answer a question, or lie to me, you are going to live five minutes longer. And you are not going to enjoy it."

She saw something move behind her. Donna whirled, gun up.

"Donna?"

Jim? What was Jim doing standing in the doorway? She'd half convinced herself she hadn't seen him when she'd pushed to see out of Thurmond's eyes.

"Don't care what you're doing here," he said. "You need to leave while—"

"Stop." She did not shout.

"Donna, what… why are you here? Do you have any idea what is going on here?"

"Shut. Up." Donna felt like her head was going to explode. The headache was back. "If you so much as take a step toward me, I will fucking shoot you."

Did he look cowed? How well had she ever known him? What the hell was going on?

"Come on, it's me, Jim." His hands were spread wide, his palms upward. "I wouldn't hurt you."

"Stay there."

"We both know you aren't going to pull that trigger. You hate violence. You don't even like action movies." He had his sympathetic face on.

"Don't," she said.

"That's not you, Donna. There's a lot going on here that you don't understand. Why don't you put the gun down and we can talk about it like reasonable people." He took a step forward. "You don't want to do this, Donna. You want us to talk it out. Share our feelings. We can come to some sort of reasonable conclusion." He took another step, confident.

Donna pulled the trigger. He snapped back, then scrabbled at the growing bloodstain on his shirt. Donna fired another two bullets into his chest, and he fell. Donna took five swift strides, lowered the gun. He was still breathing, still struggling to cover up the three bullet-holes. She looked him in the eye. He pleaded silently, pink foam bubbling on his lips. She pointed the pistol at his eye, pulled the trigger. His head snapped back and the rest of him stopped twitching.

She stopped in silence, her ears ringing from the gunshots. She should feel something. Jim, who she'd lived with, made love with, shared meals and movies and her life. Why didn't she feel anything?

Thurmond was struggling to sit up.

"You bitch how could you do that?"

She turned the pistol towards him.

"You may want to choose your words with more care."

"Jim! Good God, Jim!" Actual tears were coursing down his face.

He scrabbled ineffectually at the sheets, trying to sit up, get one last glimpse of Jim.

"Son," the word came out of him as a despairing wail.

Donna's head snapped up. "What? He was your son?" Her head spun, and she felt like she'd been kicked in the guts.

"Your half-brother," he snarled.

The Headache slammed into her, hammering at her temples. She put her hands to her head, knowing it would do no good. That couldn't be true. He was lying.

"You just bought yourself another five minutes of agony, you shit-spewing bastard." The agony was intense, her eyes couldn't focus. She was on her knees, next to Jim's body, unable to cope with the pain screaming through her head.

"Not a lie." His voice was so low she could barely hear him. He made wet sounds like he was still crying. "You've killed your brother."

She was going to fucking kill him, as soon as she could get off the floor.

"Half-brother," she grated. She got a hand on the bed, hauled herself up. Her vision was blurry, but the thumping pain was at least tolerable now. "Don't you fucking dare ignore my mother." It made sense, now. He'd knocked her mother up and left. "You weren't there when I was thirteen and got my heart broken by Clevon Dyer. When Danny the asshole cleaned out my bank account, you didn't listen to me patiently as I cried into the phone until two in the morning. In fact, I'll bet you're the damn reason I can't leave Oakham."

She faced him now, across the tubes that kept him alive. His face shrunken and etched with grief.

"There's nothing you can do about him now," she said.

His head snapped up, eyes glittering with hatred.

"You've ruined everything. Do you understand what you have cost me? How far I've had to go, only to have you shoot my only son."

"Murder is the only thing we've ever shared, and now I'm suddenly doing the wrong thing?" Donna spat through her teeth. The pain in her head screamed like a fire truck. "Did you know we were living together? Fucking each other? Your *kids*?"

"That was the plan, you stupid whore! Nothing in your life has happened that I didn't want to. I wasn't listening to your sad little voice when Dan cleaned you out? I *told him to do it.*"

The words smote her like a slap. He'd been pulling the strings on her life? How long?

"Thought you knew everything, didn't you?" His sneer was hard, his face a fleshless skull.

Where had the knife gone? Donna looked around, ignoring the pain in her head as best she could. It was still on the table.

"I'm about to," Donna said. Her head felt like a railroad worker was slamming it with a sledgehammer, but it wasn't nearly as bad as it had been. She stood, walked to the table and picked up the knife. Then she swept the rest of the equipment onto the floor. The ceramic bowls and glassware shattered, spreading brown and gray dust across the floor. Where the liquids and the powders touched, a tiny sizzle erupted, letting off a small amount of green smoke.

"You are like an elephant in a porcelain shop, you idiot!" The man she was going to kill was screaming now. "You are ruining preparations that have taken months!"

"Good." She turned, dagger in one hand, pistol in the other. "Have you said everything you're going to, old man? Because now you're going to start giving me answers."

"Child," he sneered. "You don't have the strength."

She put the pistol on the floor in the corner, away from the bed.

"What about the men we murdered together? They were sons and brothers, and some of them fathers. I was with you. And in case you missed this little piece of growing-up, I've killed your people. And more than that, I ate their flesh because I wanted them, you, to know that I was more frightening than they were. Murder? I've gone way past murder."

She pinched off his morphine drip. She pulled the tube out of his oxygen tank. His eyes grew wide. She grabbed the tube just under his nose, and yanked. His head snapped forward, but the tubes came free, followed by a slow dribble of blood. The dull red made rusty splotches on the clean sheets.

"You arranged for me to fuck my half-brother. Why?"

He looked up at her, hand to his nose to stop the bleeding. He was trying to be strong, but she could see the tremble in his hand, the fear in his eyes.

She took his hand. He tried to pull it back, but she was too strong. His fingers in her grip, she slammed the knife down, impaling his hand. He shrieked and snatched his hand back, tearing the wavy-bladed knife loose in a gout of blood.

"I killed them and I didn't want to. It was business." She loomed over him, knife in hand, seething with rage. "This is personal. I'm going to show you what I've learned from you, *Daddy.*"

Rather than grabbing at him, she tore the blankets away from him. She grabbed his hospital gown, brought the knife up to his throat, then slit the flimsy fabric. He struggled, but with only one hand, he couldn't effectively fight her. She ripped away the gown, leaving him naked and shrunken on the bed. His skin was dull, and sank between his ribs. What looked like stippled bruises bloomed here and there on his torso. His penis was a shriveled, tiny thing, hiding in a thatch of gray pubic hair.

He scrambled to get away from her, but she put a hand on his chest and leaned, letting her weight keep him down.

With the knife, she pricked the skin above his collarbone, drew a line down his chest. He slapped at her ineffectually, his cut hand leaving bloody stains on her top.

"Tell me about my brother and me."

"You can't understand…" he started.

She pushed the knife in under his ribs, stopping after three inches. He closed his eyes, grunting with the pain.

"I studied anatomy when I learned to be a personal trainer. I know where the major arteries are. You won't bleed to death for a very long time."

"I need a new body," he snarled, his eyes blazed his rage and pain. "Something that can house my consciousness. You are different enough that the Perfect Chain and Yda Stone will not link us indefinitely."

"Body thief," she said. "Without the, what was it, Key, you couldn't control my body indefinitely."

He grimaced in pain.

"What does that have to do with Jim and I?"

Those eyes bored into her. "A child would be more of my DNA. The closer to me it would be, the easier the transition."

"You sick, inhuman fuck. Manipulate your daughter into incest to create a whole new person, just so you can throw them in the trash."

"Is this your plan, then," he sneered. "Bore me to death with your small-minded morality?"

Donna let that pass, the final breaths of a dying man.

"Why can't I leave Oakham?"

"You're bound," he spit it through his teeth.

"How do I unbind myself?"

Despite the lines of pain that crinkled his eyes and mouth, he thought he had her.

"I'm not getting out of here alive. You've said as much. Why would I want to divulge my last bit of revenge, even if it's going to be posthumous? What could be worse than being trapped here for the rest of your life?"

"I *ate* people to get to you," she said. "If you think your last hours won't be in screaming agony, think again."

She shoved herself off him and stood. He looked at her, holding his hands to the seeping wound in his abdomen. With clinical efficiency, she tore a square from his discarded gown. As he struggled to pull up his feet to get out of bed, she shoved him back, then crammed the wad of cloth into his mouth.

He reached up to take the cloth out of his mouth, and Donna brought up her foot and stomped on his shin. Thurmond sat bolt upright, screams muffled by the rag. After minutes, he ran out of breath, and curled on his side, weeping, his smashed leg beginning to swell.

She let him wallow in his own agony for a few minutes. Then she pulled him back to face her.

"How?"

His eyes were blind to anything but his pain. She pulled the wadded gag from his mouth. His breath came in short gasps.

"How do I remove my binding?"

His eyes latched onto her.

"I can hurt you more. Or you can tell me."

He extended a trembling, bloody hand, pointing out the door. "In the next room, in the wooden cabinet. You will find an anchor bound with seven chains, each of a different metal. Break any one of them, and you will be free."

She took the dagger with her and, glancing once at the pistol in the corner, left. After a few minutes of searching she found a two-foot tall anchor bound with extremely fine chains. She attacked these with the wavy-bladed dagger, and pried a link open until it gave.

Nothing. It took her more time to pry off the second chain, and when that fell to the floor, she still felt no different. Had he lied to her?

Lugging the anchor with her, she stepped over Jim's body and came back to the bedroom. She put it down next to the wizened form in the bed.

"I don't feel any different."

"Did you expect a tingling in your special place?" He was dismissive, contemptuous.

She should just kill him. Put him out of her misery. Cut his throat, let him bleed out. She brought up the knife.

"You're too weak," he said.

Donna looked at the father she had never known, glaring at her. The man who had never been there for her, had never let her leave Oakham. Had arranged for her to sleep with her half-brother. Who had taken over her body in order to murder people in horrible ways. The man who had forced her to murder, who had pushed her so far that cannibalism had seemed like a good idea. He'd flushed her entire life down the shitter. He'd done it methodically, coldly.

She looked at the knife. And threw it away. She was going to regret this for the rest of her life. She knew that. But she would hate herself more if she didn't.

"I knew you didn't have the stomach."

Donna shed her coat, loosened up her shoulders.

"You should have stayed out of my life," she said, and shoved the gag back into his mouth.

With her first punch, she felt the bones of his cheek crumble. He was fragile. Well, this would take less time than she thought.

But she would have to pace herself. She swung for the other side of his head. He curled into a ball, hands covering his head. He started to speak, but a fist broke his jaw. She hit him, thump, thump, thump like clockwork, each blow also an exhalation, every inhalation a rest. His skin tore, and her clenched fists were covered in blood. She turned his face into a crushed, grisly pulp. The breath bubbled out of him in small gasps, and she kept on. Her fists were a mess, her arms beginning to stiffen up. Her rage powered her through, her hatred of the shit stain that had done so much to her, and this was the only way she could share even a fraction of that pain. Right. Left. Each impact was a meaty thump, and sometimes, the crack of bone. His face deformed, dented like a deflated basketball.

Although he was probably unconscious, bubbles still rose from the blood on his lips. After a moment's pause, Donna got back to it. One. Two. Left. Right. Until the left side of his skull splintered, stove-in like a rotten orange.

She stopped, looked at the red ruin. Blood had spattered across the sheets, as if someone had dumped a gallon of it from ten feet above. Donna's breathing was heavy, and her hands hurt. She felt free. He was dead. She could move on with her life.

Almost as an afterthought, she pulled the keys out of Jim's pocket.

CHAPTER 16

ALCOHOL

Donna was in The Horn for the first time in a month, but she still followed her evening ritual. She knocked back her first Manhattan to help erase the memory of cannibalism. Her second went to destroying her memory of incest. The third went down to help number two, which wasn't working so well. She still felt filthy. Patricidal, incestuous cannibal. There ought to be a Greek tragedy about her.

She jumped a little when Fierce sat down next to her.

"Hey stranger," Fierce was out of her collar, but the eye patch was still on. Donna felt a stab of regret. Maybe another drink.

"How you doing?"

Fierce gingerly twisted her neck. "I'm OK. My physical therapist thinks I'll be back to a normal range of motion in another month or two."

"I'm really—"

"Stow it," Fierce said. "You've apologized half a dozen times already."

"I wanted to do it in person," Donna said. And signaled Peter for another.

"You might want to slow down on those," Fierce said.

"The moment I no longer feel defiled," Donna promised.

They were quiet for a few minutes.

"How's Boston?" Fierce asked.

"It's tough. It's one thing to see a city on television, but entirely something else to be there. There's so many people, and don't even get me started on the driving. I've been through a stupid number of hoops to set up my own studio, the rent is outrageous, and not half as nice as what I had here. I'm living with Mom until I can find an apartment that's not a roach-infested shithole." She shook her head ruefully. "She says I drink too much, too."

"But it's not Oakham. I mean, Boston's a shithole, but it's not this shithole." She managed to smile at Fierce. "I go driving every Sunday. Just go out, wherever, New Hampshire, sometimes, even Maine. It's amazing."

"That's huge, Donna." Fierce's grin was unrestrained. "Have you heard anything from that tasty Nathan?"

'I'm not ready for a relationship, Fierce. Not until I start feeling less..." *mass-murderous, cannibalistic, torturer who fucked her brother.* "A little more distance, I think."

Fierce quirked an understanding smile, but couldn't think of anything to say.

"Is this seat taken?"

Donna looked up. It took a moment to recognize Officer Kutsenko out of uniform. In jeans and a T-shirt, he looked surprisingly ordinary. Next to him was a guy she didn't know.

"Go right ahead, uh, Jerry." His first name felt wrong in her mouth.

"This is Tom Boghosian," he gestured to the newcomer. Boghosian was slender, in his sixties, wore a pastel short-sleeved button-down shirt. Donna shrugged.

Kutsenko ordered a beer. Boghosian had water.

"How have you been, Donna?"

"Peachy. Can we get this over with? I've got a bit of a drive home." She looked at Boghosian. "Who the hell is he?"

"A member of the college," Boghosian said. He had a flat delivery that Donna associated with an enlightened chucklehead making money dispensing bullshit wisdom to the credulous.

"I'll tell you when I tell everyone." Kutsenko looked at the glasses lined up in front of her. And frowned.

"The back room is ready," Peter didn't say it loudly. "Rich will show you the way. Go ahead and take your drinks."

With a look at Fierce, Donna picked up her drink and followed Rich to the back room of The Horn.

"Thanks for coming," Kutsenko said. His posture was military, precise, even in his civvies. He stood at the head of a wooden table, the rest of the attendees, including Rich, sat. "Tomorrow the Oakham Police Department will make an announcement concerning the events of four weeks ago. I thought you, as people who were involved, might want to know what our conclusions are." He let that sink in. "Thus far, there hasn't been a lot of progress on the Corey estate fire. The main building was well engaged before the call went out. If it was an arsonist, then they were smart enough to cut the power to the building, which delayed the notification of the fire department."

Donna shifted in her seat trying not to look like she was squirming.

"The bodies of Thurmond Corey and his son Jim were found at the site." Kutsenko looked at his hands. "Jim had been shot by a low-caliber pistol, and was probably dead by the time the fire started. Thurmond himself was on oxygen, and that can often lead to fires, and the conflagration started in his bedroom, where he was bedridden. So far as we can tell, there was no one else in the house." Donna wondered if they had found the pistol she had left there. Even in this company, she couldn't ask the questions she had. Like if the anchor was recognizable.

Kutsenko took a pull from his beer.

"There have been some pretty wild rumors about a serial killer attempting to make Oakham his new territory. These are entirely unsubstantiated. Although there have been a few incidents of violence, and in fact more reports than there have been substantiated incidents, they seem to have clustered around some individuals hired by Thurmond Corey in the last two months. We have not yet ascertained his intentions in employing these persons, but several townspeople reported seeing them carrying pistols, although discretely. As the police did not have cause to stop and question any of them concerning their permits, the status of said permits is unknown. Following the fire, they seem to have departed Oakham. We have no evidence to connect them with the burning of the estate, so we will not be referring this matter to the State Police."

"One possible source of these rumors has been the alleged cover-up of deaths in the community. To allay public suspicions and put these rumors to bed, Tom Boghosian has stepped forward to liaise between a quiet religious order that wishes to retain its privacy, and the police. Possibly some of those rumors have started because the college often chooses not to disclose or discuss their members' lives, including their passing. The Oakham Police Department respects the college's privacy."

Boghosian nodded and smiled. Kutsenko looked down at his hands, and the assembled audience shifted in their seats.

"Police chief Peter Schenk has been relieved of duty, pending an investigation. We cannot further comment on this right now."

Donna shook her head. Out of everyone in this room, she knew how much bullshit Kutsenko had piled up. She had to admire his artistry. She wondered how long Kutsenko and Boghosian had spent working that out.

Kutsenko drained the last dregs of his beer, then looked out at his audience. "Any questions?"

Silence.

"Then hopefully, we will never have to meet again, and we can start to put all of this behind us."

Donna closed her eyes. She was free. She hadn't truly believed that Kutsenko would be able to turn a blind eye to as much as he had. She felt a hand touch her wrist, and she jerked her eyes open to see Rich.

"How are you doing?" he asked.

"Tolerable living through alchemy," she said, waving her empty glass. "Some days it's not too bad. But coming back here? It's been rough."

He seemed like he was going to say something else, but instead, he put his hand on hers. Without another word, he walked away. Everyone else had exited the room. Everyone but Kutsenko and Boghosian.

"Thank you for coming," Jerry Kutsenko said. "As the person who saw the most of all this, I want to thank you for coming to this air-clearing." He sagged a little. "How long can we expect the pleasure of your company?"

Which Donna translated as *when will you be out of my hair?*
Of course. He knew, or suspected, that she was the murderer.
And while he would cover for her, he didn't trust her to not start
another killing spree. She shook her head.

"I'll be heading out of town tonight," she said. She tried not
to hate the relief that spread across his face.

"I wish you luck in your future," he said, shaking her hand.
But she could tell, he couldn't wait to get away from her.

He turned and left, and only she and Boghosian remained in
the room. She sighed as he turned to her. Someone else wanted
to salve their conscience.

"I'm so very sorry that you got caught up in the college's
business," he said. "I want you to know that we had nothing to
do with it, and could only resist the way we did. Unfortunately,
to give in would have only made things worse."

Donna shrugged. "I still wake up with the scent of charred
human flesh in my nostrils, or the sound of starving dogs
crushing vertebrae." She paused. "I suppose I recognize your
choice, as a group, not to resist, but I can't help wishing that you
had figured something else out. Something that didn't leave
me holding the bag. You knew who was attacking you, but you
couldn't figure out any way to at least get me some information,
contain him in some way, get rid of the chains that were binding
me to Oakham?" Donna's rage was short-lived, she'd burned so
much out killing her father. She shuddered.

"Alchemy is a path to enlightenment. A purification of the
soul." Tom's irritating monotone was more habitually upbeat
than actually emotionless. "Some of our brothers were less
inclined to take the nonviolent aspect of the Art seriously. For
that, I also apologize."

Yay. Another empty apology that wouldn't help her sleep.
She closed her eyes, heard the screams of burning men, their
faces dripping fire as their fat melted and then ignited. Some
days, she still couldn't believe her ordeal was over. Sometimes
she woke in the night, not entirely sure her body was still her
own.

"Can you offer anything more substantial? Yeah, Corey
wasn't your sort, and yeah, he was rogue and all that, but I've

still got a head full of murders that I would like to forget." And incest. And cannibalism.

There was deep sympathy in his eyes. Or maybe it was empty, useless fucking pity. He spread his hands.

"There is nothing that we can do. Enlightenment involves, among other things, the complete integration of a person. All of their experiences, all of their virtues as well as their faults. As such, there isn't anything we make for the destruction of memory."

Of course not. No, they couldn't possibly be useful, helpful, or help to clean up anyone else's mess. Self-involved shit stains.

What should she say? Offer him some sort of apology? Was he looking for absolution? She wasn't offering any. None of it had been her fault. She'd been shoved into a situation she'd had no control over. Tell him the way his friends had died? That felt like what her father would have done. She couldn't blame them for the taste of human flesh that filled her mouth when she woke up, cold in her own sweat. That was all her.

"We are taking care of Olivia, the Fitzpatricks' child. There are enough of us left that we will be able to adopt her to one of ours. We take care of our own."

"Do you have any idea why…" she almost slipped and said 'my father.' "Why Thurmond only targeted the men of the college?"

Boghosian cocked his head to the side. "There are no women alchemists."

Of course not. Donna felt her hand bunch into a fist. She could take this guy down, make him beg for mercy, stab her fingers in his eyes. She relaxed her hand.

"Ah," she said. "I wish you enlightenment, I guess." She wondered what gruesome fate Thurmond had planned for him.

"Likewise," he said. Then he turned and walked away.

Fierce was still at the bar, and Donna sat down next to her.

"Did I say 'I'm sorry?'" Donna couldn't figure out any other way to start a conversation with her.

"Yeah, a time or two," Fierce sighed.

They looked at each other. Donna could do nothing but stare at Fierce's eye patch, and felt her eyes fill with tears.

"You should come have dinner with Carl and me sometime," Fierce said, ignoring Donna's tears.

"I don't think I'm coming back," Donna looked down into the empty depths of her glass. "Too much... stuff." Not even for Nathan.

"Guess we'll have to make the trip to Boston, once you find out where the good places to eat are."

She hated herself for what she had dragged Fierce into. Hated the fact that they had hurt her, hated the fact that every time Fierce looked into a mirror she had to see herself through one eye.

"You keep telling me you're sorry," Fierce said. "Maybe you're asking the wrong person for forgiveness. Not me, but yourself."

Donna thought about Jacob Stein, Jim, and Thurmond, Lawrence and Carol FitzPatrick. Not to mention all the nameless people who'd died ugly, messy deaths. Because her father was— had been—frightened. And rather than go quietly into the night, he'd dragged nearly a dozen people down with him. It wasn't her fault. Donna felt the tears tumble down her face. The first she had cried since... since she'd murdered Jim.

Maybe, just maybe, she had begun to heal.

AUTHOR'S NOTE

Books don't come fully-formed, and I'm not a good enough researcher to have done this all by myself. Enormous thanks to my trauma consultant Tara Kavanagh, Chris Irvin, my law consultant, and Sandy Stevens, my personal training consultant. Any errors are not because of their advice, but because I didn't listen to them closely.

Readers Shawn MacKenzie, Brandon Ayre, Jon Orzehowski, Tai King, Chris Knight, Dawn Piscatelli, Greg Knapp, David Nolan, Géza Reilly, and April Hawks, who all made this a better book than it would have been.

General thanks to Bracken MacLeod, Errick Nunnally, and Brian Keene for fantastic inspiration. Many thanks to Paul Goblirsch, and David Wilson, who both asked for a second helping after *Hag*.

Huge thanks to Kathleen McBrien, who has always believed, always encouraged, and always loved.

ABOUT THE AUTHOR

John Goodrich is a New Englander by birth, and again by choice. Living in the haunted green hills of Vermont, he writes science fiction, dark fantasy and horror. He has a passion for many things, including Icelandic sagas, Old English poetry, kaiju, the works of HP Lovecraft, and biplanes. Three of his books, *Dark Draughts, Hag,* and now *I Do Terrible Things*, have been published by Crossroad Press.

Curious about other Crossroad Press books?
Stop by our site:
http://store.crossroadpress.com
We offer quality writing
in digital, audio, and print formats.

Enter the code FIRSTBOOK
to get 20% off your first order from our store!
Stop by today!

www.ingramcontent.com/pod-product-compliance
Lightning Source LLC
Chambersburg PA
CBHW051431170626

46809CB00006B/2415